Heavenly Realm Publishing
Houston, Texas

When Ramona Got Her Groove Back from God

A Life Changing Novel of Spiritual Love

Stephanie Franklin

This book is dedicated to my Father,
lover, editor, writer, and best friend,
Jesus Christ my Lord and Savior.

In loving memory of the great
Hazel Myles. I love you auntie! 1931-1998

In loving memory of all the people
who died as a result of the terrorist attacks on
America. September 11, 2001. This happened
during the preparation of my book. I thank God
for: "National Prayer Day."
You will always be remembered.

Acknowledgments

I would like to thank my Lord and Savior Jesus Christ for forming me before I was in my mother's womb. Thank You for choosing me to write this novel and for allowing it to be what it is today. I pray that You are pleased, and that many people will be blessed and changed by this novel. You could have chosen anybody, but You chose me. I just want to say thank You!

To my family, I love you all! Thank you for all of your prayers, love and encouragements.

To my friends and to my sisters and brothers in Christ, thank you for your uncountless prayers. I love you all. You know who you are.

To all of those who played a part in any advice, and to Heavenly Realm Publishing, thank you for your help, revising, and the awesome printing and publishing of this book.

I would like to acknowledge all the Ramona's, all the Michelle's, and all the Tyrome's. If you fall, don't stay there, get back up and try again. God is a forgiving God. There's no condemnation…

Preface / Introduction

The Lord led me to write this book about two years ago off and on. At one time I actually put it to the side and the thought of finishing it never crossed my mind again. I know it was truly God who allowed this to transpire.

This book is fictional, however, the events and situations taken place is what goes on in many different Christians and non-Christians lives. There are so many people crying out for help on the inside, feeling as though they cannot open up to anyone for the fear that people may not understand, or for lack of trust. Ramona experienced these same things. She was saved but she allowed the enemy to make her do things that she never would have imagined she would do. And because of this, she turned away from God and gave satan the liberty to take her finances, her home, her love, her integrity, and her freedom away from her. Along with this, she battled with so many insecurities: her looks, her weight, low self-esteem, her mind, loneliness, self-pity, doubt, worthlessness, gluttony, feeling unloved, drugs, alcohol, and so much more. This is the same thing that many men, women, youth, and young adults are battling with everyday.

The good news is that Ramona over-came all of these obstacles and the wars that had her trapped in her spirit and in her mind. In the end, She got her groove back from God and had it going on again. God restored her and she ended up with more than what she had when she first started off.

As you step inside the characters while you are reading and notice that the sins that they dealt with applies to you, do not let satan tell you to close this book and throw it under the bed. Read the scriptures in the back of the book. Let go and let God save you, deliver you, set you free, and change your life forever. You can over-come any sin that may have you trapped or bound. Just like He did for Ramona. This is why God unction me to write this book, to change people's lives. The young and the old. As you read this touching story remember one thing, <u>keep it</u> <u>real</u>. God is tired of people walking around faking like they've lived a holy life from the time they were born. God is calling those who don't mind admitting that they have a problem and want God to deliver them. There are apostles, prophets, evangelists, preachers, and teachers trapped in the bellies of so many people that are waiting to be birthed out. But because of sin, God has stopped the labor. The question is, will you allow God to deliver your spiritual baby, or will you give up and allow satan to make you have a spiritual abortion? The Word of God says that satan comes to steal, kill, and to destroy. But God comes that you might have life and have it more abundantly (John 10:10).

Don't let satan steal what God has put inside of you. Arise and take up your cross and follow Jesus. He wants to give you life…

When Ramona Got Her Groove Back from God

Chapter 1

Waking up in a huge ring of sweat, I turned over to look at the clock only to notice that it's 8:30am, and I needed to be at work for 8 o'clock. O' Lord, Mr. Kevin said that if I'm late one more time, he's gon' fire me!

I jumped out of bed, went and washed my face, threw on some clothes I had lying in the chair next to the bed, and dashed towards the front door. I hate the secretarial work anyway. It's a great company that's located in the heart of downtown, but it doesn't pay enough.

The phone rings. "Who is that?! I'm not gon' answer it cause' I already know who it is." I said, as I quickly ran to the kitchen, looked at the caller I.D., and answered it as it ranged twice. "I should've known it would be Mr. Kevin! Hello?"

"Hey girl!" He yelled. "Where are you?! I got people in my face needing help! The phone is ringing off the hook! You know I can't do this all by myself! You got three minutes to get up here or I'm going to fire you! I should've kept my word and fired you like I said I was the last time! Once again it's your lucky day! Three minutes! Three minutes!!" Click…He screamed to the top of his lungs as he hung up the phone in my face.

Um', Mr. Kevin, if only he would get the Lord in his life he would be a powerful man of God. Mr. Kevin's given me so many chances it's pitiful. Lord knows I need that job, that's why he's helping me so much. But one day God's gon' make me rich to where I won't have to depend on this secretarial job. We're under paid anyway.

Traffic is so heavy on the freeways. Everybody's honking for nothing knowing that they can't go no faster than what their already going. But this is the city life.

While the traffic isn't moving, I'm listening to some gospel music on my cassette player. That music be jumpin'! I'm getting chills down my back just listening to it. "Ain't nothin' like a Holy Ghost party cause' a Holy Ghost party don't stop!" I bobbed my head to the beat.

Finally arriving at the Sky Tower Building, I already knew there wouldn't be any parking spaces left. I guess I'll go ahead and park in this handy cap parking space. Lord please forgive me this time I know I'm wrong but I'm in such a rush. You know how it is. I guess that's how most Christians do, they do wrong and want the Lord to understand. Umm...

After struggling my way through what seem like over a thousand people, I'm finally at the office with Mr. Kevin screaming in my face.

"Man, shoot girl, I said three minutes not a @$#% hour!" He started shouting and cursing.

Lord please deliver this man. He sure can curse up a storm. "God is gon' save you one day Mr. Kevin and you gon' remember that I said this years from now! Might turn out to be a powerful minister one day!" I smiled and walked over to my junky desk.

"Girl shut up and get these appointments hooked up for next week! You know we're a working corporation and if you don't wanna' work...!"

"Save him Jesus!" I blurted out cutting him off.

"If you don't wanna' wor…"

"Please save him Jesus!" I blurted out again.

"Awe' forget you with your Miss. Perfect religious wanna' be saved self!" He yelled, as he threw up his hands, walked back to his office, and slammed the door.

Thank God. Finally he shut his mouth. What am I going to do first? It's just like I don't work everyday, cause' there's always too much to finish. Boy I tell you secretaries don't get paid enough. And that lil' ol' Secretaries Day, they can save that for the birds. I don't get a raise from it no way.

Hard at work I didn't realize that it was Friday. Two days from Sunday. I love me some Sunday's, that's the time where I can go to church and release this stress, not to mention my sins too. I know I picked up a few just by being around Mr. Kevin.

The day at work is over and I'm too ready to go home. My day ends at 5 o'clock on the dot. Not before, and surely not a minute after. With weekends off, it's like a dream come true. Nothing really happens on Saturday's anyway because I don't have any friends. I normally have fun all by myself. Yea right!

Today is a hot Saturday. Since I have all this free time, I guess I'll start my diet. There's not any nutritious foods in the house. I guess I could go to the grocery store and get me some vegetables, lettuce, and some fruit. I don't know how long I'm going to be able to last on this diet but I'm going to give it a try anyway. This weight has bothered me far too long. Every time I lose it, I gain it right back. I'm tired of feeling unaccepted and unloved. To be honest, I really don't know my true potential in this world. Anybody would probably think that with my half inch eye lashes curled to the sky over lapping a set of light brown hazel eyes would have it going on. Not to mention the bushy eye brows that I just got arched at the hair salon up the street, they would probably say I'm kind of cute. I guess I could have mentioned this long out of style weaved pony tail that I like to wear all the time. If they want to call it nappy they can and trust me it isn't all that, but it works for me probably because I don't have to do anything to it.

Most people tell me I have a pretty face but I don't believe them because they turn right around and talk about me behind my back. I guess I shouldn't feel too bad, because I do the same to them. I'm still conscious of my big lips though. I should be proud because there are people out there sticking themselves in the mouth with a needle trying to make theirs bigger. My momma always told me, the bigger the better. Maybe she's right. Now getting back to me not knowing my true potential in this world. Everything and everybody seem to be passing me by. I mean, look at me, I'm over weight and I don't have not one talent to show for. At least if I could sing, that would be an excuse as to why my life hasn't moved up the ladder like it's supposed to be doing. If someone saw me who I haven't seen in years come up to me and ask what have I been doing with myself, at least I can say that I'm a singer recording some albums for an up coming concert. But no! I can't say any of that except for the fact that I'm a straight up sorry under paid secretary who has to fight satan every time I go to work. I even having to worry about somebody snickering behind my back talking about me and my weight.

The only one I have is the Lord. When I'm discouraged his spirit comes in and over takes me and immediately my heart opens up and receives it. It feels like a cool gentle breeze passing by me so gently. I always try to see if I can hold on to it and embrace it to make it last forever. O' how good it feels...

And at that point all of my worries, my heartaches, my insecurities, my disappointments, and my lonely night cries are gone. And when the cool breeze has left from me, I still have enough to hold on too. This is what gets me through each day.

Somehow I feel as though I'm supposed to be doing something in this world besides being this tired old secretary. Some people at work tell me that they bet I'm lonely because I don't have a man, and I simply tell them that I'm not lonely, I'm just overwhelmed by desire. I'm not looking for a man, I've found one. Jesus Christ, and He's right here in my heart, He's my desire. That usually scares them and they either change the subject, or walk off.

If they only knew how right they are. I mean I know where God lives inside of me, but somehow I'm still lonely. And I wish I had a man in my life to change all that. I need somebody to comfort me and tell me how beautiful I am. Right now I don't feel beautiful nor do I feel like I'm even on top of the world. Typical for a single insecure woman like me. I need to practice what I preach and know that God is my man and when He's ready for me to have a man, He'll bring him face to face to me and at that point I'll know that he's the right one for me. Somehow that's easier said than done though. It still don't change the fact that I'm still lonely. Like Pastor said the other Sunday, it's going to take us crucifying this flesh, praying, fasting, and reading our Bible's in order to get through any storm. And right now, it's going to take all that for this storm I'm in.

It gets hard sometimes, and sometime I feel like I just want to give up. But I thank God for His Spirit, cause' I don't know where I would be without Him. And I'm also glad that He's the only One who forgives me when I get set in my ways and start talking crazy. I thought to myself.

Chapter 2

Sunday's are always a life saver and a reminder of how sinful I've been during the week. When I step foot in my church which is located in the heart of downtown, I immediately feel the presence of God. Conviction sets in and when my Pastor calls for alter prayer, I'm up there before everybody, releasing this trash within me and repenting for the sins that I have so much as even thought wrong. I ask the Lord to help me with my self-esteem and everything else that I'm struggling with. Which is so awesome, cause' He never fails me. And I do realize that some things are going to take a little longer than others. Deliverance doesn't always come in an instant. It's a process.

I want so badly to feel on top of the world and to have a whole lot of money. I want to help and give to so many people who are stricken by poverty. Is that ever possible? I ask myself. Sometimes I look at the homeless and sit and think, the amount of money that the United States have, there should not be one person out on the streets. If people would simply save their pennies instead of throwing them away, a person could get rich just by sitting outside of every convenient store or grocery store picking up pennies that people have thrown away. Things can change only if we give and serve and stop thinking of ourselves and stop throwing precious things away. That is what Christ would want us to do. Let me stop. It's only my opinion anyway. One day I'll be able to help. I thought frowning to myself.

I stepped out of the car and the sun rayed down on my forehead like a hot thin stream of light. Feels like I'm in a broiling oven. I thought, walking toward the church for Sunday worship. With exception of the hot sun, I have to say it's a pretty day this morning.

Church is packed as usual and finding a seat is always hard if you get here two minutes after eleven o'clock. Service is supposed to start exactly at eleven, but you know how everybody gotta' act like they haven't seen each other in over twenty years.

Man! I thought. I didn't think about it but Auntie LolaMae is here ready to do her every Sunday shouting routine. O' Lord, and she can shout you out a house and home too. Sometime I wonder if she's faking because she shouts in the Holy Ghost the same way every Sunday. When the preacher starts singing during his sermon, Amazing Grace. It's like everybody knows what's about to happen. She always stands up, stretches her arms wide, and lets out this loud elephant roar and then falls back on the pew. She's only been through about 100 pews since the church's been built. I laughed to myself.

Now take note, Auntie LolaMae weighs about three hundred pounds. She's about five eleven and has very long coal black weaved hair. Some wonder if it'll reach the floor one day. We all like to clown around about it. She's a dark skinned, bushy eye-browed, middle aged lady with cat eyes, smooth skin, and a big butt with round hips. She really doesn't look her age. She looks great!

Anyway back to her and this church pew thang'! She has her own pew because nobody wants to sit by her. She's so loud and embarrassing.

"Let's come to order! Would you please take your seats! Church is about to begin!" Pastor shouts into the microphone.

"How many woke up wit' cho' minds on Jesus dis' mornin'?… Ain't God good all the time?!… Won't He make a way for ya'?!" He shouts to the congregation as we all shouted back.

We go through the every Sunday rituals with the same order of service. I'm not complaining but sometimes it can be too traditional. I pray that God's glory will fall down on us one Sunday and all we'll do is worship Him. I love to worship God. Praise and worship have always been my guide into the presence of God. It's like I can see Him standing right in front of me with His arms stretched wide. When I praise and worship the Lord with a pure, honest, committed, and true heart, I'm confident that my praise and worship have been accepted by Him. And because my mind is Holy focused on Him, I can give total glory to His Name (John 4:23-24). It's not about works or talents, it's about my relationship with Him. Which is important.

Pastor is now approaching the end of his sermon. "God is willing and more than able to step in yo' life and rescue you from the bondage of Satan! You can be delivered today, anybody here wanna' be delivered?!" He shouted as some threw up their hands as if to answer him. By now Auntie LolaMae is already standing up. I'm surprised she hadn't started doing her Holy Ghost dance yet. Pastor shouts out to the congregation again, "Give if you want something to be given back to you! Pray and ask God to forgive ya' from all unrighteous sins! Hallelujah!! Worryin' won't get cha' nowhere!… We need to stop worryin' bout' thangs we don't have! God said in Philippians 4:19 that He will supply all our needs… So thank God for what cha' have!" He shouts as the music followed him. "Thank God for what cha' don't have!" He shouts as the music followed him again. "Praise God that cha' have food on yo' table, cause' it's only by God's grace that we are even here today!... Do you hear what I'm sayin'?!" He starts singing with the music slowly backing him up. "Amazing grace, shall always be my song of praise…"

Not to nobody's surprise, BAM! The pew fell over with her still on it. Yep, she broke the bench again. Screaming and shouting, guess who runs over to her aide? He does it every Sunday. I think that's her way of getting his attention. His name is Mr. Walter, but they call him Mr. Freak Daddy cause' he's so lusty. He's the shortest man I've ever seen probably weighing about a hundred and fifteen pounds. Some say he's hitting that crack pipe real hard but I disagree, I just think he needs to be delivered from alcohol. Drinking that day and night will make you look like you haven't eaten in weeks, because your body don't want nothing else but liquor. Four feet five inches does justice for him cause' he really puts you in the mind of a midget. Now imagine him standing next to Auntie LolaMae—five eleven, midget, five eleven, midget. Now you know he's not no match for her. I thought laughing to myself.

Now Mr. Walter is fanning her because she passed out so we think. It's funny how every Sunday she loses conscious. We only know this because Mr. Walter tells us this. Yea' right. I don't buy it for a minute!

By now she's back conscious and Pastor is ministering salvation. "Come to Jesus before it's too late! The Bible says that we're living in the last days! There will be rumors of wars, people living immoral lives, and killings all over the world! You need to make sure that you're saved! God is waiting to make you brand new! Will you come?…"

I'm saying to myself, thank God I'm not doing worldly things and living all kinds of sinful life styles. Two people just ran by me up to the alter and rededicated their lives back to Christ. When Pastor saw this, he started dancing in the spirit! And I have to admit, I'm right with him along with almost every body else! O' how good it feels to be in the presence of the Lord after a terrible week at work. Not to mention what happened on Friday. I prayed for Mr. Kevin and told myself that I would invite him to church one day this week.

Church is over and everybody's walking out.

While pushing the front door open it's hard to ignore this loud voice shouting in my direction. Why should I be surprised? I should have known it would be Auntie LolaMae. I don't know why she always got to scream when she talks or tries to get a person's attention. It's so embarrassing sometimes.

"Hey sweet pea! Can Auntie catch a ride wit' cha'!?" She screamed as if I was across the parking lot. I love my Auntie but the last time I gave her a ride home she broke the passenger seat of my car. It took the mechanic two weeks to fix it. I'm not what you call a size zero either. In fact, heavy weight runs in our family. I weigh about a hundred and fifteen pounds. Ha! How dare I kid myself, I haven't weighed myself lately probably because I'm too scared. Two hundred and fifteen pounds isn't too bad at the height of five-five. There I go kidding myself again. I look awful and I promise myself that I'm going to lose weight once and for all. "Ramona do you hear me talking to you!?" Auntie LolaMae screamed as she asked.

"Yea' sure Auntie I'll give you a ride." Even though I wanted to say no.

As I look around at everybody driving away in their Benzes, Land Cruisers, Expeditions, Navigators, jealousy is rising up in me. Shoot Lord, when is my time going to come? They make my lil' ol' 83' Chevrolet look like a show car for the city dump.

We're ten feet from the car and now Auntie wants to talk to everybody. I have to give it to her, she does know a lot of people and have many friends. I don't hang with nobody and not because I don't want to, but because I just don't have any friends. It's been that way basically all my life. I was sheltered as a child. I guess that's normal when you're the only child. My parents didn't allow me to go anywhere but to school and back. The kids used to call me fat elephant and baboon lips because I had big lips. Sometimes I wondered if some of the teachers were laughing at me too. I would go home crying telling my momma the names they would call me. She would tell me that my lips were pretty and full and that I looked like a beauty queen. She made me feel better until I had to go back to school the next morning. And for a long time I've had this huge complex about myself, not to mention about men ever being attracted to someone as ugly as myself. O' yea' I almost forgot, I did have one so called friend name Michelle. She used to do me so bad. Maybe that's why I forgot to mention her. She would sit around everybody else at school and talk about me. But when everybody was gone, she would act like she never did nothing wrong. My momma would tell me to stop hanging around her, but I didn't listen because I felt that I would really be lonely if I didn't have nobody to hang with. At least she would come back and still try and be my friend. At one point, I tried to avoid her but it didn't work for long. I wasn't prejudice when it came to what friends I had. I was more concerned with getting to know who they were on the inside than their outer appearance.

Michelle had plenty of sense but lacked spiritual knowledge. I figured maybe she was going through a lot and just wanted to fit in with the rest of them. Even though it didn't work. She needed my friendship as much as I needed hers because nobody really wanted to hang around her either. She slept with every Bob, Jim, and, Joe. She had a reputation of being a prostitute. That's a good way of putting it. One thing I couldn't stand about her was that she would always get the hook-ups. The clothes, jewelry, men, anything you name it. I guess that's the reward she got for giving it up. Michelle could get job's my own momma couldn't get, that's how much of an impact she had on men. It's a shame too because she wasn't educated at all. I'm surprised that she even graduated. Probably had pull in that area too. I wouldn't be surprised. My heart always went out to the people that everybody else talked about and made fun of. I knew how it felt to be the victim for no apparent reason. This all happened when we were in high school. I haven't seen or heard from Michelle since then. I don't know whether she's dead or alive. She just kind of disappeared from off the face of the earth.

Chapter 3

It's Monday morning and I dreaded going to work. I made sure I was on time because I had pushed Mr. Kevin's patience enough from all the other times I had been late.

It was a hectic day at work as usual. Surprisingly Mr. Kevin was on his best behavior today. I'm shocked, he just asked me how was I doing as he walked back in his office as if he thought about what he said and regretted it. I quickly said that I was fine before he disappeared through the door. I have to say that he did put a smile on my face.

The day is going by so fast. Lunch time is approaching and my stomach sounds like a lawn mower. It's been growling all morning. I'm trying to move from side to side to make it go away, but it won't it's only getting worse. I know Mr. Kevin can hear it cause' his door is wide open. He has good ears, he could hear me if I farted silently. I thought laughing to myself. That's how good his ears are. One day I told him that he should enter into a funny book where world records are held for good ears. Of course he didn't find it very funny. I guess I didn't either, my jokes can be real dull at times.

By now it's lunch time and I just remembered that I'm supposed to be on a diet. The building goes up fifty-five floors and we're on the eighteenth floor. I'm now headed down stairs where the cafeteria and the lobby is. In the lobby, there are all kinds of big time business men and women with their expensive clothes on. All you can see is men dressed up in expensive suits, and women dressed up in dress suits and or pants suits. I feel so out of place being this lil' ol' secretary, and not to mention having on this soulful hot purple skirt and matching flowered blouse.

I just saw the couple next to our office that I see every day hugged up under each other. It's funny cause' that's not the same woman he kisses goodbye every morning when he arrives at work. I wonder what she would think if she saw that? Thank God I'm saved and don't have to worry about drama like that.

The lobby is always busy. People are walking all over the place. Some passing me leaving the building, some crossing in front of me trying to catch the elevators, and some trying to get to the cafeteria for lunch. I have an hour to eat and I'm thinking, this salad I brought is not going to do anything for me! The aroma in the cafeteria is so hard to resist. I can smell a toasted melted cheese fried steak sandwich with onions and not to mention the hula- hoop onion rings that I always like to get.

"Lord, why you doing this to me?" I'm thinking. Stupid me, I shouldn't have come way down here anyway. I put myself in this position. I guess I'll find me a seat anyway. Maybe this will help me discipline myself better in the future. I'm sitting right beside two people and one is eating my favorite hula-hoop onion rings with a fat juicy burger, and the other one has that combo that I always get. It's the smothered chicken fried steak with white gravy, corn on cob with butter on top, and your choice of either french fries or baked potato. I see right now that me and this diet ain't gon' get along. I'm too embarrassed to take out the salad I brought. It has some sliced bits of ham on top of it. I also have some French Salad Dressing in a bowl covered up with foil. I only brought about five crackers when I should've brought two boxes as hungry as I am.

It took three minutes to eat that entire salad. Sad to say, I'm still hungry. Salads aren't made to stick to you like a big juicy steak is, they're only supposed to take the appetite away. Right now I'll take that big juicy steak. I laughed to myself. See that's why you can't make a vow to do something cause' the Lord will test you every time. And I know He's testing me right now. To be honest, I'm about to lose! I can't take it anymore!

I've only been on this diet for two days. Ok I lose, I'm going to the counter and order my favorite combo I love. The one with the smothered chicken fried steak with white gravy and you know I want the baked potato. I was thinking, what am I going to drink? I need some water but I'll get a diet coke instead.

I ate all that in ten minutes. I'm sorry Lord, I let you down. But at least I'm full.

Going back upstairs was so difficult cause' I ate so much that I'm now miserable. I've made up in my mind that I'm not going to be in a good mood for the rest of the day. This is the reason why I can't get a date now. I feel so ugly and nasty. I've been on this diet for two days and lost three pounds, but gained it all back a few minutes ago in the cafeteria. How weak can I be?

As I walked in the office, Mr. Kevin is standing in front of my desk raising his wrist up at me and looking at his watch and back at me. "You're five minutes late woman! What cha' eat, a whale?!" He burst out laughing.

I can choke him. I thought, as I watched him go back into his office. I really don't care because I've made up in my mind that the rest of my day is not going to be good.

About two hours later, the door opens which isn't nothing unusual because Monday's are always slow. So I'm not going to even look to see who's coming in they probably have the wrong door anyway. That happens often.

"Are you going to ask if I need any help?" This deep dark voice asked.

I can't even look up. This voice is so deep. Before I look I'm praying that he looks as good as he sounds. Just because he sounds good don't mean he looks good. And just because he looks good don't mean he is good. Looks can be deceiving.

"Are you going to ask me if I need any help?" He asked again.

When I looked up, I fainted right on the floor.

When I came to, all I can see is these long dark hands dabbing my face with a damp towel. Mr. Kevin's standing right there waiting on something to say. But to my surprise he's not saying anything.

"Here I'll help you up." He put one hand on my waist and the other underneath my arm pits, and pulled me up.

I'm thinking to myself, if he can lift me as full as I am, I probably weigh nine hundred pounds after eating all that food.

"What's your name?"

"O' you talkin' to me?" I asked. I knew he was talking to me. It's like I'm speechless and I can't talk. He quickly sat me back in my chair.

"Are you sure you alright?" He asked, impatiently.

"O' yea', I'm alright." Trying to sit up in the chair.

"You still haven't told me your name?"

"My name is Ramona, Ramona Williams. And yours?"

"Tyrome is my name. Tyrome Jenkins."

Mr. Kevin is back in his office. I guess he saw that I was alright and left.

"Can you tell me what suite KGR and Associates is located?"

"Right here." I said without hesitation. "Right here, you're in the right place. Can I help you with something?" I asked.

"Yes I'm here for an interview with umm'… Mr. Kevin?" He said holding a piece of paper close to his face, looking at it as if he couldn't spell Mr. Kevin's name.

"Yes that's correct. I'll call him for you." I said, picking up the phone and dialing Mr. Kevin's extension.

While paging Mr. Kevin, I want so badly to tell him to hire him right on the spot. I don't even care what position he's here for. "He'll be right with you. Why don't you have a seat right over there." I pointed towards the empty chairs across the room. "What position are you applying for may I ask?"

"I'm applying for the treasurer position in the other branch on Faye Street." He followed my instructions and walked and sat down in the set of empty chairs across the room.

"That's not too far from here." I told him.

I'm melting away little by little at the sound of his voice. He has his head down and is now reading a magazine he just picked up from the side table. Now I have a chance to really get a good look at him. His skin is like smooth dark chocolate and he's wearing a suit that fits just right. Chestnut brown would be the color that describes his beautiful eyes over-shadowed by two bushy eyebrows that has no form to them. His hair is jet black with rippling waves running all over it. He looks as if he works out on a regular basis. With those running back shoulders how could a pro team have ever past him by. I see we have something in common, both of our lips are big. Only difference is, his is surrounded by his smooth goatee. I smiled at the thought. I can't really see how big his feet are because the corner of my desk is in the way. I'm not attracted to men with big feet. "But he's so handsome." I whispered to myself. I know this guy wouldn't want an over grown hippo like me anyway.

Mr. Kevin comes out by this time and motioned for Mr. Jenkins to go into his office.

After being in the office for what seemed like an hour, they both are coming out laughing and talking about something I probably don't want to know about. One of those man things I guess. I must of had this funny look on my face because Mr. Kevin is looking at me crazy. Which ain't nothing new.

"Why you lookin' all ugly in the face?!" Mr. Kevin yells at me.

Out of nowhere Mr. Jenkins speaks up and says, "I think she's very attractive."

Mr. Kevin's looking at him with amazement and I'm shocked. I have to be honest, I didn't think men found me attractive. And God knows what Mr. Kevin's thinking, I won't even go there. I'm looking like I just won a million dollars.

"Thank you for your time and I'll be there bright and early tomorrow morning." Mr. Jenkins said while walking out of the office.

Mr. Kevin turned and looked at me and said, "Don't get cho' hopes up, he's way out cho' league. He's a married man and no he's not saved! Everybody ain't so call saved like you Miss. Perfect!"

I couldn't wait for him to walk out of the office so I could pray. *"Lord, I can't take him anymore. I don't like the way he treats me and the evil things he says to me. It's hard trying to do the right thing when you have nothing but wrong all in your face everyday. It's hard being a Christian. I understand it's all for the love of Jesus, but I love You so much that I don't care what Mr. Kevin says about me I realize it's not him I should be mad at, it's satan and those spirits inside of him that causes him to act the way he does. Please allow him to experience Your saving, healing, and delivering power. In Jesus Name, Amen."*

I opened my eyes and looked at the clock, noticing that it's now fifteen after five. I had been praying and forgot all about the time. "I got to get out of here." I rushed out of the office. Traffic don't seem too bad today. It's still a little crowded on the freeways.

Thinking about what Mr. Jenkins said to me earlier brought a smile to my face. It really changed my whole day around. I was determined to have a bad day after lunch, but he made me feel like I have a chance at being an attractive woman again. I have to admit, he looked that good that I can't get him off my mind. I can't help it. I wonder what a nice looking man like him see in me? I mean. I haven't gotten' a compliment like that in years. The radio's jumping with some gospel music! All I listen to is gospel. I love how they do those back to back favorites. My head's bobbin' to the beat as the traffic's starting to move at a constant pace. It's something about Christian music. Just frees my mind from a bunch of worry.

When I got home, I slept the entire night excited about seeing the next day.

Chapter 4

Today couldn't be better! The last time I've been this excited on a Tuesday was when I found five dollars on the ground by my car. That was a trip! It's funny how everybody gets all pumped up when they find some money I guess because money is so hard to come by. Well, it found me that day.

I'm already up way before the alarm. Picking out my clothes is not hard because I laid them out last night ironed and all. I'm thinking about what Mr. Kevin said about Mr. Jenkins being married and not saved. It's like all the good looking men are either married, got a pile of kids from different women, or either their gay. And I ain't having that! I'd rather be single than to go through all that drama. I'm still excited about going to the office though. I just want to see him again so he can compliment me and make me feel special like he did yesterday. That is all! I don't mess around with married men, it's morally wrong. It says it in the Bible (1 Corinthians 7:2-3). And he's not saved either, so all the odds are against him. Look at me. I'm over exaggerating, all he did was paid me a lil' ol' compliment and I'm acting like he asked me to marry him.

Traffic is crowded and stressful as usual. I felt so bad about parking in the handicap parking space on yesterday. Something has got to be done about the long walk from the hot garage to the inside elevators. Normally I would complain, but today I feel great and I believe I'm going to have a pretty good day. Considering what happened yesterday, I'm kind of excited to see if he'll show up today. Wait I forgot his name. Let me stop playing. It's Mr. Cutie Pie. Ha! No it's Mr. Jenkins. How'd he ever get a name like that? Anyway, I'm a leave that alone.

Finally arriving at the office, I notice that my desk is piled up with paper work. I don't even care because I know I can't possibly finish all this work in a week let alone in a month. It's funny because I normally see Mr. Kevin already standing in front of my desk screaming to the top of his lungs about me being late and how he's going to fire me. I know I'm on time today and that's something new. O' well, let me go through my normal routine. Nothing! I spoke too soon, here he comes.

"Girl! Why are you just sittin' there! Can't you see you have a lot of work to do?! I get tired of comin' in here to find you not workin'!" He yelled, as he stormed towards my desk.

"Good morning Mr. Kevin. I can see you're having a great day today." I looked up at him.

"Awe' shut up, you just in a good mood cause' ol' boy said that you were attractive yesterday, which I think he's a lie! All he want to do is get in yo' pants! O' but you're Miss. Holy Then Thou, you would never sleep with a married man! Man that's funny!" He laughed all the way back in his office and slammed the door behind him.

I can't believe he just slammed that door right in my face. I take that back I can believe it. It don't matter cause' I'm having a good day and I'm not going to let nobody spoil it. No matter what. Hm'...

Could this guy have really made an impact on me? Could Mr. Kevin be right about me being in a good mood because of him?

It turned out to be a long day at work. Nobody made me mad but I'm disappointed because he didn't come by to say how attractive I am. What am I doing? I'm a saved beautiful woman, and I don't need a man to tell me that I am. I don't need a man to validate me. I wish I mean that. But the God honest truth is, I don't feel good about myself, I don't have any friends, nor do I have a boyfriend to make me feel like a woman. That's okay because God is going to send me the husband of my dreams… I still wish I had at least a guy friend though.

Lord, I had a long day at work today and with the air conditioner not working in this car, don't make it no better. That dog-gone sun is hot and traffic is at a stand still. Somebody must of had a wreck up ahead or something cause' it ain't never been this crowded. Thank God for jumbo towels, I need it to wipe this sweat from my face. One would think I was in an oven hot as it is. It ain't no big thing, I been doing this for years.

"Hey, hey Ramona!" A trebled voice screamed from out of nowhere.

Who is that calling me? I thought to myself.

"Ramona look to yo' leff', it's Mr. Walter from church. Where yo' auntie at?!" He yelled out from the back of a pick-up truck next to the car that was right beside my car.

How in the world did he spot me out in this little bitty car?

"Hey! Where yo' auntie at?! Tella' I'm a call'a when I get to the house!" He yelled again, as the truck sped off as a cloud of black gray smoke spewed from underneath it. It sped off as if it was going to drive right over the cars in front of it but stopped right in time. I couldn't help but laugh and everybody else around me.

Mr. Walter got somebody driving his truck while he's in the back with about thirty men in the back of his 79' pick-up truck. Looks like it hasn't been washed in years. They're all already drinking, you can smell them from a mile away. You would think Mr. Walter knows better but I guess you never know what people be doing when they're not in church. The biggest fakers. They all try to act like perfect saints while in church, but you creep up on them outside of church... Hm'... Thank God I'm saved and don't have to worry about drama like that.

The rest of the ride was pretty calm after I finally got out of the traffic.

Finally I'm home. I thought, as I opened the door to a hot apartment. "Man I forgot to turn on the air conditioner before I left this morning. I can't stand coming home to a hot house." I said to myself, while walking over to the kitchen counter. "Let me check these messages to see who loves me. Yea' right!" Looking at the answer machine I'm just too surprised to see that I have one message. Let me see who this is. I thought smiling to myself.

"Hey girl long time no talk too. I haven't seen you in ages! Anyway, I'm back in town to stay. I'll give you the details when you call me back! My number is 448-9132. Peace out my chick!..." click.

"I can't believe it, that's Michelle Jackson. I know that voice anywhere! I haven't seen her in over eight years! I didn't know what had happened to her." I said to myself while walking over and opening up the refrigerator.

Hm', I wouldn't have been surprised if something did happen because she was so wild. But she's the only friend, well associate I ever had. Like I said before, she was always able to get the good jobs though. I envied that because I used to burst my butt trying so hard to find a good job, and she would come right in and get hired just like that. Maybe because she was a size zero and knew

40

how to flaunt her stuff to get what she wanted. Not to mention she was kind of cute. And me, I had all the odds against me. One was, I was big and wasn't the cutest thing, but I wasn't the ugliest thing either.

I guess I'll get settled first and then call her back. She must be staying with her grandmother because her mother committed suicide when she was six. She was a drug addict. Last time I heard, her grandmother's phone got cut off. That was eight years ago. One thing I didn't like about Michelle was that she would get good paying jobs and wouldn't ever help her grandmother. And when she knew her grandmother's phone got cut off, she didn't even try and help get it cut back on. Selfish girl. They stayed in the projects on the south side of town. But one thing about it, she show took care of all her boyfriends. I always felt that that was wrong. This would make anybody mad, her grandmother had high blood pressure and a lot of times she would get sick worrying about Michelle because she wouldn't always come home. But she always managed to succeed. I had to admit, I hated it! I would try so hard to get a good paying job, but it was like nothing positive would come out of it. I'm not just talking about job's either, I'm talking about with everything. I could never understand that… And I still can't… Maybe I never will… I walked to the bathroom and ran some bath water.

This water sure feels good. Nice, warm, and relaxing! I got some of that bath and bubble works! I know it ain't the name brand stuff, but it all works the same. I wonder what Mr. Jenkins is doing? I giggled.

"Now I know that's not that phone ringing, I just got in the tub and I sure don't feel like getting out! I'll just let the answering machine pick it up. People don't understand when you're tired and don't feel like being bothered! But no they got to let the

41

phone ring a thousand times before they hang up!" I yelled as I jumped out of the tub at three hundred pounds, grabbed a towel from the rack, and ran into the kitchen to look at the caller ID. It took me bout' a good minute to get there. I'm the type that has to be covered at all times. Unlike most people, they can walk all over the house naked and it wouldn't even matter to them.

"The caller ID says it's Michelle. She's the only one who will let it ring this long anyway. "Hello?" I asked. Out of breath from running to the phone. Feels like I got asthma. From the bathroom to the living room is further than I thought it was. And I know this apartment's not that big. I normally don't get phone calls so this must be very important.

"Hey girl! O' you wasn't gon' call me back? And what took yo' a@% so long to answer the phone?!" She screamed.

"Who, who is this?!" Pretending like I didn't know who it was. Still out of breath from running.

"Girl this Michelle! You done forgot about me already?" She asked, as her voice changed to a more settled tone.

"Hey girl, no I didn't forget about you. I just got home from work and wanted to get settled before I called you back, cause' I knew we would be on the phone for a while."

"Cut the bull. So what's been going on girl? I haven't seen yo' butt in eight years. So have you lost weight or what?"

I'm about to hang up in this girl's face. She's always made rude remarks ever since high school. I should've known she hadn't changed. "Girl now you know I haven't lost no weight, you wrong for asking me that." I answered, while dropping down on the couch.

"Well, do you have a man?"

"No Michelle, I do not have a man either." She's starting to make me mad like she used to eight years ago.

"Okayyyy, where are you working at?" She asked, never missing a breath.

"Why are you quizzing me?!" I shouted with frustration. I can't believe I just did that. I have never been able to defend myself from her maybe that's why she used to pick at me so much. "I work at KGR and Associates in downtown."

"Are you on the eighteenth floor?!" She screamed to the top of her lungs with excitement. It was so loud I had to remove my ear from the phone.

"Yea, how'd you know that?" I answered in shock.

"Girl I got a job at Concept Designers. You know that big time graphic design firm on the fifty-fifth floor at the Sky Towers building? That's the same building your at. I saw your name at the information desk under your company's name. But I didn't know if that was you or not. Girl guess how much I'm going to be making?!" She asked, raising her squeaky voice.

See that's what I've been talking about, she always gets the good jobs.

"Hey, are you going to answer my question?" She blurted back in before I could answer.

"O' yea' girl, how much will you be making?"

"My starting salary will be seventy five G's a year, and will increase every year after that." She was so excited her voice trembled.

I'm about to lose my religion. I can't believe this Lord, I'm your child and I'm only making nineteen thousand a year. What's up with that? I thought You want your people to be prosperous?

"Are you happy for me?" She slowly asked.

"O' yea' girl that's a blessing you startin' out makin' that much. How did you find out about the job?" I said, lowering my voice a little. I'm trying not to let her know I'm some what discouraged and kind of disappointed.

"I got hooked up while I was in Chicago. I was talking to this guy there. He's the manager of the company and he hooked me up if you know what I mean." She said. You could tell she was smiling by the tone of her voice.

"Girl you still wild, I thought you had changed."

"You know me, I probably won't ever change especially not while this is working for me. I can get anything I want. You want me to hook you up?" She had the nerve to ask.

"No thank you. I love my job, and plus I like getting things the right way cause' that way don't last." I got up, walked to the window, opened the blinds, and came and sat back down on the couch.

"Whatever, do you want to go out tonight?"

"Now you know I don't go out."

"Awe' come on chick, you know I always went to professional clubs. I'm not going to stick you out there."

"Yea' you're right and so?" I said, sarcastically.

"So what's up? I ain't seen you in eight years. I just want us to kick it like ol' times. I know I used to say and do some really mean things in the past, but I've changed from all that."

Maybe she's right, but somehow I still don't trust her. She used to be real manipulative and controlling. But then again she's really the only friend I've ever had. Maybe I'll give it a try.

"What cha' say girl?" She asked, excited.

"Now you know I'm a Christian?" I said, walking back to the bathroom.

"There will be Christians there."

"I mean it Michelle!" I said, raising my voice.

"I mean it too, it's not like everybody there is going to be having sex. Some will be dancing, some will be talking, and some will be drinking. But you don't have to indulge yourself in all that. Just go dance and have a good time. Christians need to have fun too, and you know I'll be doing my thang'! So get in where you fit in!" She said talking and laughing at the same time.

"I'm sure you will... Yea', I guess I'll go. What time are you talking?"

44

"O' we can leave about eleven thirty. Of course the club don't start jumpin' til' about twelve thirty. But that'll give us time to talk and catch up on old times." She answered quickly.

"Alright girl, and you better not leave me when we get there." I said reminding her of how she used to do.

"Now you know I'm not gon' do that silly girl. How do I get to your house crazy?" Her voice faded away as if she removed her mouth from the phone.

"I live at 1342 Holly Rd. number 431. Do you remember your way around town?" I asked, as if she'd never lived here before.

"Do I remember? You just be ready at eleven thirty. Do your apartments have a security gate?"

"Yea but it's always broke so don't worry bout' calling when you get here. Just come through the back gate, trust me it's open." I laughed to myself.

"Okay I'm out chick, see you then."

"Alright, bye." I said, as we both hung up the phone.

That girl haven't changed a bit. She's still crazy. I got upset at the salary she'll be making but after hearing how she got it makes me real thankful for my job. Lord, please forgive me for saying what I said earlier. And forgive me if I'm going against Your will by going to the club. I'm just going to have a good time, that's all! You know my heart and that's all that matters. I got back in the tub, soaked for awhile, then got out.

Okay let's see what I'm going to wear. I want to make sure all my flesh is covered. I'm thinking, I probably won't have a good time anyway. And I probably won't see anybody I know either. I guess I'll wear this pink and green outfit that one of my sorority sisters gave me when I was in college. It's funny because, I remember when people would ask me how did I become one because of how big I am, and I would simply say, yes, big women can be a part of sororities too. Most of the time it was funny because I looked at how stupid it was for them to ask me that. But all that took place before I got saved. A lot has changed since then. Thank God!

North Cloud University wasn't a bad school I guess, until they started taking all my money. Thank God for financial aid. And thank God that He blessed me to graduate with honors. It helped me with my self-esteem. I actually felt like I could accomplish something. Momma and Daddy were very proud. Some may ask why I don't have a good paying job since I got a degree. Well, it's not the degree's fault, it's my fault. I'm not brave enough to go out and get a good paying job like Michelle is. But the difference between she and I is that I get my jobs the right way. I also learned that just because you have a degree doesn't mean that you will get a high paying job after you graduate, let alone getting one at all. Things happen. That's why it's very important to watch what you choose as a career. Some of them can't do nothing for you. But that's what life is, trial and error. I'm not trying to see mine like that though. I want to be rich one day. So I can bless the church, bless my family, bless the poor, bless myself, and bless the world! And one day it will all happen, I just got to keep on believing! I yelled within.

This outfit fits a little snug but it will have to do. Let me see, where's my favorite pinkish cream pumps? O', there they go. This is going be cute. Now I know that phone's not ringing again? I never had this many phone calls in one day. I thought smiling to myself. "Hello? O' hey Momma, what are you doing?" Not surprised that she called, cause' she calls all the time asking me when I'm going to go out and meet somebody, get married so she can get some grand kids. Typical mother for you.

"Why are you soundin' so chipper?" She asked concerned.

"Because I'm goin' out tonight."

"You goin' out?! Ha! I can't believe this, wait til' I tell your Daddy, he's gon' flip out!" She screamed to the top of her lungs.

"Where is Daddy?" I asked, as she brought her tone down.

"He's at work; you know he works at night now. They changes his hours around too much for me. But anyway, who you goin' with? You done found a boyfriend finally? Momma's po' baby." She said lowering her voice to a whisper.

"No Momma, please don't start with the pity parties. Hey! You won't believe whose back in town?"

"Who?" She asked.

"Michelle!"

"Michelle? Umph' where have she been?"

I know when Momma's tone changes and her conversation gets serious, that tells me she's not pleased with something. "In Chicago. And that's who I'm goin' out with tonight."

"You better be careful, you know how she used to do you along time ago." She said.

"I know Momma but Jesus said to love everybody despite what they say and do to you. You also taught me that."

"I know baby, but I just don't want her to hurt you like she used too. It's been years so hopefully she's changed."

"Alright Momma let me go and finish gettin' ready and I'll call and tell you what happened tomorrow." I said, walking towards the kitchen to get me some water from the frig.

"Okay babe, bye. I love you."

"Bye, I love you too Momma." I said, as we both hung up the phone.

I looked at the clock and can't believe its eleven fifteen and Michelle is supposed to be here in about fifteen minutes. I need to see how I'm going to fix this hair. Time seems to pass so fast when you're running late. I didn't realize I was on the phone that long.

Now I know that's not Michelle knocking at the door, she's fifteen minutes early. Let me just pin my hair up real quick. "Coming!" I shouted as if she could hear me from way in the room. My room from the front door is about a good fifteen feet, not including all the mazes from the furniture I have to walk through just to get to the door.

Opening up the door and looking at Michelle, I feel like a big whale compared to her. She's gorgeous! She lost some more weight off of that size zero body she already had.

"Well aren't you going to give me a hug and let me in?!" She shouted. She smiled so hard you could see all thirty-two teeth.

"Hey girl! Long time no see!" I shouted, while looking her up and down trying to find something wrong with her but couldn't. I feel like bursting in tears as we both reached to hug one another.

"Yea', I know! Girl you did lose some weight, look at cha'!" She smiled, looking me up and down.

I can't believe it, she actually paid me a compliment. I can see where she's changed, at least so far. "You think so? I've been dieting." I said, closing my eyes and raising my head up towards the ceiling.

"You sure are doing a good job!" She held my arms up while looking me up and down again.

"Thanks! Are you ready to go?" I asked, walking towards the room to turn off the light.

"Girl now you know I'm ready to get my groove on!" She said, following me to cut on the lamp by the sofa.

"I'm ready too, just not ready for this kind of groove." I said, as we both walked out together.

Michelle has a spanking brand new fully loaded candy apple red convertible Mercedes Benz. Typical for a girl like her. She has her convertible top down and we're ready to roll.

The sky line is so beautiful. The clouds are scattered in random order. They all seem to have this shinny glow to them. Peace is what I feel. If you've never felt God's Spirit, you can look up to the sky and actually experience Him for yourself. The wind is blowing across my cheeks and through my eyes. An eternal dream can only be the answer. It's more than a glamour girl in Hollywood. And more solid than any greatest football player that have ever lived. God's presence is just that awesome! To be honest, a look in the sky just won't do.

"Girl you're acting like you don't come out at night." She said, turning the corner with one finger on the steering wheel.

"Huh'? What did you say? O' girl I really don't be going nowhere." I answered, thinking if she only knew where my mind is right now.

The scenery quickly changed as we finally pulled up in the parking lot of the club. I feel somewhat uncomfortable but I'm determined to have a good time anyway. Let me stop kidding myself. I'll just go in and sit down while Michelle gets all the guys and have such a fabulous time.

As we walked in, the music quickly got my attention. Not because of what's playing, but because it's so loud. I'm not surprised though, I had already imagined that it would be this way before we got here. They're a lot of people here. All different kinds of shades of colors everywhere. Some Black, some Caucasian, some Chinese, some Hispanic, and some even mixed with many different races put together. It's nice to see all these different colors cramped up in this building like a can of sardines. I thought, smiling to myself. Michelle was right when she said that it's a very classy jazzy club.

"Wow, there's some big time people here girl." I said, looking around.

"Just like I told you, I don't go to no trashy clubs! You can't meet a rich man at no boot-leg club!" She shouted over the music as we walked further inside.

The music is so loud I can't even hear myself think. Just think some of these people do this every week. Poor ears ought to be ruined. People are dancing, talking, and some even drinking just like Michelle said they would be doing. After being here for a minute, I'm not feeling so uncomfortable anymore. I guess because I realize I don't feel pressured to get a drink. I only feel pressured to have a good time. And not to mention, the music's not so bad after all. But something in the back of my mind is saying: "Don't be luke warm…" I hope I'm doing the right thing.

Michelle spotted this empty booth from way across the room that over looks the dance floor. You can tell she's a pro at this. I never would have spotted it even if I had been standing right in front of it. But Michelle is more out going than I am anyway. And her body shows it. With her size zero waist line, hair layered down her back, make-up so perfectly done, you would think she went to school for it. Not to mention those six inch heels and short leathered skirt outfit she's wearing that would turn any man's head. Most men would say she got curves or babe got back. I guess that's why most women envy her. I'm sure I can be added to the group cause' just looking at her sometimes makes me sick to my stomach. And I know God created everybody different but I guess I haven't gotten' to that point of view yet. Which is another reason why I'm not uncomfortable anymore because I see some big women are representing tonight. Even though I wouldn't wear what their wearing, but it feels good to see that I'm not alone.

"Girl are you going to talk to me or what?! You haven't said two words in over fifteen minutes!" She said, shouting from across the table.

"Um'… O'! I was just checking out the scenery, trying to see who I want to approach first!" I said, shouting as I looked into the crowd.

"For real?! I didn't know you had it in you?!" She said, smiling as she reached over and looked in her little strap over purse.

If she only knew. I probably won't move from this seat for the rest of the night. I've basically made up in my mind that she's going to have all the fun anyway. So I'm preparing myself for the upset. And maybe that's why I'm faking so hard.

"Hey girl, you wanna' virgin drink?!" She grabbed a ten dollar bill from her wallet.

"Yea sure just as long as it's virgin!" I shouted back smiling.

"Okay, I'll be right back chi'!" She shouted, as she got up from the table and walked away. I can see some very handsome men checking her out. I shouldn't expect her back any time soon. If I know Michelle, she'll probably be gone for the entire night leaving me here all by myself just like she used to do.

Blue and red lights are flashing so bright you would think the cops were here to take us all in. I don't know what I would do if I was to get put in jail. I've never been, and don't plan on ever going.

Everybody's getting their mingle on and poor me left out once again. I don't know what's taking Michelle so long to come back with the drinks. I should've known she wasn't going to come right back. She always used to do this to me that's why I didn't used to like going anywhere with her. Shoot my butt is starting to hurt. All that food I ate at lunch is doing something terrible to my stomach. Maybe that's the punishment for cheating on my diet.

I don't know why my mind just went to Mr. Jenkins and how he gave me such a wonderful compliment the other day. I was kind of hoping I would see him again. He probably wouldn't even notice me. Basically I just want him to say to me again what he said the other day. That's all! Nothing more! I don't fool with married men and not to mention he's not saved either? Not a chance in this world!

"Is anyone sitting here?" This prodigiously deep voice penetrated through my ears and was somewhat recondite. It had this hidden treasure quality of a gold mind that could only be secretly found in somebody's heart. Then going straight to my imagination. But before all that can happen, I must see how he looks. I've got to hear him say something else. If I never see how he looks, I would be satisfied with just getting to know that voice. Shoot! It's hard being saved! Nah', I take that back! I thought smiling.

"I said is someone sitting here?" He asked again. This time a little impatient.

"No! No one's sitting here." I said, looking up to match this astonishing voice with this astonishing face. O' my God, I can't believe it's him! It's Mr. Jenkins! I can't believe my eyes it's really him. I hope I'm looking alright. Knowing me, I'm probably looking tore up from the floor up! I thought grinning a little.

"Where do I know you from? O' yea', that's right, you're that beautiful secretary I met at KGR and Associates! That was the same day Mr. Kevin hired me!" He shouted over the music.

I am in ah'! I can't believe that he remembered me so clearly. He remembered where he met me and everything.

"Um', yes, you're exactly right!" I answered, shouting over the loud music. I can hardly talk for looking into his chestnut brown eyes. And not to mention those beautiful white teeth. They're sparkling every time he opens up his mouth. And not one tooth is out of place. Some men just don't care though, they'll come up to you with yellow caked up teeth with a little piece of lettuce in between and try to talk right in your face. Looking like an uncle Jetthro'. I know everybody got an uncle Jetthro' in their family who tries to talk to everybody no matter if there kin or not. How gross! I thought, laughing to myself. This is the kind of stuff that most Christians think cause' most try to act like they've been saved all their lives and never had not one bad thought to run across their little bitty minds. NOT! Don't even try it! Keep it real! I mean don't get me wrong I'm saved, but I too have to tell my flesh to die daily(1 Cor. 1:29, 15:31). I too have to be cleansed and purged so that I can be pleasing in the sight of God (Psalms 51). This is actually the reason why I was created, to serve Him and not myself or others. I thought, looking around to see if anybody noticed me pondering and hoping they don't see this solemn expression on my face.

But anyway, back to those teeth. Perfect. Just perfect. And he has a good grade of hair too. The club lights are reflecting off of every wave he has on his head. It's gorgeous! I can tell he takes good care of it. This is natural stuff and not some kind of wave kit either. He looks better than when I saw him the first time. I didn't really get a good look at him considering the circumstances that happened that day. But something about him tonight just seems different. By looking I can't really tell how tall he is. One thing's for sure, he's towering over me like he's at least six nine or something close to it.

"Are you going to let me sit down?" He asked, as if he had been waiting for several hours.

"Sure you can!" I reached my arm in the direction of the seat across from me.

The music is starting to take over. I can feel myself bobbing to the beat. I kind of want him to ask me to dance. I haven't danced in years. Especially since I got saved. Everybody seems to be having such a good time. There's nothing that would make me feel uncomfortable now. Some Christians would say that I'm a backslider cause' I'm here at the club, but I beg to differ. I don't know. Maybe. What ever I'm just having fun.

"I can't believe your sitting across from me?" He said.

"Why not?" I asked.

"Because I never see anybody from my job. The last time I saw you, you fainted on the floor and all I remembered next was saying how attractive you were!" He said, still shouting over the loud music.

Now I know he's not trying to charm this dress right off of me? He did look cute saying it though. Giggling to myself. And I must say that it felt good hearing the compliment again. I thought as I smiled to myself.

It feels weird to hear somebody say something sweet to me. I always thought I would pass through this world not ever being a part of someone's life; nor feeling special because of the sweet words that someone could ever say to me. At one point I wouldn't believe them because of how negative my life as been with men. They never looked my way. And the names they would call me, I'll never forget. In my dreams I saw myself killing every last one of them. But that was because of the anger and unforgiveness I had in my heart. Thank God I'm passed that now. There were so many things that used to run through my mind. I can't recall all of them, and most I choose not to because of the pain of remembering is just too much. I know within myself I need more deliverance. But one thing's for sure, I'm definitely not in denial. The night I accepted God as my Lord and Savior, was one that I'll never forget. Anybody who is truly a Christian knows exactly what I'm talking about. I'm sure there are some that have forgotten where the Lord have brought them from. It's funny, sarcastically, because if you ask them what have the Lord done for them lately, they would simply tell you either, I don't know or nothing, or let me think about it. And I fail to understand why those that don't go to church try and label those who are going to be perfect. I'm far from perfect. In fact, I experience more of the devil's tricks than I did before I accepted the Lord into my life. I wish people would stop judging and just pray for each other; and realize that once we accept Him as our Lord and Savior, we are a threat to the devil because he doesn't own us anymore. And he's going to try anything he can to destroy us. But the good news is that he can't touch us because we are God's children and we are covered by the Blood of Jesus. And no devil in Hell can touch us. That's why God gave us His Whole Armour so that we can stand against the strategies and tricks of satan which is what I'm trying to do (Ephesians 6:11-19). But I don't know if I'm doing a good job or not because I'm in this club. I thought.

"Why are you so quiet? I came over here because I saw this fine sexy lady sitting all by herself and I decided to come and talk to her. But look, I can leave if I'm taking up space? You seem like you're enjoying your thoughts more than me anyway." He got up from the table as if he was about to walk off.

"No! Don't leave I am enjoying your company. I guess I was just wondering what was keeping my home-girl. She was supposed to be going to get us some drinks and she hasn't come back yet. I'm gettin' a little worried about her." I hope he'll change his mind about leaving. I feel bad about the little lie I just told. I'll repent later. I'm glad he can't read my mind. I'm trying not to burst out laughing.

"I guess I can understand that. How long has she been gone?" He sat back down on the bench across from me, putting both of his arms on the table.

"Well, she's been gone about forty-five minutes." I said, pretending as if I was really worried. If I know Michelle, she's probably sitting some where with another guy watching us and laughing.

"Man, you a really good friend. Most wouldn't even be worried. I can buy you a drink if you like, or do you want to wait for yo' friend?" He raised his voice as the music got louder.

"O' no! I would love for you to buy me a drink." I smiled.

"What chu' havin'?"

"I'll have a virgin strawberry daiquiri!" I shouted back as the music changed to another song.

"Aright, I'll be right back!" He got up from the table and walked towards the bar.

My eyes were fixed on him until he vanished into the crowd. All I can see is this tall dark tower. I just can't believe what I'm seeing. He got to be about six-nine or something like that. He has these set of arms that's as big as a body builder. His muscles pushed outward every time he moved them. And he don't have this feeble lil' chest either. Very toned and well put together. With his tan slacks, silky emerald green button down shirt with tan designs in it to match, and rounded off with some black boots. The cologne he's wearing smells like a fresh man straight out of the shower. It had this sweet but musk smell that I love. Lord please have mercy on my soul. I bet-cha' Michelle is somewhere with a nicer looking man. I'm sure I'll envy her when she's taking me home and tells me that she met some police officer or some engineer. Everything's so perfect with her. From her men, to her figure, to her line of work, and I'm sure more than I even know about. It truly shows that men cater towards women that are size zeros before they would a woman that's a size fifteen or sixteen. Or even bigger than that for that matter.

"Hey, do you want cha' drink or not?" He said, as he placed the drinks down on the table and sat down across from me.

"Of course I want my drink, thank you." I answered grabbing the cold drink and taking a sip.

One thing I'm noticing about him is that he likes all the attention. And he also likes to pick with you. I guess that could be a good thing. I've always been able to feel things about people before they would tell me. Good and bad. My Momma always told me that I have a gift from God. Some would call it psychic, but I call it prophesy. Which is a gift that only God can give (1 Corinthians 12:10). And my Pastor also confirmed it in one of his sermons one Sunday. He said that I have a calling on my life. I know somehow that that is supposed to play a huge roll in my life. But sometimes I wonder because it's like nobody likes me. I've never done anybody wrong. I love everybody and I long to be of help to everybody. And if I'm supposed to have this special assignment, somebody has to like me sometime or another. I know God has much in store for me.

I've learned when people talk about you and treat you mean for nothing, that means that you're someone special. The devil's not going to mess with you if you're not a threat. And I believe that more and more as the days go by.

"There you go being quiet again, am I that boring?"

"Huh? O' no, you're not boring. I just daydream a lot."

"Why do you need to daydream when you have me sittin' here?" He asked.

"It's not that at all. It's just that I've been doing it for so long that it's kind of a habit." I answered.

"What?! I don't understand that?!" He shouted over the music as it got louder.

"Look I'm kind of like a loner. I've never had any friends so I'm used to talking to myself and daydreaming because of not having anybody to talk too." I took the straw, stirred my cold icy drink, and took a long sip.

"I understand, but you say you don't have any friends, but what about your home-girl you came here with? I thought you said you and her were close?" He took a sip of his drink. "Look I'm not tryin' to pry in yo' business."

"Trust me, you're not. She's the only friend I have and sometimes I wonder if that's true." I said. I'm thinking, this man sure does ask a lot of questions. Kind of nosy.

"What does she do that would make you wonder if she was yo' friend or not?" He bewilderedly asked.

"Look, now, you gettin' too personal, I don't even know you to be telling you all my business." I looked out towards the crowd.

"Hey look, as I said before, I don't wanna' sound like I'm pryin' in yo' business but I really don't understand?" He said, with a little smirk on his face.

"Okay, look, after I explain this I hope this'll be the end of your curiosity. As a child I've had bad luck with friends. They never really wanted to be my friend and I never did anything to them. So to make a long story short, I've been by myself practically all of my life. So that's why you may wonder why I'm day-dreaming so much. And two, I never had anybody that I could actually open up to and talk too. Trust me you don't want to be feeling what I'm feeling right now."

"I understand now, you can talk to me though?" He said, smiling as he stretched his opened hands towards me as if he wanted me to put my hands with his.

"Look I don't know you to be talking all my business too." I said, as I drew my hands back so he couldn't grab them.

"That's fine maybe someday if you give me a chance to see you again?" He asked, looking confident as if he knew I would agree.

Deep down inside I really want to but he's looking too confident I need to make him wait. "Well, I'm just gon' have to think about that." I said, hoping he wouldn't say whatever and walk off into the foggy atmosphere.

I guess my biggest fear is being alone. Shoot I'm tired of being alone. Maybe he can become a good friend and nothing more. I thought.

"Yea' I guess we'll see about that, hum." He answered back with all the confidence in the world. By this time the music slowed way down. He has this look on his face as if he wants to ask me to dance. He's staring me straight in my eyes, but somehow I can't stare back. Which is weird. I'm asking myself, why am I wasting my time? Maybe it's because I need a friend. A woman has needs too. I don't know, he seems so nice and he was the first guy to give me such an unforgettable compliment. I've never had a man to sincerely say something like that to me and mean it. Maybe he just want to be my friend too. Everybody needs a friend. "Hey! I guess you day-dreaming again. You wanna' dance?" He asked, still looking straight into my eyes.

"Um', well, not really." I answered.

"Sounds like to me you don't know what you wanna' do. Come on, you'll be alright. I'll take good care of you. Is it that you can't dance?" He got up from his seat.

"Well, yes! That's what it is. I can't dance." I quickly answered, hoping he would get the picture that I felt uncomfortable dancing to secular music. I don't know why I just can't tell him that I'm saved and that God has changed my life from all that?

"I don't believe that! I think you just tryin' to play hard to get. Come on girl let me sweep you off yo' feet!" He grabbed my hand and pulled me up out of my seat towards him.

I can't say a word. My mouth won't open up for nothing in this world. Looking into those beautiful light brown eyes of his made my body num. The smell of his cologne would drive any woman crazy. Not to mention how handsome he is. I'm enjoying just being this close to him. This is all new to me, but somehow it feels so right. I can't lie, I'm lonely but I'll live and repent later.

"So are you ready?" He pulled me closer to him.

"Yes, I'm ready." I answered back.

He turned and guided me to the dance floor. It was a maze just getting there. It's so crowded. They're all kinds of aromas in the air. Some smell okay, while others smell like they need to shower before they leave the club. And it's hot too. Lord! I'm actually holding my nose. All and all, this is a nice club though, and the environment is very professional and clean. I really like it. But somehow, I can still hear God telling me to leave. It's so much action going on in here. Looking up, I can't help but see this sparkling silver ball hanging from the ceiling, surrounded by red and blue disco lights in the center of the dance floor. All of them are going round and round, seems like to the sound of the music. There's this foggy haze moving towards the ceiling like thousands of misty clouds. Everybody's on the dance floor moving in their own way to the sound of the beat, while Tyrome's pulling me like I'm already his. I have to admit, it feels good and for a moment I feel secure with who I am. I can't lie, I did forget how to dance though. I thought, laughing to myself.

We danced what seemed like forever. Sweat's pouring down my face.

"All the lovers stay on the dance floor for the last song of the night!" The D.J. shouted through the microphone.

The dance floor is packed. Its funny cause' my mind isn't on them, it's on Tyrome. Somehow I feel that that isn't a good thing. He turned my body face to face with his. His breath even smells good. I'm hoping that mine smell the same. I laughed to myself.

He softly whispered to me and said, "I meant every word I said when I first saw you in that office. You were beautiful then, and you're even more beautiful now."

"I really appreciate the compliments and it feels good coming from a handsome man like yourself." I whispered back.

He moved his hand down my back which made me jump because my mind just came back to reality that I'm a saved woman, and I can't fall into sin. I'm not married and the sad thing is that he is. There's really no hope for this to go any further.

"Is somethin's wrong?" He smiled.

"No, nothin's wrong." I smiled back at him.

I can feel the old me trying to rise up and it feels terrible. I'm starting to realize that I'm in the wrong environment and I'm getting very uncomfortable. My flesh is telling me, take him home and have it all night long. Whereas, my spirit is telling me the opposite, get rid of him before he makes you sin. Don't be tricked by satan. I don't have to wonder which voice is the right voice to listen to. But how can I jerk away from this feeling? It feels so good. I'm just going to enjoy the moment; I'll get rid of him later.

His hand suddenly grip the back of my shoulder. I opened my eyes only to notice that we had been so captured by one another, that we didn't notice that the lights were on and almost everybody had vacated the club. A short Hispanic corpulent but brawny guy shouted to us with a Hispanic accent, "Ya'll need to take that outside, we need to close up the club!"

I turned and looked at Tyrome and he motioned for me to walk towards the front door.

Feels like it's 20 degrees below out here. The club was just that hot and I had sweated just that much. People are still standing around talking to one another and playing loud music. I had gotten' so caught up that I forgot that I came to the club with Michelle. And I'm glad too because I had a good time without her. I hadn't seen her all night, which I'm not surprised. I knew she'd leave me just like she used to do a long time ago.

"Can I walk you to your car?" He asked, looking like he want to come home with me.

"Yea', you can." I quickly answered.

"Where's your friend?" He asked, following me in the direction of the car.

I shook my head. "Your guess is good as mine."

We parked along the street which seems like a mile away because when we arrived at the club, the parking lot was already full. It don't matter cause' I'm enjoying just being around him anyway. I've never had anybody so in to me like he is. Compliment after compliment. I hope this never changes. I thought.

The walk to the car seemed like forever, however we finally made it only to realize that nobody was in it.

"Where's your friend?"

"I really don't know."

"Can I take you home?" He smiled, stuffing his hands in his pockets. I threw my hands up in discuss.

"No, I'm sure she's somewhere around here."

If I know Michelle she's probably in some guys car doing something she ain't got no business doing. I wish I had the key's to her car I'd drive off and leave her right with who ever she's with. Anyway, Tyrome could come with me. Wait a minute, I got to get a grip on myself this is not the will of God for me. I've been living right this far. I'm going to keep on doing right. I've saved myself for the right one and that's who I'm going to continue to wait for.

Forty five minutes have gone by.

Here comes Michelle out of nowhere with some nice looking guy. "Girl where have you been?! Are you crazy leaving me out here waiting on you this long?! And why did you lie to me talking about you going to get us some drinks and never coming back?!" I yelled at her. Michelle and I've been friends for a long time and I've never had the courage to stand up to her when she talked to me crazy. Her mouth is wide open. I'm sure it's because of how loud and aggressive I am with her. Hm', tonight is a new night! I'm tired of people talking to me any kind of way and getting away with it! No more will they do this to me!

Maybe it has something to do with Tyrome standing right here. I don't know. Maybe.

"Girl you ain't never came hard on me like this before. I'm shocked. What have you done to this woman?" She turned and frowned at Tyrome as if he had the answer.

He shrugged his shoulders as if to say that he didn't know.

"Anyway it don't matter what he's done! All you need to worry bout' is why you left me in the club and why you left me standing out here all night?! I know you knew this cause' it ain't not one car left in the parking lot! I always wondered if you were really my friend because of the way you have always treated me in the past! And me like a lil' wimp, would never say nothin'! But not, no more! I'm sick of you! And right now I don't even want to be around you let alone even look at you!" I yelled, pointing my finger at her. "Will you take me home?!" I turned and asked Tyrome.

"Yea' sure." He quickly answered as if his life depended on it.

As we turned and walked away towards his car, I didn't hear her say a word. Nor did he say a word.

When we got to his vehicle, all I can see is this huge dark navy blue 2002 Lincoln Navigator, with sparkling chromed rims and dark tinted windows. The light from the moon is sparking off of every grain of the paint. It looks like they sprinkled glitter all over it.

He opened the door for me and closed it after I got all the way in. Before I could reach over and unlock his side, he was already getting in. I forgot about power locks. I've had my 83 Chevrolet for years and ain't never had no working air conditioner or power locks. I don't even think they made power locks back then for this hooptee! I laughed to myself. "Hey, I really like your truck." I said smiling, looking at him for his reaction.

"You like it? Well I tell you what, you can use it anytime you want too." He said, putting the key in the ignition.

The streets are deserted. There's not a car in sight. Things were pretty quiet between us as I showed him the way to my apartments. As we pulled up in the driveway, I see they haven't fixed the security gate yet. These apartments are alright, I don't have no trouble over here everybody pretty much do their own thing. But it's just some things that needs to be straightened up. Like fixing the security gate for one.

"Well here we are. Do you mind if I come in and talk?" He asked.

"No, maybe some other time. I really appreciate the ride though." I answered, grabbing the door handle.

"Are you sure you don't want me to come in?" He grabbed my hand before I could open door to get out.

"Like I said before, maybe some other time but not tonight." I answered, opening up the door, getting out, and closing it behind me.

"When can I see you again?" He asked, raising the passenger window down.

"Sooner than you think." I said, smiling as I turned to walk toward the apartments. "Is there something wrong?" I asked, turning and walking back to the truck to see why he hadn't drove off yet.

"No, just the fact that I want to come in and talk to you and you won't let me." He smiled so hard I could see all thirty-two of his beautiful white teeth.

"Well, I guess you can come in. You're probably not going to leave until I say yes anyway." I stepped back so he could go and park. I admit, I kind of wanted him to come in the first place. Maybe that's why I turned and went back out to the truck. Men have a way of reading women's minds. He knew all the time that

I wanted him to come up to my apartment. I figure this is not no amateur I'm dealing with. This is all man and he knows the right words to say at the right time to make a woman feel good.

He's out of the truck now and walking towards me. The apartments supply us with a lot of light so I'm able to see just where he parked. I stay towards the back of the apartments. It's sort of like a maze from the parking lot to get to my apartment. First you pass four huge trees, walk down three different halls, turn right on the last one, hike up two flights of stairs; and last, walk down one last hall and my apartment is on the left. My neighbors are pretty quiet. Most of the time everybody's in their own world doing their own thing and minding their own business.

"So how far is your apartment?" He asked, walking towards me.

"Not too far, you got cha' tennis shoes on?" We both laughed, turned, and started walking towards my apartment.

I'm glad I cleaned up yesterday. I would be so embarrassed for him to see my dirty place. I thought, as we finally made it to the apartment. Now I see what Momma was talking about when she would say you always want to have your house clean, cause' you never know who's coming. I think that's an old folks saying that goes way back to the grandma's and the grandpa's. Big Momma from North Carolina would get a switch after us if we didn't clean up before we went out to play. That's when you could get whipped without your parents going to jail.

"You have a nice apartment." He said, as I opened the door and closed it as we walked in.

65

"Thank you." I said, motioning for him to sit on the couch while I turn on more lights and the TV. He went and sat down on the love seat and crossed one leg over the other.

"Can I get you something to drink?" I asked, as I sat on the long sofa across from him.

"No that's alright. Hey why don't you come over here and sit with me?" He patted his hand on the couch.

"I hadn't thought about it."

"Do you want me to come over there?" He asked.

"You sure don't give up do you?"

"Nope, I'm not supposed too, I'm a man." He said, as he got up, came over, and sat down beside me on the couch.

"Where do you go to church?" I turned to look at him. I hope this question'll help calm him down some.

"Where'd that come from?"

"I'm just asking you don't mind me asking. Do you?" I smiled.

"No. Not at all. I go to St. Matthews Baptist Church."

"Where is that located?" I asked.

"It's on the south side of town."

Somehow I know he's lying but I'm not going to push it any further. "Can I ask you a question?" I turned my body towards him.

"Come on wit' it." He answered.

"Are you saved?"

"Yes mam' I sure am." He answered, nodding his head yes.

Lord have mercy, if he gets this next question right I'm going to be on cloud nine. I thought, as he scooted away from me and lowered his head.

"To be honest with you it's been along time since I've been back to church. I guess you can say I'm a backslider. It's been just that long. See I'm a foster child and the only life I ever knew was going from house to house. And at every house I experienced some kind of abuse. The worse thing that happened to me was when I was about six years old. I was locked under the kitchen sink for a week with no food. And my father told me if he heard one pot or pan move, he was going to kill me. For my sake I never did. All this happened because one day my room wasn't clean when he got home from work. The only way I was able to get out of that situation was by the school calling looking for me cause' I had missed several days. Shortly after that I was in another home and from there I was going from home to home. I been in a total of thirty-eight different homes. I experienced seeing too much as a kid from watching one of my father's kill one of my mother's right in front of me. It was something that nobody should ever have to see. Blood was everywhere. After he had finished beating her, I ran over to see if she was dead because she wasn't moving. Just as I was about to touch her, he came back in the room with a shot gun and shot and killed her. I'll never forget standing there helpless and scared to death. Not being able to do nothing to help her. I don't think I'll ever be right, I mean on the inside. Sometimes I can still hear the gun shots. That took something out of me. No fool's gon' put their hands on me!" He yelled, as his countenance changed to anger.

Tears and sweat is running down his face. His fist is balled up and he's leaning back and forth as if he's about to explode.

"In another home I was molested by my momma's sister for about three years straight. She used to keep me while my parents went to work. They couldn't get out of the driveway good before she was all over me. She would force herself on me for about three hours. She made a man out of me real early. She would make me do all kinds of stuff and threaten me not to tell anybody and if I did, she would kill me. When she had finished and fell asleep, I would go in the bathroom and throw up until there was nothin' left in my stomach. And because of this experience, I hated women. I saw myself leaning toward men because I was scared that another woman would do me the same way. I had a fear and a hate for women all because of what she had done to me for years. But one night I was asleep on the couch in another foster home. And I heard somethin' fall in the kitchen so I jumped up to see what it was, only to notice that nothing had fallen. As I was walking back towards the couch, I could hear a voice comin' from the TV talkin' bout' letting God deliver you from any sin that has had you trapped or bound. He was sayin' all kinds of stuff like, if you have a problem with sex, God can deliver you. If you've been raped or molested and you haven't let it go, God wants to heal you. And because of this, you're living an immoral life style like, fornication (sex before marriage), or homosexuality (being attracted to or sexual intimacy with the same sex), or even adultery (having sex outside of marriage), and so on. God wants to heal you from this perverted life style (Romans 1:24-32). All sins are the same in the eyes of the Lord. He has no favorites (Romans 2:11). And if you want to be delivered stand to your feet, lift up your hands in total submission! No matter where you are. Here in the station, in your homes, on your jobs, receive your healing...!" He said, demonstrating with his hands and changing his voice to fit there's. "From that night on, I haven't had a feeling for the same sex since. Because of what happened that night I do believe that God can heal you if you let Him." He turned to look at me. "But anyway, things quickly changed after that, I mean I haven't felt for another man but I was still mad on the inside because of all the abuse that I received from home to home. I had been delivered from one thing but there were still so much more that needed to be dealt with. There was a war going on inside my mind. When I hung out with my friends, it didn't take long for me to click. I would beat them up for nothin'. We would go out and gang bang businesses and homes and then go get high to celebrate. Drugs and alcohol was the lick. If you wasn't wit' it, you would either get beat up or popped. Cause' then we would know that you was a snitch. By the time I reached eighteen, I was a mad man." He turned towards the television as if it was me. "I was on my own and didn't have to answer to nobody. Yea' I had a couple of girls from around the way but none of them I got along with. It was hard to get a job cause' my self-esteem was so low which caused my attitude to be bad. I would jump people for nothin', just for a dollar. I was practically homeless and was also a male prostitute. I slept with women twice my age for cheap money. I gotta' admit, I ain't never slept with no young girls and never will. I didn't believe in robbing the cradle. I'm the only child. My biological parents died when I was too young to remember. And they were the only children with both of their parents dead. So I had nobody to depend on after they were gone. That's why they put me in a foster home. The real world helped me grow up fast though. There were a lot of hungry cold nights. I do remember one day walking and hearing these people shouting about some free hot meals. It came from this Baptist church. They were giving away free meals to the needy. And that's the church I ended up joining. But that was two years ago and I haven't been back since." He laid his hands over the back of his neck and pulled his head down in his lap.

"I'm so sorry that all that had to happen to you." I said, as the tears feel from my eyes. Just by looking at this nice looking man nobody would ever think that he had been involved in so much in his life time. I'm shocked. I don't know what to say but thank God for deliverance. And I know God's going to deliver him even more when he gives his life back to Him.

After a moment of silence he reached over and slowly kissed me on the cheek, then on my neck. I can't believe he's doing this. My spirit is telling me to pull back and make him leave. But my flesh is saying let him have his way. This is all new to me. I'm a virgin. I've never been touched like this before. It feels so right and nothing could keep it from being wrong. Lord please let this man leave right now before something bad happens. He's starting to take off my blouse...

69

Thank God the phone just ranged. I thought, as I threw him off of me and quickly reached over to answer it. "He-hello?" I asked, looking back at him.

"Hey Ramona, girl I can't stop thinking about what happened tonight and I just want to apologize for what I did. I know we haven't seen each other in along time and this was supposed to be our celebration night. I was wrong, do you forgive me?" She asked.

I can't believe she's actually calling to apologize to me. She's never done this before. I don't know how to react. "Yea, I forgive you. But just don't do that to me again. It's cool, we still cool."

Tyrome's beeper went off. He looked at the number. "Let me use your phone."

"Hey Michelle, let me talk to you later everything's cool between us."

"Alright, do you wanna' hang out at the park later on today? Everybody hangs out at the park on Sunday evenings."

"Yea' I guess so we'll talk about it later."

"Alright then, bye." She said, as we both hung up the phone.

As I hung up the phone, he quickly reached over and grabbed it out of my hand and went to the other side of the room. I guess he don't want me to hear his conversation. Sounds like he's fussing at somebody about some money at 3:25 in the morning. It's not my business so I'm not going to ask, I'll just pretend like I'm doing something. I thought, buttoning my shirt back up and grabbing a magazine from the coffee table.

"I gotta' go!" He rushed out without waiting for me to say bye or at least walk him to the door.

He looks to be mad about something. Hm', that was low down and dirty. I see right now I'm a have to stop this before it gets started. Really, I can't be mad because I just asked the Lord to make him leave. Well, it looks like He answered my prayer. And I'm glad because it was about to be real ugly up in here.

Chapter 5

C hurch was good as usual. Auntie LolaMae showed out once again. For some reason I felt different. Could it be that I was convicted for what I allowed to happen on yesterday and this morning? Pastor taught on temptation. I was sinking in my seat. I had never had to sink in my seat before. It felt like Pastor was speaking directly to me. It even looked like he was looking straight at me too. Maybe it's just me but I wondered if other people felt the same. I was so uncomfortable. What would I do without the word of God? I certainly wouldn't be here that's for sure. I know I wouldn't. And what I allowed to happen this morning was because I haven't been fasting and reading my Word like I should, and so my flesh was in total control with no submission to God. I'm so sorry Lord and I repent. Please forgive me? I've got to be stronger than this. But I'm so lonely, could it be that I'm losing my mind? Something's telling me that the battle is not in my body, it's all in my mind. I can feel myself pulling away from You Lord. Why? I'm so confused but I'm sure You'll help me find the right answer...

I'm so glad I don't have to give Auntie LolaMae a ride home anymore because she finally got her car fixed. Thank God! I saw her riding home and one side of the car was leaning to the left. I wanted to laugh but it's different when it's your own ken-folk.

This house is a mess! I don't know why I always feel like it's never clean. I just cleaned up two days ago. Nobody lives here but me. This is crazy for me to feel this way. Anyway, I guess I'll just wash these few dishes. That'll give me something to do. I don't know why that phone likes to ring right when I'm in the middle of doing something. "He-Hello!" I asked, rushing to the phone with dish suds all over my hands.

"How's Momma's baby doing?"

"Hey Momma, I'm fine."

"No hangovers huh'?" She laughed.

"Hangovers? Now Momma you know I don't drink." I said. I hope she don't ask me no questions about what happened this morning.

"So did you meet a fine strong Christian man?" She sounded so excited.

"As a matter of fact I did but he's not a Christian though." I grabbed a towel, wiped the water off my hands, and went and sat at the kitchen table. I need to wipe off my fake center piece, I see it's gotten dusty.

"What! Are you serious?! You mean my baby finally found somebody nice?! Now can I get them grandchildren I've been waiting for?!" She said, screaming to the top of her lungs.

I don't know why Momma won't let me grow up. And I'm getting sick and tired of this grandchildren stuff. She didn't even hear me say that he wasn't a Christian because she screamed before I could even get it out. "Momma you're going to get you some grandchildren in due time!" I disgustingly answered.

"I'm sorry baby, I just want you to find somebody really nice. I'm tired of seeing you all by yourself." She said. Mother's always have a voice that nobody can ever imitate.

"I had a fabulous time though. He bought me a drink and we talked. After that we both danced. It was a little uncomfortable for me at first because I hadn't done that since I got saved. O' well, probably won't be doing that again. Momma he was so nice! The weird thing about it was that he said something really sweet to me last week at work."

"At work? So you had met this guy before?" She said.

"Yea! It was so weird how it happened. I wasn't even expecting it. He just showed up at the office the other day out of nowhere! He came for an interview with Mr. Kevin. And you know how Mr. Kevin is, he kept him in his office forever interviewing him. Wait, I'm getting ahead of myself. He came in the office to apply for the treasurer position at our other branch down the street. And Momma, when he came through the front door, he was drop dead gorgeous! He is so handsome! You talk about a nice built, handsome, well put together man. That he is! He's very tall and shaped up like a professional basketball and a football player. The good looking one's that is." I said, as we both laughed. "He took my breath away. When he and Mr. Kevin had finished with the interview, they both came out of the office and Mr. Kevin said something smart as usual and Mr. Jenkins corrected him. I couldn't believe my ears! What he said was so sweet! I mean…"

"What did he say?!" She blurted in before I could finish.

"Wait Momma, stop cutting me off!" I shouted with excitement. "It was so sweet. To make a long story short, he told me that I was very attractive!"

"What? He told you that?" She asked, inquisitively.

"What do you mean he told me that? Why, he can't tell me I'm very attractive? So are you saying I'm not?" I playfully asked.

"Now baby you know I'm not implying anything."

"Momma you know that ain't never happened to me before? That made my day! But wait until you hear this! About a couple days later, which was last night at the club, he just showed up at my table out of nowhere. Michelle had supposedly gone to get us drinks and during that time when she was gone, he just popped up. It was a trip!" I laughed.

"Hm'. That's different. That only happens with destiny." She chuckled. "So have you two kissed yet?" She asked. Momma can be so nosy sometimes.

"Now Momma, you supposed to be a Christian. But to answer your question, no we haven't, but we almost did. It was my fault I'm not ready for that. If ever with him. I mean, we had a good time at the club but…"

"Lord what's wrong with my child? I don't understand you always dreamed of meeting somebody nice and handsome and you gon' let him get away from you…" She said, as I cut her off.

"Momma hold on, you don't…" I said, and then she cut me off.

"I'm really trying to figure my child out Lord."

"Momma, can I say somethin'?"

"Lord knows I tried to raise her good…"

"But if you would listen for once you could…"

"What! What child, what is it? And don't be cutting me off when I'm talking either. I'm still yo' Momma!"

"What I'm trying to say is that he's married!"

"What?! Now I know you not going with no married man?!" She shouted as her tone seriously changed.

It's funny because before I told her that, it was like he was all that. And now it's like he's a nobody. That's real funny.

"Are you gon' answer me?!" She asked.

"No, I'm not dating him." If she had just listened to me in the first place, all this could have been avoided. "And that's why I didn't kiss him either." I threw my arm up and then let it fall.

"That's my baby. Momma taught her well." She whispered. Which made me feel about two years old. But that's my only

Momma, and I'm her only child. So what would anybody expect? Nothing else.

"You need to leave him alone because he's nothing but trouble. I just feel there's something about him that isn't right." She raised her voice.

You know what they say about a mother's intuition. Maybe she's right and just maybe she's wrong. Momma can be a little judge mental at times though. And plus, she's never met the man before. She don't know nothing about him. I shouldn't have told her. It don't matter no way because I've decided that I'm not going to go any further with him. Especially the way he just got up and left this morning. "I hear ya' Momma." I said, hoping she'll change the subject.

"Well your Daddy is working hard as ever, I probably won't see him until way later own tonight or tomorrow. And don't worry you'll find somebody real special. Momma promise. On that note I'll talk to you later on, okay?" She said, sounding exhausted. Can't be too tired, it's just her and daddy and he's the only one that works cause' she's a house wife.

"I know Momma, and thanks for all your advice, I really appreciate it. I know you think I don't, but I do. Hold on, somebody's beeping in." I clicked to the other line. "Hello?"

"Hey girl, why haven't you called me yet?"

I should've known it would be Michelle. She's been hounding me ever since I got on her last night. She didn't even let me get in the house good before she started calling. This is all new to me. Maybe this is the new me, maybe this does have something to do with Tyrome. I don't know and I don't want to think about it.

"Hello, are you still there?" She hysterically asked.

"I'm still here Michelle."

"Did you just get home?"

"As a matter of fact I did, and I haven't even taking my clothes off yet so let me call you back." I waited, holding my finger on the flash button.

"Okay. Hey, don't forget that we're supposed to hang out at the park later on."

"O' yea', how can I forget?" I regret that I told her I would go.

"So I'll be by there to pick you up in about an hour." I know she'll come earlier.

"Alright girl, bye." I clicked back over to Momma.

"Who in the world was that?! I liked to hung up; you don't do that to your mother that's rude!"

"Momma chill out, you're trippin'. I see right now it's time for me to get off this phone. Bye Momma, I'll talk to you later. I love you."

"Bye baby, call me later." She said, as we both hung up the phone.

That's one thing I love about my Momma, she knows when she's about to get on my nerves. And she don't mind giving me my space at least now that I'm out on my own. I really don't feel like going to no park today. To tell you the truth, I really don't feel like being bothered with nobody. But I said I would so I'm a go ahead and go. Lets see what I'm a wear. I guess I can wear these baggy red shorts with this green and purple shirt. I think that's going to be real cute. I'm trying not to look like a diva, but I can't help it. Yea' right, that was so funny. I already know I'm not going to meet nobody so I won't get my hopes up.

Michelle is not a minute late. In fact, she's way too early. I thought, walking to get the door while looking at my watch.

I could barely get the door open before she burst through as if somebody was chasing her. "Hey girl I know I'm a little early but

76

I want to get there before all the freaks take all the fine men." She smiled.

If she only knew what they think about her. Probably saying the same thing. I hope and pray that she get delivered from those lusty spirits living inside of her. "Girl you so crazy, let me put on my sandals and I'll be ready." I walked back towards the bedroom.

After putting on my sandals, I stepped outside the door only to meet the sun as it beamed down on my forehead. It's so beautiful out here. It's a great day for the park or the beach after all. The sun's shinning straight down on her two seated candy apple red 2002 convertible Mercedes. I must admit, I am kind of jealous. Look like she just got it detailed. She spends money like it's nothing and here I am struggling just to make ends meet.

Michelle's car drives so smooth it feels like we're not even moving. I'm sure that's why it cost so much. Passing through the neighborhood, it's not hard to notice everybody out enjoying the awesome weather. Some are sitting out on their porches, some are mowing their yards, or washing their cars in their driveways, and kids are everywhere playing with one another.

"Hey girl you heard from that guy you was with at the club?" She turned to look at me.

"Sure haven't." I wonder if she knows I really don't want to talk about it?

"It looked like you two really had something sparking up." She smiled, looked at me, and then back at the road.

"Whatever, that's a married man and plus he's not saved either." I looked out the window in the opposite direction.

"Girl for real? He's married?" She asked, with a devious jealous smirk on her face.

"You're asking like you're happy he is."

"Now you know I'm not happy. I just thought you guys were going to really hit it off. I don't see what the big deal is, so what he's a married man. Have you seen his wife?"

"No."

"Were you and her ever good friends?"

"No. What kinda' question is that? And what are you getting at?" I asked, kind of curious as to what she's going to say next.

"I mean if she and you were never friends you shouldn't have nothing to worry about." She said, never looking over at me.

"I still don't know what you're talking about." I turned to look at her.

"Girl you are so silly, why is it so hard for you to understand? What I'm saying is that you and him are just friends and nothing more right?"

"I really don't know because he stormed out of my apartment the morning he brought me home from the club." I said.

"Now you got me confused. How is he going to storm out of your house when all he was doing was dropping you off?" She snickered underneath her breath.

"He did come in and he did stay for a while. We didn't do anything we just talked and I must admit, I really enjoyed his company. We were talking and all of a sudden you called and for some reason his pager went off while I was on the phone with you. He asked me to use the phone which was the reason why I got off the phone with you. Next thing I knew, he stormed out without saying bye or anything. I really didn't understand it." I said.

"So did you call him to see if everything was alright?" She curled her lips and looked at me as if she already knew the answer.

"Well, no I didn't, was I supposed to?" I reached down, picked my purse up off the floor, and put in my lap.

"Now I know you already know the answer to that. And I expect something like that to come from me. I'm surprised in you." The wind blew through her hair. "Just because he stormed out of the house don't mean he don't like you. I mess with married men all the time. They take me out to eat and wine and dine me but all we are is just friends, nothing more. And you know if a man's gon' buy me a meal, I'm gon' take it. Momma always told me not to miss no meals." She said, as we both laughed.

"I'm not saying that I don't like him, maybe I really do and don't realize it? I see what you're saying now. That was wrong of me not to call him to see if everything was alright. But I just don't feel comfortable messing with no married man though." I looked at her for reassurance.

"Like I said before, you and him are just friends and nothing's wrong with just being friends." She said, as we turned off on the road leading into the park.

I must admit ever since I got on her at the club, she haven't been the same. She's acting like somebody who cares now. Maybe she's right about me and Tyrome. I mean we are just friends. I think. Maybe not considering how I didn't call and check on him. He probably don't want to talk to me anymore. I feel better since Michelle put it the way she did. It's nothing wrong with messing with a married man just as long as you two stay just friends. Even though the Bible says that it's still wrong. Well, it don't matter no way cause' I haven't heard from him. Maybe he's still mad at me and don't want to talk to me anymore. He's the first real man I've ever had in my life and I really enjoy his company. Oh' well, so much for dreaming.

The park is peaceful, with exceptions of the loud music I can hear whispering in my ears from a distance. It seems to be getting louder the further we drove into the park. Wow. It must be a million people out here. All you can see is different shades of black, brown, yellow, and white colors all mixed together. The color of people is so beautiful to me. I have to wonder what God was thinking. It's amazing how He can put so many different shades of colors at one gathering and they all mix together so perfectly. I thought, as Michelle drove a little further and then parallel parked into an empty space.

"Alright girl! Let's get out and mix with all these fine men out here!" She put on some lip stick and got out the car.

I'm really not used to being around all these people. It feels kind of uncomfortable. Maybe it's because I'm a little intimidated and insecure about how I look when I'm around them. I know it's not them, it's me and I'm not confused about this. I hope they don't notice my insecurities. What if a guy comes up to me, what will I say? I'm not going to worry about it because nobody's going to approach me anyway. So much I can say for Michelle, she'll probably pull about twenty men at one time. She's just that stunning. She always knows how to dress for every occasion. She's wearing some short blue shorts with a halter top and sandals with a little heal. Her long hair is pulled up in pin-curls with stringy pieces hanging from the sides; with her make-up looking like it's been professionally done.

I could never look as beautiful as she is. I thank God for who He made me to be, I just wish I felt this in my heart.

"Girl you coming or what?" She got my attention as I got out the car. "Are you alright?" She asked, as we started walking towards the crowd.

"O' yea, I'm fine." I'm trying to hide the way I really feel.

"Girl what if you see Tyrome out here?" She smiled, waiting on my response.

"I don't know. What should I do if I see him?"

"I think you should play it cool like nothing ever happened just to see where he's coming from. And if he shows that he don't want to talk to you, then go ahead and apologize." She said, as we maneuvered our way through the crowd.

"Girl you got all the answers when it comes to men." I smiled at her with comfort. "I already know I won't see him, and probably won't ever see him again." I'm looking around hoping that I would see him in the crowd anyway.

We walked what seem like two or three miles into the park. Trees and barbeque pits are everywhere. Kids are playing all through the park, people are barbequing, listening to loud music, eating water melon, and drinking liquor and smoking up some marijuana. It's so much smoke you would think it's a forest fire out here. I'm getting high just by being around it. I'm starting to feel really uncomfortable. My Momma didn't raise me to be no crack head nor a weed head. And plus I'm a child of God and this don't set right with my spirit. "Hey Michelle, are you ready to go?" I asked, defensively.

"You ready to go? We just got here? Look over there can't you see there's still more people coming out here?" She pointed towards the entrance.

"Yes I am ready to go. You can drop me off and you can come back out here. All I know is that I'm ready to go." I said, walking back towards the car which was too far to see.

"Why, what's wrong? You were okay when we first got out here? What's the big change?!" She raised her voice.

"It's the smoking and the drinking Michelle. You know how I feel about alcohol and drugs. Why would you bring me to this environment knowing that I would be uncomfortable?!" I answered back, raising my voice over hers.

"I didn't know that they would be drinking and smoking!" She tried out yelling me. "All these years we've been friends have I ever taken you to unsafe environments?! Huh?! Huh'?! No! I didn't think you would disagree! If I would have known that there would be all this out here, trust me I sure wouldn't have brought you! I've just got to be honest with you Ramona, you judge too much! Just because they're drinking and smoking don't mean you got to join em'! You are your own person and you make your own decisions! Yo' Momma and Daddy got you spoiled into thinkin' that this world is perfect and that you're never going to see worldly things! That don't mean you partake in em'?! See your problem is that you ain't never been there when all you felt like you had left is a high. And no I'm not talkin' about the high of Jesus! I'm talkin' about getting stone high off of satan's drugs. And all you thinking about is if I can just get high, my problems would be solved. And you always talking about praying for people. Well here's where the praying starts. I do know that the Bible speaks about going out there where the problems are and leading them to God. But how are you going to do that if you running from them?! That's what's wrong with all these Christians, they think they too good. They think they better than everybody else! And what they don't realize is that they were once out there too! And still can go back out there! I'm tired of you judging everybody and blaming it on me! If you still ready to go home, I'm too ready to take you!" She yelled, storming towards to front entrance.

It also says not to be partakers of evil. But she is right about going out there where the problem is and leading them to Christ. That much is true, I haven't thought of it that way. Maybe that's why she's in my life. I mean she is right, I can't judge nobody for what they do wrong. I make my own decisions and it's nothing wrong with being around it but just don't partake in it. But something is telling me not to partake in evil works. O' well, I might as well stay anyway. We got this far, a little more time out here won't hurt.

"Are you going to answer me?" She stopped, turned around, and looked at me.

"No, no, you don't have to take me home." I answered, looking down at the ground as if to be ashamed of acting the way I did. But for some reason I still feel that I'm right about my opinion.

"That's my girl. I was worried about you for a minute there. Hey, let's sit over there on that bench." She said, already walking across the side walk and sitting down.

Michelle can be a little controlling at times but she's right about me judging though. If all these people wasn't out here, boy it would be real peaceful. And it would be destiny if Tyrome showed up in my face right about now too.

"Girl look up, guess who's at the park?" She said, poking me in my side with her boney elbow.

I glanced to the left, and sure nuff' it's you know who, Mr. Tyrome himself walking towards us with some friends. My heart is beating so fast. I'm not nervous though, at least I don't think I am. Tyrome looks nice as ever! His pro football figure is a knock out! I know I said basketball figure, but looks like he's been working out lately so he's got a football figure now. Either way he looks nice with his turquoise shorts on, with a tank top to match, showing off every muscle in his body. I feel like I'm a faint just looking at him.

"Girl look, they're coming this way! I think he see you! I got to give it to you, you lucked up with that cause' he got it goin' on. Too bad I didn't catch him before you did, cause' it sho' would've been somethin' serious! Umph', umph', umph'. You better watch him somebody else might take your place."

I admit I am kind of jealous. If she ever think about taking him away from me. I'll kill her! O' Lord these thoughts aren't me. I can't believe I just let my mind go that far. Just to think such a thing. I think I'm getting off focus and I just can't, not over no man. "So what do you mean by that Miss. Thang?" I gave her this I'll knock you out look.

"Whatever. Now you know I'm just playing." She said, laughing as she threw her hands up in the air and gave this devious look out the corner of her eye. "I know somebody not getting jealous, especially from what you said earlier." She looked at me.

"What? What did I say earlier?" I said, smiling back at her.

"You remember what you said. You said you really don't care whether or not you see him."

"Well that may be true for the other day, but this is a whole new day so just drop what I said. You shouldn't pay so much attention to me all the time anyway silly girl!"

"Yea, I see you. You just liking what you see right now and wanna' try and act like everybody's crazy around you and not supposed to remember what you said the other day. But that's okay cause' I'm feeling ya'." She said, as we both laughed.

Tyrome and his friends are about ten feet from us and moving closer as we speak. It's funny because he won't even look this way. He's so busy playing and laughing with his home-boys. Maybe as he gets closer he'll see me.

"Girl, no they're not just gon' pass right by us without speaking! What's wrong with your boy, he don't like you anymore?" She said, laughing uncontrollably and running across the side walk and back.

I can't say nothing. No he didn't embarrass me? One minute Michelle is so supportive, and the next she's like a witch from hell. I guess that comes with not being saved. I'm too embarrassed. I just knew he saw me and was on his way to speak to me. Maybe he's really mad at me and don't want to be bothered with me anymore? Or maybe he just didn't see me? But how could you miss a big woman like me? O' well, I'm too ready to go now. "Michelle, you ready to go?" I said, holding back the tears. It feels like I just swallowed a brick. I guess I'll go home and eat up the house.

"Yea we can go ahead and go, I'm supposed to be getting a phone call right about now anyway." She smiled like my feelings don't matter. She's probably happy. You just never know people these days. One minute they're supporting you, and the next they're your worst enemy.

It was a long quiet ride home. Michelle dropped me off quick. I guess to get to that phone call she has waiting on her. I'm not going to let it bother me because one day I'll have somebody and won't have to worry about being around her.

Chapter 6

The sound of a sizzling television is all that I could hear as I jumped up from the couch. My ears are making a loud hissing noise from the TV. Shoot! It's 11:23 at night! I didn't realize I had been sleep that long. I put a movie on about five hours ago, and I guess I fell asleep after eating a whole gallon of ice cream, a pack of cookies, and a whole pack of snicker's. I was depressed at how Tyrome did me at the park. I'm so hurt. I didn't think I was that rude to him that night for him to treat me like that? I'll never find nobody. They wouldn't want me because I'm too fat and ugly. That's why Tyrome didn't speak at the park because he probably was too shame. I still have his pager number. I should page him and ask him why he high-sided me in front of all his little ol' friends. He probably wouldn't call back. O' well, forget it. I didn't realize the phone is ringing. Let me turn this TV down. "Hello?" I answered, trying to hide the depressed tone.

"Hey you." He said. His voice sounds like it's gotten' deeper. Which is very dangerous right about now because I'm alone, I ain't got no man, and I'm tryin' not to lose control. So what's next? "Who is this?" I asked, trying not to scream, pretending not to know who it is.

"You know who this is girl." He replied, with a slight whisper.

"Look I'm about to hang up in your face if you don't tell me who you are!" I smiled trying to sound frustrated.

"Hey look you don't have to get hostile. This Tyrome." He answered, lowering his voice even more. "Hello, are you going to talk to me?" He made his voice deeper than it was from the beginning.

"Sure. Why are you calling me so late? Are you okay? Is everything alright?" As nervous as I am, I feel like I'm about to drop the phone. I hope he doesn't notice.

"As a matter-a-fact, no I'm not okay." He answered. "Do you mind if I come…"

"No, I don't mind come on over." I said, cutting him off. I can't believe I just said that. I'm not worried cause' nothing's going to happen anyway. He probably just want to talk again. And anyway I love the Lord too much to let this man take advantage of me in my house. I'm going to take Michelle's advice, we're just friends and that's what I'm going to be. Just a friend.

"I'm on my way don't fall asleep on me." He whispered, while hanging up the phone.

I can't believe he's coming to see me. I'm excited! I thought he gave up on me. I oughta' wake Michelle up and tell her. I bet not, she might try and come over and get in the way. I got to watch her.

Let me get this house clean before he gets here. All I need to do is get this room cleaned and the kitchen cleaned. That shouldn't take long.

After about twenty minutes he's finally knocking at the door. "Who is it?" I shouted, smelling his cologne through the door.

"Open the door beautiful." His voice snuck through the cracks of the door.

Opening the door and to my surprise is a dozen of roses staring me in the face. I ain't never got no roses before. I don't know what to say or how to act. "How sweet, you sure know how to please a woman." I said, motioning for him to come in.

"I'm a man I'm supposed to do this. You like em'?" He asked, walking through the door towards the couch.

"I love em'. Thank you that was really sweet of you." Of course I want to scream not because of the roses, but because of his handsome body. Lord have mercy! I got a clean cut man staring at me, looking good, and smelling good. He's going to make me lose my religion.

"Where do I sit?" He asked.

"O', right over there on the love seat."

"That's funny because I was sitting here the last time I was here." He sat down on the sofa. "We got a lot to talk about. I've been having some things on my mind lately." He crossed his legs.

"Hang on, let me go put these roses in some water, I'll be right back." I cut him off, walked towards the kitchen, placed the roses in a vase, and came back and sat on the couch.

"Hey you mind if I turn off some of these lights, you got every light in town on in here?" He turned off the lamp next to him.

"I guess I don't have much of a choice since you already did it. I kind of like my light. I don't take to good to the dark if you know what I mean?" I said, hoping he would get the picture.

"There's nothing wrong with a little dark every once in a while." He smiled.

"Well it depends on how you look at it. Hey lets change the subject."

"Yea', you ain't ready for that no way." He mumbled under his breath.

"What did you say? Why are you mumbling under your breath? If you got something to say, why can't you say it loud so I can hear you I'm not going to bite?" I smiled, as I got up, got the roses, and set them on the end table by the couch.

I'm a leave that alone. Look woman I didn't come way over here to debate with you. There's been some things on my mind and if you don't mind listening, I'd love to share what I'm feeling with you. Is that alright?" He looked me straight in my eyes without blinking.

"Sure. I'd love to hear what you have to say." I sat back down on the couch.

"Well first of all I want to say thanks for listening to me the other night even though I left on a bad note. I apologize for that." He looked down at the floor.

I can't believe he's actually apologizing to me.

"You know Ramona, when I first laid eyes on you I thought you were the most beautiful woman I had ever come across. I mean I had my share of fine women but something about you was different when I first met you. When you fainted and I held you in my arms until you came too, was a whole different experience all together for me; and I'm just being real about it. What I'm trying to say is that I really care about you, and I'm looking for a chance to really get to know you. If that's alright?" He said, slowly looking up for my answer.

"Wow, I'm lost for words. Tyrome I have to be honest with you, you are a very handsome guy and I admit I am very attracted to you but I hardly know you. It hasn't been that long since our first meeting at the office and I don't want to take things too fast. If you don't know already, I am a Christian and I love the Lord very much. So much that I'm not looking to get caught up with no married man." I said, sitting on the long sofa across from him.

"Married man?! Who told you that?!" He raised his voice.

"Mr. Kevin said that you were." Lord, I hope Mr. Kevin was lying.

"Well I mean, I am married but we've been separated for about two years now. So that's like I'm not married I just haven't gotten' the divorce papers yet. All these years I felt like I didn't need to as long as I didn't see her face again." He scooted down in the sofa.

"I hear what you're saying but on paper and by law you two are still legally married and anyway that's a sin to God. Adultery is wrong (Galatians 5:19-21)! And I'm tired of people trying to sugar-coat wrong for being right! I can't do it!"

"Look just hear me out before you start bashing me, and you really don't know what you're talking about. I can see if we were still living together but we been broke up for not just two weeks, but for two whole years! Don't that mean something to you? I can give you the world if you let me. You said it yourself that you ain't never had a man. So I'm here to change all that. And I know that if you ain't never had no man, I know you're still a virgin." He gave me this quick glance with a smirk in his grin. I don't know whether to take it offensively or not. "I'm not trying to come hard on you but I just want a chance. You know all my personal business. I've never told that to nobody, so it's something about you that I got to have. You're beautiful. Fine. Spiritual. Got a job, and know what you want out of life. And that's the kind of woman I need. Will you be my lady?" He said, turning and holding out his hands.

"I don't mind being your friend Tyrome but I can't be your girlfriend because you're still married." I said, grabbing the remote and turning on the TV.

"I understand I won't bother you no more. Sorry I kept you up." He got up and walked out the front door.

"Lord, I just want somebody that's going to love me and I think I just lost him. Why can't I have somebody special in my life? I'm tired of being lonely and depressed. I want to be accepted, and he seems to be the first guy that really accepts me for me. I don't understand do every Christian go through this? I feel like I'm about to lose my mind!" I screamed, while running towards the bathroom. "I know you didn't have us on this earth to be alone and right now I feel like I'm all by myself! Look at Michelle she has it all! The men, the looks, the car, the big house, and the big job! What more can she need?! I'm sick and tired of getting the short end of the stick! That's why I'm just going to take all these pills and then all my worries, fears, doubts, and insecurities will be gone! I don't even care anymore!" I threw myself down on the floor and shoved the pills in my mouth. "What in the world was that?!" I spit the pills out and ran towards the front room. "O' my God how did this big lamp fall off the corner table? What was I thinking? I almost swallowed a whole bottle of pills. How stupid can I be for losing control of myself over a man?" I said, crying hysterically as I threw myself to the floor. "Lord I'm so sorry, please forgive me!" I yelled as I got on my knees, bald up my fist, and pushed them into my face. "I repent for even thinking about killing myself. I realize that suicide is a sin and I don't want to go to hell! I want to go to Heaven! Lord please deliver me from all these strongholds that are trying to destroy my life! My flesh is weak! I really need you right now!" I threw my hands up towards the ceiling with tears falling hard from my eyes. "Please help me Lord! I need You to deliver me! I can't wait until sun break I need You right now!! I feel like I'm losing my mind! I have no one to turn to! I can't call my parents, they would never understand! I'm calling on You Lord! I need Your peace! Please send me Your peace! Send it Lord, send it! Send it Lord! Take the pain away, it hurts too bad...! Thank Lord! I feel Your Spirit! Thank You for Your peace... Thank You for Your forgiveness... Thank You for answering my prayers..."

Chapter 7

Today's a rainy day and I sure don't feel like going to work. I thought, as I grabbed my keys and umbrella and walked out to the car.

Traffic is backed up as usual. It's amazing how a little rain can change everybody's normal routine. Last night was a trip! I almost killed myself. I ain't never done nothing like that before. What's happening to me? I guess if I really think about it, every Christian goes through a little temptation every now and then. I thought, finally arriving at the job and parking in my usual parking space.

The lobby is crowded as usual and the elevators seem as if they aren't ever going to open up.

"Hey Ramona! Ramona!" Somebody shouted behind me. Turning only to notice that it's Michelle looking gorgeous as ever. Makes me so sick to look at her at times. I promise I'm going to lose all this weight once and for all. "What's up girl?" I said, as she got close enough to hug me.

"I don't have time to talk. I'm late for a meeting with the CEO so I'm going to take the emergency elevator." She walked off towards the elevators across the hall.

"How are you going to do that, the alarm's going to go off?! I shouted back at her hoping she would hear me.

"He knows I'm using it! He's going to open it for me! I'll meet you for lunch!" She shouted back as she vanished into the crowd.

"Must be nice to have it like that?!" A Caucasian man behind me shouted as the crowd laughed. If they only knew. The elevators have finally opened up and it's a war trying to fit inside before it gets too full. I never have that problem because I basically just smash everybody into the wall as I make my way in.

It was a long ride up to my floor with everybody stopping on different floors. "Where's everybody at?" I said, literally talking to myself as I walked in the office to find nobody in sight.

"Why you lookin' so beat up? One of those nights huh'? I bet you had it all night long with your stuffed animal!" Mr. Kevin came out of his office laughing and then walking back in.

I shoulda' known he would be some where around here. That man is never going to quit. I pray that God will really change his life one day. If he can heal a serial killer, I know he can heal him. All I can do is laugh because it isn't him, it's what's inside of him that needs to come out. And one day it all will.

I feel really good this morning. But for some reason I feel bad that I rejected Tyrome last night. I just can't see myself messing with no married man. All this thought about him I didn't even see these dozen of roses sitting on my desk. Let me read the inscription cause' I don't have a clue as to who would send them. They may belong to Mr. Kevin. I don't know who would bring him anything. Let's see what it says. "*...I'll keep trying until you are my lady...*" The inscription read. Now he got me blushing. I can't hide it. I can really start liking this. It's funny cause' I always see women trying to be all that when a man is chasing after them, when really they're just as weak as a child taking candy from a stranger. Hopefully I won't turn into that little child. I can't help but smile…

Nothing happened in the office all morning. My lunch break is in about 2 minutes. Shoot. I'm supposed to meeting Michelle for lunch downstairs. But I told myself I wasn't going to eat lunch today. Maybe I'll just drink a diet soft drink. Yea' that's what I'll do. That'll get rid of these hunger pains.

The lobby is less crowded unlike this morning. I guess people decided to go out for lunch today. We have such a beautiful lobby. It has a huge water fall that showers towards the ceiling when you first walk in. It's so beautiful, makes you feel like you're at some resort on the islands. There's a huge open cafeteria that's located on the right side of the building. With a bookstore sitting next to it. The ice cream shop pretty much sits in the corner by itself. It reminds me of the food court area in the mall. There's two escalators located on opposite ends of the elevators, which is located in the center of the building surrounded by cream patent leather sofas and chairs. And all around the building, there are floor modeled windows that leads from the floor to the ceiling. I think they're kind of bare. Me personally would have put some swinging curtains, gathered by some gold curtain rods. But my opinion don't count one way or the other. One thing I do like is that they're overlooking downtown and most of the city which looks beautiful at night. I'm sure they had one of the top interior decorating companies to come in and do their thing. I don't have to guess that they got paid a lot. O' well, I ain't mad at em'. If I had that talent I would definitely be doing it too. God's Word says that our gifts will make room for us. Well I wish He would show me my gift so it can make room for me.

Michelle is sitting over on the opposite side of the cafeteria at a table for two. I really don't feel like walking way over there. I wish she had sat closer. "Hey girl how long have you been sitting over here?" I asked, finally sitting down in the chair across from her.

"I'm having a marvelous day so far. I got a hot date tonight and you know I'm excited! I'm a get me some money if you know what I mean?" She said, smiling, ignoring my question and taking a bite of her hamburger.

"Girl what are you talking about?" I asked, looking at what she had ordered.

"You don't know what I'm talking about? Man are you that dumb or what? I'm talking about having some good sex tonight! I haven't had none in about a week. My supervisor was doing a good job of taking care of my needs but he done lost his touch. I need a real man that's gon' do it right! The only difference is, I'm getting paid. And it don't matter cause' I've gotten' paid before." She smiled. Closing her eyes as if she could imagine it in her mind.

"Michelle, I don't mean to get in your business or anything but are you truly thinking about what you're saying?" I hope she's just joking.

"Yea' I do know what I'm saying and I'm very serious, I'm going to get paid!"

"But Michelle you don't even have to do that. I mean it's not like you're struggling or starving for money? You know what you're doing is wrong. It says it in the Bible. (Galatians 5:19-21) It says, when you follow the desires of your sinful nature, your lives will produce these evil results: Sexual immorality (adultery, fornication), impure thoughts, eagerness for the lustful pleasure... and anybody living this way will not inherit the Kingdom of God. "This is what the Bible says. And I'm not making this up so it's up to you."

"I'm not trying to hear what you got to say right now Ramona! You something else with this Bible stuff! And I don't know what makes you think cause' you quoting me some Bible verses is going to make me change my mind?! NOT! I'm going to live my life and you live your life. Okay? Thank you case closed!" She said, raising her voice to where everybody around us could hear.

"Alright Michelle you don't have to get loud. We can just drop the subject but just know that what you're doing is wrong and don't say that I didn't warn you. You're now accountable because you've been told." I turned to look at the people walking by.

"Whatever, I know exactly what I'm doing. And besides I used to do it all the time before I came back in town. Anyway, what did you do after I dropped you off yesterday?" She said, changing the subject.

"Girl I came home, kicked off my shoes, and watched me some TV. No let me stop lying. I had some company last night about 11:30. And guess who it was?"

"What?!! You don't even have to tell me cause' I already know! So what did ya'll do and why did he come over so late Miss. Christian girl?!" She puckered her lips, took one of her french fries, and threw it in her mouth.

"I actually gave him permission to come over but he didn't stay long."

"So what happened?" She scooted her chair closer.

"Nothing happened but the fact that he asked me to be his lady." She burst out laughing. "What's funny? You are so silly!" I pushed my chair from the table and folded my arms.

"He asked you to be his lady? So did he tell you why he didn't speak the other day?" She threw up her hands and took another bite of her hamburger.

"You are so messy Michelle. Actually we didn't even talk about that and he didn't mention it, so I'm assuming that he just

97

didn't see me. Because if he did, he wouldn't have come over last night begging." I smiled at her as if to say, now take that.

"He was begging?!" She covered her mouth in amazement.

"Girl like I had him wrapped around my finger."

"So what happened after that?" She asked, trying to scoot her chair even closer but couldn't.

"I'll just put it this way he wants me to be his lady."

"Are you serious? Are you going to be?" Her eyes widened.

"Now Michelle, you know me better than that. I told you that I don't mess with married men."

"Whatever, you'll give in. So is he living with his wife?"

"No he's not living with his wife. They've been separated for about two years."

"Well, that's just like they're not married anymore. Ramona you're just too stuck on this religious thing. I think you really need to loosen' up. I mean it's not like he asked you to have sex with him. You might even enjoy that type of company. You know you haven't ever been rubbed on so he may help you to relax." She said, laughing.

"Girl shut up with your silly self. I don't care what you say, just because you're not living right don't mean I have to engage in immoral acts like you."

"Whatever Miss. Religious Thang. What I got goin' on works for me." She laughed even louder and took a sip of her drink.

"When I got to the office this morning there were a dozen of roses staring me right in the face."

"What? There's more to the story? So what did you do, throw em' away?" She said, finishing off the hamburger she was eating.

"Now why would I do that?" I said, taking one of her fries she had on her plate and eating it.

"Now wait a minute! That's wrong! Now you're the main one saying that you don't mess with married men but you're accepting gifts from him. So what cha' gotta' say to that?" She sarcastically smiled.

"Nothing. I'm keeping my roses and I don't care what you say." I said, as we both laughed.

"Well it's about that time." She threw her napkins on her plate and took one last sip of her drink.

"I know and I sho' don't feel like going back up there to hear Mr. Kevin's mouth."

"You? I don't feel like sitting in that big ol' office of mine doing nothing. My secretary finished all my work yesterday so I don't have anything to do but sit on this large check that I'm about to get in two days. And I sure can use it." She got up from her seat and started fixing her hair.

I don't know why Michelle always got to brag. She sure knows how to spoil somebody's day. Maybe that's her purpose. I won't let her do it. "Alright girl, I'll talk to you later." We both started walking towards the elevators.

"Bye, this is where I turn off." She said, as she went into the opposite direction towards the emergency elevators.

I could waste my time getting mad and upset but it's not even worth it because the luxury she got going on right now won't last because it's all done the wrong way. I'm not hatin' at all. My time will come. I'm thinking, maybe she's right about Tyrome though. He hasn't been married in two years that's a long time. I'm sure he's gotten' over her. I don't know and I really don't want to think about it.

Finally making it back up to the office. There is a huge crowd standing in the door way. As I pushed my way through, which didn't take much, I can see Mr. Kevin holding up something in front of my desk. I can't make out what it is. "Mr. Kevin, what's going on?" I yelled over the crowd.

"You the dumbest person I've ever seen. You didn't know you was getting these?! Must be from yo' dog cause' you ain't never had no boyfriend!" He said, as everybody laughed.

He held out his hand and two huge diamond earrings jumped at my eyes. I think I'm about to faint. They look like two gleaming lights from Heaven. The size would have anybody astounded. They had to have cost a fortune. I don't have to wonder who sent them. Now he's starting to scare me. Am I now obligated to talk to him? I don't know what to do? Maybe I do need to give him a chance. Then that would give him a reason to divorce his wife. Look at me. I'm thinking stupid now. Let me stop. I got to play this thing off. "Is this for me?!" I grabbed the earrings from his hand.

"Hey you ain't gotta' be snatchin' nothin'!" He smiled deviously and walked back into his office. I guess that's a sign for everybody else to leave to because they're all going back to their offices.

I'm standing here with the biggest smile on my face. I feel like a movie star. I can't believe these are for me. Hm'. The box is even elegant looking. What's this? All this excitement I didn't see the little card inside. Let's see what it says:

"It only gets better if you give me a chance to make you feel like a real lady."

He sure knows how to make a woman feel special. If I was weak and full of pleasure, I could really fall for him and allow my imagination to run wild but I won't because I fear God. I've got to give it to him though, he's already made me feel like a real lady.

Traffic was crowded as usual but surprisingly I got home pretty fast. Lord, this house is a mess. It won't get cleaned today. I've got to get me some rest. Seem like I haven't rested in two months. Now I know somebody ain't knocking on that door. I can't get in my own house good. "Who is it?!" I shouted. I raced to the door as if they could hear me. "Who is it?!" I shouted again. I peeped through the peep hole with one eye and squinted with the other one.

"It's the post man mam'! You have a package!" This squeaky voice called out from behind the door. I can imagine what he looks like. Short, thick, and scanty with red hair.

I can barely get the door open. I'm so excited to see who would send me a package. I opened the door and all I can see is this cart with this enormous box sitting on top of it.

"It was too large to put inside of your mail box and it was too heavy to carry. Normally I would put a notice on your door informing you to come down and pick it up. But I knew you were here because I saw you coming up to your apartment. Someone must be real special." He squint his eyes and gave this stupendous smile. His face suddenly turned red. I guess he's blushing or either red from the hot sun. I'm trying to figure it out. I thought, gritting my teeth just to keep from laughing.

"How am I supposed to get this in my apartment?" I asked, walking towards the package as if to examine it.

"I'll bring it in and set it on the floor if you will help me?"

"Sure."

He brought the package in and we're both picking it up and setting it on the floor next to the coffee table.

"Thank you. What do I owe you?" I asked, walking him back to the door.

"Nothing. It was all paid by the sender. You have a good day mam." He said, vanishing down the hall.

Thanks, you do the same!" I yelled out to him, closing the door and rushing over to see what's inside.

This got to be one of those old TV boxes from one of the department stores. My heart's starting to palpitate. My anticipation is rising as I tore open the box. O' my God it's a foot-stool! I never told him I wanted one of these?! In fact I haven't ever told anybody! I wonder how he knew? Every woman wants her own foot-stool. It's an old fashion thang. Both of my grandmother's had one. They used it for reaching high places in the kitchen or in other parts of the house. He sure has good taste. It looks like a big pillow sitting on top of four short thick wooden legs. Each leg is specially carved. It had to be some kind of master carpenter to design something like this. The material has a flowered pattern that's surrounded by so many beautiful bright colors. It looks like a fluffy flowered garden. My very own foot-stool! I love it! I'm really lost for words. This man really knows what he's doing. I need to call him and at least thank him. I mean we're still friends and that's the least I can do. I'm praying that he's there by it being the time of evening and all. If I can only find his number... O' yea! I forgot he gave me his pager number. I'll just page him...

The phone immediately rings after a few seconds of waiting. "Hello?" I answered, hoping it's him.

"Hey you. You finally decided to give in huh'?"

"No." Shaking my head. "Actually I'm just calling to thank you for the nice gifts. Even though I can't have a relationship with you, I really would like for us to be friends if that's ok?"

"I don't understand you. At first you were saying that you don't want to have a relationship with me, but you want to be friends?!" He raised his voice.

"Why is that so hard for you to understand?"

"Forget it. I'm through talking about it. Let's talk about something else. So can I take you out tonight? Friend?" He chuckled underneath his breath. The phone is quiet... "O' I guess you can't do that huh'?"

"Yea I guess I can do that." I answered back.

"What?! Cool! I'll be by your crib to pick you up about 7pm. Be ready I got to go. I'll see you then my friend." He laughs as he hangs the phone up in my face.

I'm glad he gave me a chance to say whether or not that time would be alright? Anyway, I guess it'll do. Let me get out what I'm a wear so I can iron. It's almost 6 o'clock. I got right at an hour. I need to take me a quick nap so I won't be so tired. I have to admit, I'm kind of excited because I've never been taken out on a date before. I wonder where he's taking me?

There's a knock at the door. I can't believe it. I was just about to get in the tub. "Hold on! I'm coming! Who is it?!" I screamed, running towards the door.

"Girl it's me open up the door!" She screamed and laughed at the same time.

Now why did she have to pick this day out all days to come by and visit? I hope she don't stay long. "Hey girl what's up?" I asked. "I'm surprised to see you." I opened up the door.

She looks stunning as usual. Makes me so sick to look at her at times. Got the nerve to be wearing a sky blue body suit with some black 6 inch heals laced with the same blue matching her outfit.

Anybody would think she'd look like a hoochie in that but because she's a size zero with a big butt, it fits her well.

"I thought you wasn't at home at first. It took you so long to answer the door. Who you got up in here? Some nigga'?" She said, looking around and laughing as she forced her way inside of the apartment. Almost pushing me over. Yea' right. "Let me look in this room to see if what's his name is up in here!" She rushed towards the room.

"You are so silly! What did I tell you about saying the n word in front of me? You know I'm not down with that talk. We're not Niggas, we're African Americans. I thank God that He doesn't see us in color. He accepts us just the way we are."

"Look I didn't come over here for some sermon. You know that was just a figure of speech. I didn't mean no harm. Ok forgive me. I'm sorry to who ever. You or God. Now tell me where he is. I know he's hiding in here some where?!" She threw back the covers on the bed almost throwing off my clothes. She then walked in the bathroom and came back out with her hands up.

"Girl would you stop?! I don't have anybody up in here! Come out of here I haven't cleaned up yet!" I followed her.

"Oh' no this room is a mess! I see you got some clothes out on the bed like you got a hot date or something?" She looked at me and squinted.

"Thanks to somebody, they're all wrinkled up." That girl is so smart. Smarter than what people give her credit for. She already knew I was going out. "Those are some clothes from last week. You are so crazy. Anyway, as a matter of fact I do have a date tonight."

"With who? Oh' let me guess, with Mr. Tyrome right? Is that his name?"

"Yea you got it right. He's coming to pick me up at 7."

"Ok so we got to get you looking sharp cause' you know sometime you act like you don't be caring at all."

"What do you mean?" I put my hands on my hips and shrugged my shoulders.

"I'm saying the way you be dressing sometimes be needing a little help. Before you say anything, I'm not trying to rag on you. You know I love you girl. I'm just telling the truth." She smiled.

"Whatever! So if you think I can't dress then why don't you find me something to wear?" I dropped down on the bed.

"Fine. I can do that." She walked into the junky closet and started pulling down all kinds of clothes, and then drapes them over her shoulder.

She came out with stuff I didn't even remember I had. "I forgot I had that pants suit with those matching shoes." I said, as

I got up off the bed and walked over to the closet to get a closer look.

"So what cha' think? Do you like this get up? Now this is the way you should be dressing all the time girl."

"I do like it! So do I need a scarf?"

"No, you wear it just like it is." She came out of the closet and laid the outfit across the bed.

"Now I'm getting jealous. I'm a have to go and get laid tonight." She walked back into the front room.

"How many times do I have to tell you Michelle? Stop talking like that in my house!" I followed her.

"Ok chick, once again I'm sorry!" She quickly turned around with a sneaky smirk on her face. "But I'm still going to get me some tonight." She chuckled to herself as she walked over and sat down on the recliner. "Who's that box for?" She got up and walked towards the huge box. "And what's inside of it?" She opened it. "A foot- stool?! Girl, not another gift?! This is ridiculous! If you don't want him, let me have him! I could care less if he's married! I want a foot-stool to! I've been wanting one of these for a long time. I think every woman wants her own foot-stool!" She took the foot-stool out of the box and set it on the floor.

"Get a load of this." I stuck out my hand and showed her the box of earrings. "He sent these to the job earlier today."

"Diamond earrings Mona?! Now I'm too through! You can wear those with your outfit tonight. You crazy for not getting with him. Girl you're getting all these gifts and you haven't given him none yet? This is hard for me to believe." She handed the earrings back to me.

"Look don't hate. You already know me. I'm a woman of God. I don't have to sleep with a man in order to get some gifts. And anyway, my mind is way passed that sex stuff. My mind is totally focused on the Lord."

"Yea, well, we'll see how long that lasts." She smiled and whispered underneath her breath.

"What? What did you say? Forget it I don't even want to know. I got to go get dressed. It's a quarter til' seven. You made me lose track of time. I hope he don't decide to come early."

Sure nuff' as I said it he knocks at the door. "Shoot that's him! What I'm gon' do?!" I ran towards the bedroom and started throwing off my clothes.

"Girl just calm down! I'll answer the door while you finish getting dressed." She slammed the room door. And ran to the front door. "Who is it?"

"Open the door sexy, it's me." He whispered through the door. She opens the door like he's talking to her.

"Hi. How you doing? I'm Michelle. I'm Ramona's friend, she's in the room still getting herself together. She'll be right out. Come in and have a seat." She opened the door wider and motioned for him to come in, and closed it behind him. Her voice trembled at the sight of him.

"So how you doing?" He asked, staring at every curve on her body.

"I'm fine." She smiled, making the stare mutual.

"I can see that." He smiled back.

"So do you live around here?" She sat on the couch.

"I live close enough." He plopped down on the recliner.

"Would you like something to drink?" She got up and walked to the kitchen.

"Na', that's alright I'm taking your girl out so I don't want to lose my appetite, but thanks anyway."

"She should be on her way. Let me go see what's the hold up." She walked towards the bedroom.

His eyes followed her until she vanished behind the corner.

"Girl what is taking you so long? You got one fine sexy man out their waiting on you. You better hurry up before I kidnap him." She waved her hand towards the door.

"Whatever, I'm ready." I brushed passed her and went into the front room.

His eyes met mine the minute I came from behind the corner as he got up off the recliner. I feel on top of the world. And for once I feel prettier than Michelle. His eyes are only on me. He looks so handsome. He's wearing some loose dark green slacks with a tight black shirt showing off every muscle of his upper body, some black boots, and a black shinny belt. He's one man that can easily make it in the modeling industry.

"Hey, how are you? You look nice as always." I reached up and gave him a hug around his neck.

"You look great, and you smell good to." He bent down to meet me, wrapped his arms around my waist, and softly kissed me on my cheek.

"Well I see that you and Michelle met?" I asked, looking at them both as we released one another.

"Yea we did but I remember her from the club. So are you ready?" He walked toward the front door.

"I'll talk to you later Miss. Ramona, and nice seeing you again." She said, twisting hard towards the door. "Is it Tyrome?" She had the nerve to ask. If she twists any harder, her hips are going to pop out of joint.

She is so flirty it's pitiful. That lusty spirit has got to go. "Bye girl." I said, pushing her out of the door. "I'm ready, let me leave on one of these lights so it won't be dark when I get back." I turned the lamp sitting next to the door on and then walked back to the door.

When we got to the parking lot, there were some women standing by Tyrome's Navigator. They seem to be waiting on somebody, hopefully not us.

"Do you ladies need something?" I asked, walking towards the door.

"No mam' we're just admiring his screens he has on the inside of his sun visors." One of them answered. They all apologized and went on their way.

He quickly opened my side and walked around to his side. The smell is one that I can sniff all night. It has this new fresh smell to it. With a little cologne aroma added. I can't help but to notice the tight fitting shirt he's wearing and the fresh cut. He has long side burns and a thick goatee which makes his nice thick lips stand out even more.

"So how you feel? I can't get over how beautiful you look tonight. That outfit really looks nice on you and I see you have those diamond earrings on. They look good on you." He smiled, while gazing into my eyes.

I quickly turned my head looking towards the apartments as he started the truck. I don't want him to think he stands a chance. In other words, I don't want to lead him on. But for some reason or another I think I already am. What am I getting myself into? I'm not worried about it. Nothing won't happen unless I want it to happen. "Thanks, you look very handsome yourself." I turned and smiled back at him.

"I picked this nice restaurant. If I'm not mistaken you did say you loved Chinese food right?" He turned to look at me then quickly turned back to watch the road.

"As a matter-a-fact I do. So where do you have in mind?"

"Don't worry just sit back and enjoy the ride with those beautiful eyes." He grabbed my hand and pulled it to his lips.

"Tyrome, what did we talk about earlier?" I slowly pulled my hand away, hating inside that I did.

I want so badly to enjoy this moment for what it is. But I can't get caught up. I feel you God tugging at my heart telling me to end this before it goes too far. But I feel as if I can handle it. At least for right now. I'm not ignoring the conviction. I know it's there.

"That's cool, I understand. I love it when you play hard to get." He said, keeping his eyes on the road.

Pulling in the parking lot is a whole new experience for me. As long as I've been living in this city I've never seen or heard of this restaurant. It looks to be very expensive. Everybody's dressed like they're at a grand ball or something. This man has a lot of class. He definitely knows how to treat a lady.

"Don't open your door. I'll open it." He got out, walked over to my side, and opened the door.

I feel like a movie star getting out of her limousine. I can say no wrong. Everything is going so right and not to mention it feels right to.

We were seated fast. Most of the time it takes a while especially when it's crowded. And tonight it was. It's funny because it's almost like Tyrome knew the right words to say to get us seated so quickly. He and the manager seemed to be really good friends.

"So, do you and the manager know each other?"

"As a matter-a-fact we do. Why?" He asked, as if he got offended.

"Because right when you whispered something to him, he motioned for us to be seated in front of about twelve couples who were waiting before us."

"Yea, well, I got it like that. Why you worrying about nothing woman?"

"I'm not worrying. Just curious to know how you got it like that." I said, looking at the menu.

"It's nothing. He's an old friend from High School." He smiled.

Something seems real fishy about that but I'll leave it alone.

Dinner was great. The drive back to the apartment seems far. Maybe because I'm full and sleepy from eating such a great meal. I notice something different about the apartments; they started painting them another color today.

"Can I walk you to your apartment?" He pulled in a parking space.

"Yea I guess you can, but you're not coming in so don't even ask." We both got out of the truck.

"See, I wasn't going there because I already know how you feel. You need to stop jumping into conclusions. And stop being so hard up. Let loose once in a while, you just might have a little fun. Come on let me go ahead and walk you to your door." He took off walking sort of fast.

The walk to my door seemed rather long considering the fact that we weren't in conversation with one another. I think he's a little upset with me. I have to admit, I do feel bad for saying what I just said after all he's already done for me. The least I can do is relax more and stop being so stuffed up. I thought, as I opened the door and turned to face him. "Maybe your right. I have been kind of hard up. I really don't mean it. It's just that I've been hurt too many times and I don't want to get hurt anymore. It hurts too bad." I looked at him for his reaction.

"Let me tell you something. Your hurt is nothing like what I've been through. I will never do anything to hurt you. I really care for you and I want to become apart of your life." He put his hands on my shoulders and slowly backed me into the apartment.

"I hear what you're saying but do you understand where I'm coming from to? You can't just see only your side. You have to see my side too. I'd love to be with you but first you got to take care of your business. I'm saved now and I can't sin against God. He's done too much for me. I've made it this far and I can't turn back and get caught up. Why is that so hard to understand?" I broke away and sat down on the couch.

"I'll be lying if I said that I understand where you're coming from. I want you so bad you can't even imagine what I'm feeling right now." He sat next to me.

"I just want somebody to love me and never leave me." I said, resting my head on my thighs as the tears fell.

"I'm that man that's going to be all that you want in a man. You don't have to worry about my love. It would all be yours." He started rubbing my back with one hand and caressing my hair with the other. "And I promise you I'll never leave you. Just close your eyes and dream while I make you feel like a real woman." He bent over and took off my shoes. I don't want to think about what he's about to do to me next. I just want to dream.

I can't believe I'm letting this man take advantage of me. I have never in my life felt anything like this before. I don't know what to do? Should I respond? Should I resist? This feels too good to be wrong. I can't stop him now. I just can't.

He took off my jacket and my blouse and slowly kissed my forehead. He's so gentle. It's like he's thinking before he makes his every move. I'm now exposed. No man has ever seen any part of my body except God, the One who created it. I feel so uncomfortable now. I think he notices in my expression. I can't believe this is happening to me. I said that I would never let this happen. I slipped. I don't want to know what God is saying right now.

"Don't worry I won't hurt you." He whispered. The rest of the night was one that I'm far from proud of...

Chapter 8

I **opened my eyes only to notice** that its twelve noon and no sight of Tyrome. The sun is shinning so bright through the window that it's hurting my eyes. I'm aching all over and afraid to move. I have never felt this way before. I actually feel different and don't know why. Is this the way I'm supposed to feel afterwards? Where's the man that took my virginity? Is this how it goes? I thought I was supposed to open my eyes only to find him in my arms like they do in the movies? My flesh totally got the best of me. I'd gotten so caught up that I forgot who I was. I forgot all about God and what His commandment says. "Lord please forgive me for what I fell into. I fell into temptation. I was drawn away by my own lust and enticed by desire and not by what You were pleading with me not to do. I realize that we are not tempted by You because You're not tempted with evil (James 1: 12-13).

I just laid with this man and is guilty of fornication and adultery. And now I got to deal with the shame and the guilt. I'm sorry Lord how could You ever forgive me? I was supposed to be an example of how a Christian should live but instead I chose to be a hypocrite. I can never tell anybody about this secret. Could You ever forgive me? Please forgive me. Please…" I whispered to myself. The tears are falling down my checks like a streaming river. I just want to run and hide. I wonder if Tyrome's in the front room. I want to go see but my body is saying no, leave me alone. I'm so sore. I wonder if he's lost respect for me?

The phone rang.

I sure hope this is Tyrome with an explanation. "Hello?"

"Hey you. How you feel?" He asked.

"I feel alright, where are you? And why weren't you here when I woke up? Is this the way it's supposed to go? Just get it and go? I can't believe I…"

"Wait! Slow that noise down! I don't want to hear all that!" He had the nerve to raise his voice. "Why don't you give me a chance to explain before you tear me apart like that! Look, I had to take care of some important business early this morning. I would have loved to have been there in your arms when you woke up. But I figured there'd be other nights. You seemed to have enjoyed it." He chuckled.

"So it's a joke that I gave my virginity up to somebody who could not stay, and hold me and make me feel like I just done the right thing?! Which I didn't! And furthermore, I won't be doing that again so you won't have to look forward to other nights. My flesh may have enjoyed it last night but I'm convicted because of it now. That was a terrible mistake I made last night! I can't sit here and act like the Lord was never in my life!" Even though I did anyway, I thought.

"Look I don't want to fuss with you. And I'm not going to stay on the phone to do it. Can I take you out again tonight to get you a bite to eat? Or are you going to stay mad at me forever?"

"Did you hear what I just said? You just totally ignored me? I guess it don't mean nothing to you huh'?"

"Woman I heard what you said and your wish is my command. But I do want you to know that you are a very special lady, if you know what I mean?" He laughed.

I can't believe this, he's taking this whole entire night like a big joke. I knew I should've listened to my first mind and sent him on his way instead of letting him walk me to my door last night.

Maybe I'm over reacting a little. He didn't argue with me and he is being understanding, so why am I being so hard on him? It's not his fault, it's my fault.

"Hello?"

"Yes, I'm here." I answered.

"What did I tell you about that quiet stuff? Are you going to give me an answer or what?"

"Yea I'll go with you to dinner. But this time you won't be coming up to my apartment. When the night is over it's over."

I put my hand over my eyes blocking them from the bright sun that's shinning through the window.

"That's my girl. I can't wait to show my new woman off to the world. You are my lady right? Right?"

"Umm… I…I…"

"What you mean umm… I…I…? So what you're saying is that all we shared last night don't count for nothing?"

"Yes it does count for…"

"Well what's taking you so long to answer?"

"Yes I'll be your lady! There. You feel better?!" I shouted into the phone.

"That made my day baby. Now that you're my lady, they're some rules that go along with that. But don't worry about all that now. I'll see you at 7 tonight be dressed and look sexy. Bye baby…" He said, quickly hanging up the phone in my face.

He hung the phone up so fast I didn't get a chance to say bye back to him. I wonder what he meant by some rules? He said don't worry about it so I won't hurt my brain trying. He was probably playing anyway.

Let's see, what should I wear this time? I'm so excited to be going out to eat again. Oh' Lord just that quick I forgot about church tomorrow. This is not like me. I never forget about church. I always look forward to Sunday morning worship service at church. What's happening to me? I'm not going to worry about it now. I'll worry about it in the morning. Maybe I can ask Tyrome to come with me? That would be great.

Now I just committed to something I didn't mean. Why did I tell him that I would be his lady? He was talking so fast it's like I was manipulated into saying what he wanted me to say. So I said it. And now I regret it. He's still a married man. I can't be with him? What have I just done? How can I tell him I made a terrible mistake? I can't let Satan trick me into something that I know isn't right. I've got to find a way to tell him that I didn't mean what I said about being his girl friend. What I can't understand is why he won't get a divorce from his wife? That's the only thing that's stopping me from going any further with him. But anyway, I'm not going to worry myself about it. I'll just talk to him about it at dinner tonight. I'm sure he'll understand.

Its 6:30 and I still feel like I'm not ready yet. What's missing? Should I re-polish my nails again? I know he's going to come with nothing but the best on. I've got to give it to him, he always seem to look good in anything he wears.

There goes the phone.

"Hello?"

"Hey bay, how you doing? Are you busy?"

"O' hey mama, actually I am sort of busy. I'll call you back later on tonight. Is that alright?" I hope she don't ask any questions and understand.

"That's fine baby but why do you have to call me back later? Are you that busy?"

"Yes mama I am very busy right now."

"You must be about to go somewhere?" She asked.

"Actually I am and I'll call you when I get back ok?" I shook my head. I'm starting to get real impatient. Mama can be so nosey.

"Where are you going if you don't mind me asking?"

116

"Why do you always have to know where I'm going and what I'm doing?"

"Because I'm your mother. And you're mama's baby and I have to keep up with you. That's why. And what is wrong with that?"

"Mama you've been treating me like a baby since I was born. I'm now thirty six and you're still treating me like I'm a baby. When does it end?!"

"Never! And as long as I'm your mother I'll never stop because you will always be my baby and that will never change! Now do you understand me?" She screamed. My ear drum's about to explode. Mama always have to raise her voice to get her point across. Which isn't necessary.

"First of all you don't have to scream at me! I can hear you just fine! I know you're my mother and that you will always be my mother but you need to stay in a mother's place! I'm tired of you treating me like a new born! Now can't you understand that?!" I screamed back at her, picked up a shirt from the bed and throwing it across the room. I'm standing here with my fist balled up and moving it back and forth as if that's going to release the anger. I felt something that was built up inside of me explode and I had no choice but to release it. It must have been there for years.

"What is wrong with you?! You have never talked to me in that way, and surely you have never raised your voice at me either! Ever since you met ol' what's his name…"

"That man got a name mama!" I said, cutting her off.

"Ever since you met that man your whole attitude has changed! And I'm gon' tell you this only one time and one time only, don't you ever get to where you think you can talk to me any kind of way. Just like I brought you in this world I'll take your behind out!" She screamed louder slamming her fist down on something. The sound penetrated through the phone piercing my ear.

"Whatever mama, all I know is…!"

"Hey!" She cut me off. "Say no more! I see right now you don' got out there! You acting of the world! You just remember one thing, the Bible says in (Ephesians 6:1-2), *to obey your parents in the Lord: for this is right, (2) and to Honor thy father and mother; which is the first commandment…* And when you can do that, then you call me back. Do you understand me?! I said do you understand me?! I'll just let the Lord Himself deal with you!"

"Yea mama, whatever…!" I said, hanging the phone up in her face. I can't believe I just done that. I have never in my living life talked to my mother like that. Nor have I ever hung up the phone in her face. What's wrong with me? It's like I have this burst of anger in me now. Anger that has accumulated. Oh' well she shouldn't have said what she said and I wouldn't have went there on her. Anyway, I don't have time to worry about that. I have enough problems. I need to figure out how I'm going to tell Tyrome I made a mistake in saying that I'd be his girl. I'm sure mama will get over it and call me later. It's almost 7 and he should be here any minute now.

Time kept passing and no sign of Tyrome. It's been over an hour and still no sign of him. He should have been here by now? I hope everything's alright? He needs to come on I'm starting to cut a sweat in this pink dress suit. Michelle really helped me out when she went in my closet and showed me all my clothes I forgot I had. And fortunately this was one of them.

I can't figure out what's taking him so long? My patience is running out. He's never done this before. Should I page him or just continue to wait? I think I'll page him, something may have happened.

His voice mail sounds very professional. Only flaw is the loud music in the background. I can't really hear his voice. My cue to leaving my message was the beep.

It didn't take him long to return my page.

"Hello?" My voice trembled.

"Did somebody page me at this number?" He's acting like he never met me.

"Tyrome, it's me boy! Ramona! Why are you acting like you don't know me? Never mind all that, where are you? I've been waiting here for you for over an hour." I said, raking my fingers through my hair as if to comb it. Where is he? That music in the background is way too loud. Sounds like he's at a club. Probably the same club we were at. Men are so simple minded. Now I know he haven't forgotten that he asked me out to eat tonight? That's some crazy stuff. How can anybody forget that quick? "I think you owe me an apology, Tyrome."

"I don't owe you nothing! Look, let me tell you something! First of all you don't be hollering at me! And second of all you don't be paging me unless I give you permission to do so woman! And third of all, you wait til' I get there! You don't run me, I run you! Now wait til' I get there and you better be ready!" He hung up the phone.

I know he didn't just hang up in my face! And I know he didn't just talk to me like that! I ought' a page him back and tell him I'm not going. And what's this you don't run me I run you business? Wait til' he gets here, I'm a tell him that I'm not his girl and that I don't want to ever see him again. I ran to the bathroom, threw off my pumps, and sat in the corner chair.

God has totally left the seen. It's weird because I used to feel that unconditional love for people. Even when they would talk about me and my weight. I would still love them. I don't know what's happening to me. Is this a dream? If so, somebody please wake me up. I feel like I'm slipping further and further away from

God. It's best for me not to think about it, and then I won't get depressed. Now I know what it feels like to get into something and not know how to get out of it. I always had answers for everybody else but never would I have dreamed that I would need to put some back for myself. I'm sure everything will be alright when I see Tyrome face to face. He was probably showing out in front of his boys. Men are like that, they like to front in front of their boys but when you see them with their girls, it's a whole different ball game.

I walked in the front room, got me some juice from the frig and plopped down on the couch. I wonder what's on TV? Probably some shows that ain't funny. Now days you can't watch everything on TV because everything seems so perverted. All they show is naked women in bikini's, who wants to see that stuff? Maybe I'll just get a book and read. I haven't done that in months. I used to do it everyday before Tyrome came into my life. What a joke.

It's now 11:30. The book I was reading is on the floor. I didn't realize I had fallen asleep. Where is he? He must think I'm some tied ol' woman sitting in front of the TV all day and night waiting on him? NOT! I'm going to bed and if he knocks, I'll just ignore him.

A few more hours have passed and still no sign of Tyrome.

It's 1:27 in the morning and there's a loud knock at the door. Sounds like somebody's trying to beat the door down. The loud noise startled me so much, my ankles are shaking. There it goes again. Who in the world is that?

I jumped up out of the bed, got a stick from behind the dresser, and ran and stood on side of the front door.

It sounds like they're hitting it with a bat or a two-by-four.

"Open the door Ramona!" It's Tyrome and he sounds so drunk. He's shouting so loud he's going to wake up the neighbors. Maybe if I let him in we can get to the bottom of this, and so the neighbor's won't call the police.

"Ramona would y…"

I opened the door.

"Would you come in and stop shouting, you're drunk!" I closed the door behind him.

"Why wouldn't you open the door woman?!" He pointed his finger in my face. I wanted to slap it down his throat, having the audacity to come in my house drunk and full of the devil!

"Tyrome you're drunk and I think you need a reality check. Because you don't be putting your finger in my face!" I screamed back at him. Stepping back from his hand as he waved it closer to my face. His breath smells horrible!

"What did I tell you bout' bossing me around?! Don't no woman boss me around! I done told you that already and if I got to tell you one mo' time I'm a…"

"You gon' what?! Huh'?! What you gon' do? You ain't scaring nobody!" I yelled back. I've never experienced this side of me before. I didn't think I could ever get this bold. Fear and anger has totally taking control of me. This was once a nice, tall, intelligent, respectful, nice looking man. But now he looks like a walking beast. And he's acting like a drunk from off the streets. They always say, what's in you will going to come out. And what was in him all along has surfaced. "Ain't nobody scared of you! Get out of my house!" I pointed towards the door.

"What?! What?! I'm not going nowhere…!" He ran up and slapped me right in the face. It was so hard all I can see is stars.

I have never been hit by anybody before, not even by my parents. This is the man I gave myself to. He stole a part of me and now he's scarred me for the rest of my life. I'll never forget this. "What is wrong with you?!" I yelled, as I tried to run to the room.

"You're not going nowhere!" He pulled me by the hair, picked me up, and slammed me on the floor like a man.

All I can do is scream. I can't believe this is happening to me. "Stop hitting me! Why are you doing this to me?!" I screamed louder hoping somebody would hear me. The more I screamed, the harder his punches got. It's like I'm his personal punching bag. Finally I stopped screaming, my face is numb, and can't feel his punches anymore. I think every bone in my face is broken.

"Shut up! I told you don't no woman own me, I own you! Do you understand?!" He hit me again. It's like he's possessed with demon spirits. His eyes are blood shot red from what my swollen eyes will allow me to see. And he looks like a totally different person.

Finally I agreed so he would stop. I figure if I say what he wants to hear, he would eventually stop. I see now, it's a controlling thing. I never thought I would get with an abusive man. What in the world have I gotten' myself into? What does my future hold? All I wanted was to be happy. Not tortured.

He finally stopped. He got up and ran out of the house as if something was after him. The only noise in the room was my crying from the hurt of my wounds he had created. There's nowhere to run and nowhere to hide. I'm scared to even move.

I finally got the courage to turn my head and try and see where he was but both of my eyes are closed shut. Blood is all over my face. God, is this the punishment I get from sleeping with a married man? Yea I messed up, but why would You allow this to happen to me? I don't understand? It's early Sunday morning. I can't go to church looking like this? I'm not even worthy enough to set foot in Your temple after what I've done.

When I was finally able to open my eyes, it was 3:00 in the afternoon. I'm still on the floor in front of the door of my bedroom. My body ached as I tried to pull myself to sit up. I wrestled to my feet and staggered to the bathroom to see what damages were done. My head's as big as a basketball. My face is so puffed up. It feels like my eyes are about to pop out of my head.

I turned and walked back into the front room only to find blood all over the floor, and the door wide open. The door was open all night. I wonder when he left? I thought, as I closed the door, staggered back into my room, closed the door behind me and laid across the bed.

I know what I'm going to do, I'm going to call mama and tell her to tell daddy to go get him. As I started dialing her number I remembered our last conversation on the phone and it wasn't a good one. They probably wouldn't want to talk to me anyway. I don't have anybody to turn to. My parents don't want to talk to me, I'm all alone, and I just got beat up by this man that I thought loved me.

It's like for a moment I had the whole world in my hands. I was on cloud nine. What happened to my praise? What happened to all the things I was believing God for? What about my morals and values? What happened to the Holy Spirit that was living inside of me? I used to be excited when Saturday nights came because I knew that it wouldn't be long before Sunday was here. All that has left me. That scripture is so true, *the wages of sin is death* (Romans 6:23). And right now I feel spiritually dead. All because of what I allowed myself to get involved in. All because of my flesh. There's nothing good about this flesh. Nothing. I'm so embarrassed for people to see me like this. Especially when I'm supposed to be the example at my job. The people at work have always disliked me because of my relationship with the Lord. And there was a time when they tried to get me fired. But God said different. He did say that we would be persecuted, because He was. And we're supposed to be following in His footsteps but look at me. I'm going in the opposite direction. I can remember at work when my co-workers would come against me, God would fight my battles every time. He said that *He would make our enemies our footstool* (Psalms 110:1), and he has made them all my footstool. They don't like me but they don't have a choice but to respect me when they're in my presence. But what made this time so different? This is when I needed you the most. Why did You allow the enemy to put his hands on me? Is it because of what I done? I slipped, I know. I'll never be able to live with myself. All I wanted was to feel like somebody. Maybe it was my fault? Maybe I drove him to hit me? I mean I was running my mouth too much. I feel like I've lost control of who I am. I'm just a fat ol' whale with no future and surely no chance of having a real family. Don't nobody want a fat woman. O' well! It don't even matter anymore… I guess the devil has won. He's the real reason for all of this anyway.

Oh' my God, I've over slept. It's going on 1:30 in the afternoon. I hope Mr. Kevin don't get mad because I didn't show up for work today. I thought, as I rose up to look at the clock. I'm surprised. He didn't even call like he normally does when I'm running late. But today he didn't, I wonder why? Whatever, I'm not going to worry about it. I'll see him tomorrow. Maybe.

The phone is ringing so loud it's piercing my ears.

"Hello?" I answered, after struggling to the phone beside my bed.

"Girl where were you today? You know I missed seeing you this morning and for lunch? This is not like you. You never miss work. Are you alright? I didn't like the way you said hello when you answered the phone. That didn't sound like you. You have a cold?" She asked. Michelle has the nagging type of voice that would sometimes get on your nerves if you let it.

"No I oh', don't have a cold." My face and my mouth are still swollen. I hope she'll just leave it alone and don't press the issue.

"No um' um' something's not right and I'm about to come find out what it is. I'm on my way over there." She quickly hung up the phone.

It wasn't long before I heard a knock at the door. Every knock sounds like the bamming he did on last night. I'm almost too scared to look, it may be him again.

"Ramona! It's me girl open up the door!" She shouted, through the door.

Good it's her. I guess I'll go ahead and open it.

"Oh' no! Wait a minute, what in the world happened to you?! I know that low down dirty animal didn't put his hands on you?!" She grabbed my shoulder to get a closer look. She had this expression on her face that I have never seen before. For once I felt like she cared about me. She's so upset. Her eyes got redder the more she opened her mouth.

"I can't lie to you. Tyrome and I got into a fight last night. He asked me out to dinner but never showed up. He was supposed to pick me up at 7. But when 7:45 rolled around and he hadn't showed up, I got worried and paged him. I left a message on his voice mail. When he called me back he acted like he didn't even know me. And when he figured out that it was me, he went off and started yelling and told me that I better not ever page him again until he gives me permission to. He also said that he owned me or something like that… and… and…"

"Girl I am so sorry for you. Don't cry. I'm right here. I'm your friend and you can trust me. I don't know why tied ol' sorry wimps like him want to hit on a woman. Why can't they just fight a man?" She walked to the kitchen, got some ice from the freezer, put it in napkins, and brought it and put it on my face. "Cause' they're weak lil' ol' punks that's why." She said, as she went to the bathroom, wet a towel, and came and wiped off the blood that had dried on my face.

For the first time I truly believe her. I know I can trust her and I feel really confident about being her friend. I know she got my back. I hope that never changes.

After about fifteen minutes of silence she finally asked me what was I going to do.

"I really don't know what I'm going to do. I don't have an answer to that question. It's weird because my flesh wants to call him and see where he is and in my spirit I want nothing to do with him. It's like I'm tied to him. Once you sleep with a man you become one. You are soul tied together. And that's basically how I'm feeling right now. My flesh wants him to come over and have sex with him all night long. But my spirit is saying leave him alone. He's no good for you. Which one will I listen to? I don't know because my flesh is weak, and I can't control it. This is crazy, I know. I only slept with him once. But I guess that's all it takes. I know you're surprised that I'm talking like this because I'm usually the one telling you to do right. Well hey, I messed up Michelle. Judge me later."

Her eyes and her mouth is so wide open It's like she just seen a ghost. She finally says, "Actually I'm in shock. I don't know what to say." I figured she'd say that.

"I don't know either."

"What do you mean you don't know?" She stood up beside me and put her hands on her hips.

"You want me to be honest with you?" I looked up at her then looked down at the carpet.

"Yea I want you to be honest with me but not stupid. Do you want him pounding on you again?!" She raised her voice. "Look at cha', you don't even sound like yourself. Where's the Christian woman that I once knew? I'm the one that should be sounding like you. Not you sounding like me? Ok so what, you made a

mistake get over it and move on! I'm not going to judge you!"
She went and sat down on the couch.

"I don't think he's going to do this again."

"Girl please if he done it once, he'll do it again."

"No, really, I don't think he'll do this again because he was
real drunk when he came over last night. He probably don't even
remember what he did which is probably the reason why he
haven't called yet." I said, putting the ice pack that Michelle made
down on the floor, because the melted water was running down
my arm.

In my heart I want so badly to believe that. And I want
Michelle to believe it to. It's almost like I'm being controlled by
him and he's not even here.

"Well, that's you. Look, I'm about to go but whatever you
choose to do, I'm going to support you." She got up off the
couch, walked over and picked the ice pack up off the floor, took
it to the kitchen and then went and opened the front door.

"Thanks girl I really needed to hear that."

"Alright, I'll call you later to see how you're feeling ok?" She
turned to face me.

"Thanks for everything Michelle. I'll talk to you later."

"No problem. Bye." She turned and closed the door behind
her.

I couldn't hardly wait for her to close the door before I broke
down crying. I can't stop crying.

I've made up in my mind that I'm not going to go back to
work until my face totally heals up.

I stayed out of work for 2 weeks. My wounds have totally healed
up and I'm back to work tomorrow. I couldn't find it in my heart
to tell Mr. Kevin what really happened so I just told him that it
was female problems. Or course he didn't want to hear about it

so he told me to take as long as I needed. Two weeks have gone by and I haven't even seen a church. In fact, I never came out of the house. Michelle calls constantly but sometimes I don't even pick up the phone. She comes and knocks on the door and I don't even have the strength to get up and answer it. I'm so depressed and lonely. I want so badly to page him. Not once have he came by or even called. I should be happy because the relationship wasn't right in the first place. How can a dysfunctional relationship work out? It can't. There's no way on this earth. It all seem fantastic at first but then as time goes by, that's when everything starts to go wrong. Starting with jealousy, leading to fussing and possessiveness. Then to control, to manipulation, to domination, and then to beating the brains out of each other. Sounds like a Jezebel spirit to me. Unfortunately the woman always seems to lose the battle. But not in all cases. Sometimes it's the other way around. Either way is wrong. I read in the Bible about a Jezebel spirit *(1 Kings 16: 30-34, 17-22)*. Jezebel was a very evil and controlling woman. She was the wife of Ahab and the daughter of Ethbaal king of the Zidonians. And the spirit that she operated in was more than one spirit. They were all a controlling spirit, a manipulating spirit, a dominating spirit, and a seducing spirit. I believe that Tyrome is operating in those spirits. But I can't talk about him because I'm operating in some body's spirit myself. We all need help. That's all I can say right now.

I guess I'll go get ready for tomorrow. It'll be my first day back and I know I got a pile of work all over my desk which I don't look forward to.

Chapter 9

Everybody screamed with joy when I walked in the office. I'm shocked. There's even a big smile on Mr. Kevin's face. Hum. I need to stay away more often. You never know how much you can miss a person until they're gone. "Thanks for the warm welcome. I just want to say, thank you for your support and for your encouraging words." I walked towards my desk and sat down. Some had more encouraging words to say as they all returned back to their offices.

Mr. Kevin came up to me runnin' his mouth and ready to be negative. "Alright girl, you got a lot to do! I saved all the work for you and it's piled up on your desk as you can see. And next time try not to stay away so long you hear?" He walked towards the door of his office. "And another thing, you need to do something about your friend. He came in here everyday looking for you! And tried to get an attitude because I wouldn't tell him where you were! How I look telling another man you can't come to work because you got female problems?! Huh'?! You better be glad I like you cause I was about to hit your friend and I know you wouldn't have liked that! So you better talk to him before I get with that head!" He yelled as he laughed, walked into his office, and slammed the door.

I can't believe it. Why didn't he just come by my house? I was so busy I didn't notice all the cards he's left on my desk. It seems to be about ten or fifteen of them which one do I read first? I guess I'll read the one with the latest date on it.

I see he got a Christian card. I wonder why when men mess up, they always want to resort to the Lord? If they would just do right in the first place they wouldn't have to do all this buttering up. I guess he think these cards is going to make me jump at his command. I admit, I want to talk to him but I just can't right now. I just can't. He's not good for me.

It's only 11:30 in the morning and I don't get off of work until five. Which seem so far away. I can say that I miss being at work considering all the work I have to do. I think back to the times when I talked bad about my job, and the minute I wasn't working it felt like I was unemployed. So it made me appreciate it real quick. Especially when I thought I wasn't coming back.

Lunch time is almost here and I'm meeting Michelle for lunch. I can't wait! I miss eating lunch with that girl, and having to listen to her run her mouth.

The phone rang.

"Hello, KGR and Associates may I help you?" I asked, while tapping my pen on the desk.

"Yes you may by letting me apologize for what I did to you the other week. I don't really remember what happened, I was too drunk. But I do remember some of it. And I just want to say I'm sorry. Will you forgive me Ramona, I'm so sorry."

"I don't want to talk to you, and don't call my job again!" I slammed the phone down in his face.

Why did I do that? Maybe he is sorry and don't really remember what he did? I mean, when you get drunk you do lose conscious of everything. I hope he calls back. I've been waiting to hear from him and I don't want to miss this chance again.

"Hey! Did you hear what happened?!" Mr. Kevin came running out of his office screaming.

"Did I hear what?"

"Somebody broke in our other branch office and stole all the money that was in the main safe! Can you believe that?! Who ever did it must be a professional thief cause' that's the hardest safe to break into. They're cameras all around the place! They had to have known what they were doing! I wish I knew who did it I wouldn't even tell on em'. I'd just make em' give me a lil' cut on the side and my mouth is shut!" He laughed as he went back into his office without waiting on my response.

I admit, I had to laugh too because Mr. Kevin is so silly. The sad thing about it is that he's serious. I wonder who would do something so bold? It couldn't be their first time either. Just like Mr. Kevin was saying, it had to be a professional. Anyway, I have bigger and better things to do than to be worrying about that.

It was a long and very hot ride home. My air in the little Chevrolet still doesn't work. But that's ok cause it's going to be my time one day.

When I pulled up to my usual parking spot, I noticed a brand new 2002 Lexus Land Cruiser sitting in the way. What a beauty. I love its champagne color. I always wanted one with that same color. Now. Let me see. I know almost everybody in these apartments, and I can't think of anybody who could afford something like this? Maybe it belongs to that new girl who stays right around the corner from my apartment. She's very quiet and unfriendly. I have to pass her apartment to get to mine.

Something about her just doesn't seem right. Anyway, I wonder if this brand new truck belongs to her? I'll soon find out. I thought, as I got out of the car, walked to my apartment, and went in.

It's nice and cold in here. Just the way I like it when I get home from a hard days work. "What? I have four new messages?

131

I wonder who could they be? I know one of them is probably from Michelle. But I have the slightest idea who could've left the other three. Let me see."

"...*Message one*...Hey Ramona I have to tell you something. Call me chick! This Michelle." The phone clicks.

"...*Message two*...Click..." The phone hung up.

"...*Message three*...Click..." The phone hung up again.

"...*Message four*...Um', he- hello, hello, look Michelle like I was trying to say earlier, I'm truly sorry. I know you probably don't want to talk to me but I remembered you said a long time ago that you wanted a Lexus Land Cruiser and I thought, what better way to make it up to you. I know by now you've seen the brand new Land Cruiser sitting out front..." The answering machine cut him off. "As I was saying before I was cut off. I parked it in your parking spot so you'll know it belongs to you. Why don't chu' go outside and get in, it's yours baby! The keys are on top of the front left tire. Surprise! I hope you forgive me! Let me go before this thang hangs up on me." Click... The phone hung up.

"What? I don't believe that. I know he's lying." I said out loud. Should I go out and see if it's really mine? I guess I better before somebody drives off in it. I thought, as I ran out laughing.

Tyrome is a really nice person inside I just wish he could do right. I now realize that he didn't mean to hit me, he's a really good hearted guy. I just have one question, how in the world could he have gotten all this money to get this type of vehicle? Oh' well I'll think about that later I'm a enjoy this right now before this dream ends. I laughed at the thought.

When I got to the truck I felt under the left tire and sure nuff' the keys are right there. I screamed. "Let me go call Michelle so we can go cruise around town!"

I ran up to the apartment, and went straight to the phone.

I wonder what she's going to say. I thought, pushing the buttons on the phone. "Hey girl what are you doing?! Guess what?! You'll never believe it?! I have the biggest surprise for you! Can I come over right now?!"

"Girl what?! Your timing is so off! I'm busy right now with some company, if you know what I mean? What's the surprise? You know I support you in anything you do?" She laughed.

Um' yea' right. I'm not going to go there. "Oh' girl don't worry about it, I'll show you later. Go ahead and entertain your company. I'll talk to you later."

"Alright bye." She quickly hung up.

It's just like she didn't even hear what I was telling her the other day at work about the men she's sleeping with. Oh' well, the pot can't talk about the kettle.

I got a brand new truck sitting outside and nobody to celebrate it with. I guess I'll celebrate all by myself. I walked back out to the truck, got in, started it up, and started driving down the street. The interior in this thing is so computerized. I can't believe it's actually mine. And it rides smooth too. Anything's better than that old Chevrolet. This is my dream truck. I just got to go back and beg Michelle to come and ride with me! She won't believe this! If I had a cell phone, I could just ring her from inside the truck.

It was a quick ride back.

I got to admit, I was speeding a little. Wait a minute that looks like Tyrome's truck sitting in my parking space. I thought I'd never see him again.

I pulled beside his truck.

"Hey sweet thang, I see you couldn't wait could you?" He smiled.

"Is this mine or did you borrow it from somebody, and late tonight when I'm sleep you plan on coming back to steal it from me?" We both laughed.

"No, now you're talking crazy. You know I would never do you like that. Especially not at a time like this. I'm too busy trying to make up for what I did to you baby. I guess you accept my apology because you all in the truck and thangs. What's up?"

"Well I can't say that I haven't thought about you but that doesn't mean that I'm still not mad at you."

"Look, why don't we take a ride in your new truck? I've never been in a Land Cruiser before."

"You don't waste no time, I haven't told you that I forgive you yet?"

"You don't have to, it's all in your eyes. So like I said what's up? Are we going to do this or what because I got things to do?" He asked with confidence.

He always has a way of trying to rush me for an answer. Some people would ask why am I even talking to a guy who just not too long ago beat the brains out me? Well, all I can say is that I don't have an answer for that. It's hard to say no to him for some reason. I don't know why? And besides, I do miss talking to him. So why not? We're just going for a ride. "I guess, but I'm not going far because I have things to take care of to."

"Cool, it doesn't matter because I'm not doing the driving." He got out of his truck and got into mine.

The hot breeze blew hard on our faces as we drove down the street with the windows down.

"Let me show you how to work the air because this hot breeze is not working for me." He pushed the button to raise the windows up, and then turned the switch that controls the air conditioner on.

"So that's how you turn it on?! O', ok! That feels so much better!" We both laughed.

"Say girl you going mighty fast, won't you slow down? You didn't drive this fast in that ol' hoopty sitting at your apartments." He threw his hands up and laughed.

"You right, I didn't even notice that I was driving so fast. This thing rides so smooth."

"Yea' but you got to control yourself because I'm not going to jail for nobody."

"Who said anything about jail? I'm not going that fast Tyrome? And why are you so paranoid?" I looked over at him.

"Woman just drive we're having a good time, don't ruin it."

"Hey, wait a minute! I can't believe this?! Look in your mirror! It's the police!" I slammed my hand on his thigh.

"What?! What have you done you crazy woman?! Keep driving, don't stop I know some back roads, they'll never catch us! I've done it too many times!" He yelled looking back.

"Why not stop, we don't have any warrants?! It's just a speeding ticket?! It's my truck, I can pay for it!" I slowed the truck down.

"No! I said don't pull over!" He reached for the steering wheel and took his foot and slammed it on top of mine. The truck sped up to 90 miles per hour down a two lane road.

"Are you crazy?! Let go Tyrome! You're going to make us run into something! Let go and move your foot! Let go! Move! I can't control it, we're about to crash!" We wrestled as I slammed my left foot on the break bringing the truck to a screeching stop, throwing Tyrome into the front glass.

It was silent for a minute. I thought Tyrome was dead but he gained conscious. The right side of the window is shattered. Blood is running from the huge gash he has on his forehead. He wasn't wearing a seat belt.

The police voices echoed from the loud speaker. "Hold your hands up where we can see them and don't make any extra moves or we'll shoot! Get em' up!" It must be a hundred cops behind us. I threw my hands up and Tyrome did to.

"Now get out slowly with your hands on top of your heads, and lay down on the ground face down!"

"What in the world is happening? I've never been in trouble before. All I was doing was speeding? Why are there so many cops after us? I don't understand?" I turned and looked at Tyrome for an answer.

"Shut up and open the door. Don't say anything to me ever again. If it wasn't for you we wouldn't be in this position right now." He opened his door with blood still running down his face, and threw back up is hands.

"No. No you will not blame this on me. It's all your fault. And furthermore, it's only a speeding ticket." I opened my door and put my hands back over my head.

If it's only a speeding ticket then why do we have to get on the ground? Maybe because we sped up and didn't stop right away. I don't know. I thought.

"Now get out and lay on the ground, facing the opposite direction. Slowly!! One false move and we'll shoot you!"

They ran up to us so fast I thought they was about to beat us up. Two of them jumped on top of Tyrome, put one knee in his back, and pulled his arms around his back to lock the handcuffs. Not caring about the cut on his head. "I'm not understanding this, what's going on officer?! All I was doing was speeding?! I realize that I didn't stop right away but we shouldn't be treated like this?!" He pulled my arms around my back and fastened the handcuffs.

"We don't have time for games! You know why we stopped you!"

"I'm sorry officer, I really don't know why we're being arrested?!"

"Ok let me put it to you this way, aggravated robbery with a deadly weapon, theft, possession of narcotics, resisting arrest, speeding, need I go on?!" He pulled me up, walked me to the car, and put me in the back. "Stop acting like you don't know what we're talking about!" He slammed the door.

They put Tyrome in another car. I can't believe he did this to me? The truck was stolen all along. How could I be so stupid?

"Why did you do this to me?!" I yelled, cried, and kicked the back seat.

"Do you want more time for taring up my property?! I suggest you stop right now!" The police yelled from outside the car.

It was a long ride to the police station. I had plenty of time to think about what in the world I got myself into. Lord what did I do to deserve this treatment? What did I do to be put in this position? I don't even care anymore, it's over for me. My kinfolks and I aren't getting along so I have nobody to call to bail me out. Wait, I forgot all about Michelle I know she will with all the money she got. Good I'll just get up here and be in and out. I'll explain it to them that they got the wrong person and that I didn't have anything to do with none of this drama.

The police station was full of people. It took forever to get me enlisted and forever for me to use the phone. They took me straight to the cell. It's horrible in here. I always saw this kind of stuff on TV never in real life. It's actually worse. The toilet stinks, the cell stinks, and the whole jail stinks.

"Hey you, you fat girl! Can I come sit by you?" This tall skinny Caucasian woman yelled from across the cell.

I figure if I act like I don't hear her, she'll leave me alone. I looked the other way.

"Say, you don't hear me talking to you?!" She came up to me and slapped me right in the face.

I screamed and threw myself to the floor. This is a flash back from the damage that Tyrome had just done.

"Ha! Look ya'll she's a wimp!" She looked around as the other inmates laughed. "Get up!" She kicked me in the stomach, knocking the air out of me.

"Please stop, I can't breathe!" I tried to scream but couldn't.

"No, don't cry now you big baby! Can't nobody save you!"

"Leave her alone!" This woman with a husky scratchy voice came up behind the other tall woman and pushed her in the back, knocking her to the floor. They wrestled for a minute, and then the tall one ran to the other side of the cell.

She pulled me up off the floor and set me on the bench. "Thanks for what you just did I really appreciate it." I said.

"It's no problem, I do this for all my women. You can thank me later. Remember you owe me one."

"Hold up I don't know what you're talking about but I don't roll like that. I thought you was just being nice?"

"Nobody's nice in here. You better get with the program or you'll be beat up or killed in a matter of days." She walked off.

What in the world am I going to do? I have never been in this kind of situation in my life. It doesn't look like they're going to let me out soon. I can't let these women humiliate me and my body. "Let me out! Let me out!" I yelled through the bars. They won't even look in my direction. I'm not calling on God, I'm sure He doesn't want to have anything to do with me anyhow. All the damage I've caused. And all the disappointments I'm sure I've caused. It's all Tyrome's fault, if I hadn't been fooling with him all this wouldn't be going on right now. Well I can't put all the blame on him. It's really my fault because, I allowed myself to get involved with a married man that probably didn't love me in the first place. When I met him he was already living in sin, so what was left was either for me to go down, or for him to come up. Unfortunately, I was the one to go down. This all happened because I lost contact with God. Basically I've backslidden from God. I got caught up with somebody who was never good for me. That's why they always say, a saved person should never hook up with somebody who's not saved, because you two will be unequally yoked. You would be on one level and they would be on a whole different level. Your mindset would be totally different. Either you're going to think like him, or he's going to think like you. You wouldn't have anything in common. But I allowed myself to get involved anyway and look what happened. I'm in jail and my life is shattered.

"Ramona Williams, let's go!" The guard yelled as the cell bars opened up. "Right this way." He directed me towards a small room.

A detective met me at a small table. "Come in Miss. Williams… Have a seat."

He's sitting on the opposite end of a small table, two more detectives are standing up on each side of him, and the room is full of cigarette smoke.

"Hey you want a smoke?" One of them asked.

"No, no I don't smoke." I wonder why all the attention is focused on me? I was just speeding? I don't have a record cause' I've never been in here a day in my life.

"Are you ready to talk?" He pushed the button on the tape recorder that's sitting on the table, took a long puff of his cigarette, and leaned back in his chair while putting his hands behind his neck.

"What are you talking about? All I was doing was speeding." I answered nervously.

He jumped up out of his seat and leaned over the table. "Look we don't have time for games you stupid lady you know exactly what we're talking about!" He came over and pointed his finger in my face. "Now talk!"

"I'm sorry but I don't know what you're talking about?!" I moved my head away from his finger.

"Stop the bull! We know you're apart of them. We've been watching you two for a while now. So when are you going to talk to us, or do we have to settle this in the court room? Look we'll make a deal with you, if you talk to us, give us names of those involved, we'll let you go free with only probation." He went and sat back down.

"I still don't know what you're talking about. I can't give you names because I don't know anybody."

"Where did you meet Tyrome?" One of the officer's standing asked as he pushed the tape recorder towards me.

"We met at my job."

"First of all you know the truck you were driving was stolen, and you know we found boxes of drugs underneath your truck? We know you already know that. Now tell us where you got it from? Who are your sources? If you tell us, we'll let you go with probation. We've been trying to get Mr. Jenkins for a while now. He's the biggest drug dealer in this state. And now he's behind bars! We really don't believe that you're totally involved, but we believe that you do know some important information that we need to get the rest of them locked up. If you would just cooperate, we'll let you go. Simple as that! If not, you will be in here for a long time! Now you choose!" He turned and looked at the rest of the detectives for their agreement.

Wow, this is serious. I didn't know Tyrome was wanted for drugs. And I didn't know he was the biggest drug dealer in this state. How could I be so naive? That's how he was getting me all those gifts. I wonder if he was responsible for the money that was stolen from the safe at work?

"Are you going to answer us Miss. Williams or do we need to go ahead and do what we're going to do with you?!" He slammed his fist down on the table.

There's a huge lump in my throat. I feel as if my whole life depends on my answer. I don't know who they're talking about, so I don't know how to answer. If I lie I'm in bigger trouble. I'm already in enough trouble with the Lord anyway. "I'm sorry, I can't give you an answer because I don't know who you're talking about." I lowered my voice.

"Ok fine! You wanna play stupid! We'll take care of that, somebody get her out of here! You'll have plenty of time to think about it!" The guard came over, pulled me from the chair, and shoved me out.

My entire life has just ended. I can't stop the tears from falling from my eyes. The guard took me all the way back to the cell. I used to say I would never go to jail and that would never be me. But I've learned to never say never.

I guess this is called the holding tank. The room can fit about ten or fifteen people. There's one toilet that sits in the corner with no sink. The noise is unbearable. People are screaming and cursing and the guards act like they don't even care.

Where in the world do I go from here? I know if mama and daddy knew I was in here, they would probably disown me. It doesn't matter because it's like they disown me now anyways. I can't remember the last time I talked to them. And I know it's going to be a long time when I'll be able to see or talk to them again. I shouldn't have talked to mama like I did. How could I be so stupid and disrespectful? I wasn't raised like this. I let a man come between our relationship. We were always close. If I could turn back the heads of time, I would turn it back just enough to apologize to my mama and tell her that I'm sorry. I used to be so close to the Lord. Nothing could make me fall. How could I have strayed away from you Lord? I was sold out for Him. I felt like nothing could come between us I… I rested my head on my legs and let the tears fall.

"Ramona Williams!" The guard yelled through the cell bars as the they opened up.

He walked me to the telephones. "You got five minutes so make it quick." He turned and walked away.

The only one I have to call is Michelle. I wonder what she'll say? "Hello? Michelle?"

"Yea girl what's up? Why are you calling from the jail? And collect at that?"

"Look I need your help. I got into some trouble with Tyrome and I need you to come bail me out. I'll explain it all later when we get home." I turned towards the wall so nobody could hear me.

"I can't do that!"

"Why, what's wrong?" I tried to whisper. "You got all the money in the world? I'll pay you back."

"Look that doesn't mean anything. Is that all you want me for?"

"No Michelle you know I have never asked you for no money nor have I ever needed you in any way."

"Well anyway, besides I got a date tonight and I mean I've been trying to get with this guy for along time. Let me get back with you. I can't miss this one. I've been waiting too long for this handsome thang'!" She tried not to chuckle but did anyway.

"Get back with me? Michelle this is not a joke, I really need your help. I'm in some deep trouble, and the sad thing about it is that I'm innocent. So are you going to help me or what?"

"Look I told you I'd get back with you, it's not like you're going anywhere?" She chuckled.

"Are you serious? I hope you're drunk and not thinking about what you're saying?"

"I'm not drunk!" she yelled. "In fact, I haven't had a drink all day! Look you got in this mess by yourself, so don't make it seem like it's my fault! You're the one that's supposed to be Miss. Perfect Christian. So get your God to bail you out?! You the main one preaching about this stupid word call faith, so let faith bail you out! I'm glad I don't run around running my mouth about some God I've never seen nor felt! You better off living like the way I live, at least you don't have to worry about things happening like this! What I do is working for me. Got a good paying job, got good men coming to my house when I want, and got money coming to me from every direction. So Miss. Thang, I think you better get with the progra…"

"You know what Michelle let me cut you off!" I raised my voice as the guards looked my way. "It sounds like to me you never was my friend in the first place! You're nothing but a big front. You look good on the outside, but all torn up on the inside! You can't have no peace while living in sin! There's no way! The sad thing about it is that you're not saved and don't even care to be! God is still doing so much for you even though you don't want to know Him! It's only because of His mercy! But remember, you reap what you sow. You sow evil, you reap evil. The reason why I slipped is because I got too close to this friendship and let you entice me to do things that I knew I shouldn't have done! Going to the clubs, stopped going to church, and fornicating with a married man! And the reason behind all this is because I was trying to please you and not God! You never really accepted me as your true friend in the first place!"

"That's not true!" She yelled.

"Yea, it's true! In high school you used to talk about me behind my back! But when you came back in town years later I thought you had changed! But I see right now that I was wrong! You were starting to be like the sister I never had! I put my trust in you when I should've been putting my trust in the Lord! I'm sorry I ever bothered calling you! I promise you, you will never hear from me again!" I tried to hold back the tears, but I can't they're too heavy. My throat feels like it's about to explode.

"Whatever Ramona, you're not going to make me feel like it's my fault you're in jail. I don't care what you're saying about me! And that's fine, if you don't want to be friends there's more where that came from! So whatever, bye, you'll need me before I need you!"

She hung up the phone in my face. I slammed the phone down right behind her as if I was hanging up in her face, leaned against the wall and slid down to the ground. Everything's happening to me all at once. First I get into it with my mama and now we're not talking, then I get hooked up with this married man that I allowed to ruin my life, and now the only friend I thought I could trust has just betrayed me. What have I done to deserve this? I know they're a lot of people that sin all the time and nothing happens to them like this. Maybe Michelle's right, I'm always preaching and teaching and look at me now, I'm the one who needs help. And like she said about the word faith, deep down inside I agree with her. I mean look at me, I was going to church doing all the right things and still was broke. And now I'm in trouble and more broke than I was in the beginning. I'm so sick of this whole world, I'm better off killing myself because if I stay up in here I'm going to die anyway. But somewhere in the back of my mind I can still hear the Lord saying: *"Don't give up. I want you to come back to me and I will forgive you. I'll rescue you from all of your fears. I never turned my back on you, you turned your back on me with your sins. I love you, but I hate sin, and I punish sin. If you repent and come back to me, I'll deliver you and save you from all of your troubles..."*

All I have left is to talk to Him. How could You ever forgive and rescue me? All that I've done wrong? I'm not worthy to be forgiven. If You're really speaking to me, then confirm it. Confirm that I'm going to be alright. I said within myself.

"Ok times up! Right this way!" The guard slightly grabbed my arm and directed me back towards the cell.

"Mr. I feel real weak, it feels like I'm about to pass out." I stopped and leaned against the wall.

"I'm not buying that, lets go I got other inmates to tend to!" He reached over and pulled my arm.

When I woke up it seemed like I had been sleep for about a week.

"This light's too bright in my eyes." I covered my face. "Where am I?" I asked the woman standing over me.

"You're in the hospital. You're going to be fine." She said. Her voice is so soft and full of wisdom. It makes you want to trust her with your life.

"How did I get in here?" I looked up at her.

"You passed out in jail."

"Why do they have these handcuffs around my arms? I'm not a criminal?"

"Calm down, I'm here to help you." She said humbly.

"Look, I didn't ask to be up in here. My stupid ex-boyfriend got me into all this mess. I'm innocent and they won't believe me! This entire thing is crazy! And I feel like I'm going crazy!"

I tried to get up but the handcuffs stopped me. Their latched around both of my wrists, with the other half around the bed posts.

"Quiet down it's going to be alright, the Lord is with you." She gently held me down on the bed.

"The Lord?! If He love me so much why did He allow this to happen to me?!"

"He didn't have anything to do with what happened to you. You took your eyes off of Him and allowed the devil to take control. See, God loves you more than you will ever know." She said softly. "He would never do anything to hurt you. What destroys us is our sins, because God hates sin. It says in James 1:15 that *'when lust hath conceived, it bringeth forth sin: and sin, when it is conceived, it bringeth forth death.'* And it also says that *'the wages of sin is death.'* But *'the gift of God is eternal life through Jesus Christ our Lord'* (Romans 6:23). If you turn back to Him, He will rescue you from all this pain, suffering, and hardships. But it's your choice. Hell is real and I'm sure you don't want to go there. There's so much in-store for you, so many blessings to receive. Just turn back to Him that's all He's waiting for." She softly rubbed my hand with comfort.

She's a Caucasian woman that looks to be in her late sixties. She has long beautiful shinny grey hair. Looks like she weighs about one sixty at about five nine. She's breath taking, she looks like an angel. Her eyes twinkled as she looked into my eyes and spoke with words of humility. Her skin is even glowing. She looks so pure. The presence of God is all over her. I know she's a real woman of God. It's like I'm at peace with all of my problems and about this situation that I'm in right now. Her touch is one that I have never experienced. My mama always said to be careful how you treat people cause you could be entertaining angles unaware (Hebrews 13:2). I believe she's a messenger sent by God. Thanks for confirmation. "I feel better now, since you're here." I hope she never leaves me but for some reason I know she won't be staying long.

"Good I'm happy for you, you're going to be alright. Remember to trust in the Lord with all your heart and lean not to your own understanding, and in all your ways acknowledge Him and He will direct your path (Proverbs 3: 5-6). Don't give up on Him, He loves you and is waiting for you to come back to Him. You are very special to Him and one day you will see. But first you must endure these hard trials and in the end you will be victorious. Don't let the cares of this world make you miss your blessings. My assignment is up. Would you like something cold to drink?" Her smile lit up the whole room as she walked towards the door.

"Yes, please. Some water." I never took my eyes off of her as she left out of the room.

Fifteen minutes have passed. No sign of the doctor. I wonder where she went?

"Hi senora, here's your cold drink you asked for." Another doctor came in. She's a short Hispanic lady with beautiful short black hair with streaks of blonde running down the sides.

"Where's the doctor that was in here earlier?"

"What other doctor? I'm the only one that has been assigned to your room." She looked at me strange.

"I know I'm not crazy. There was another doctor that was just in here."

"I'm sorry senora but I'm the only doctor on this floor. And it's been this way all day." She put the drink of water on the table next to my bed. "If you need anything else just push the button right beside your bed again." She walked towards the door.

"Again? Did you say again? I never pushed the button for you to come in the first place. How did you know I needed service?"

"Because the bell was ranged from this room for service." She looked at me bewilderedly and then left out of the room.

"Hey, I didn't..." I stopped myself because she closed the door while I was talking.

Could that really have been God sending his angel to tell me that? I've heard of things happening like this in movies or people testifying in church about them. But never in my wildest dreams would I have ever thought that that would have happened to me. Maybe God is looking down on me? Maybe He's going to get me out of this mess. I don't know but I'm worried about what's about to happen to me and how long I'm going to be in this place.

Chapter 10

I was moved from the hospital the same day that doctor came and visited my room. It's been three days since I've been in jail and no sign of a trial. They got me a Lawyer. I've been talking to him. They won't let me out on bail. This is something serious. I'm taking the wrap for something that I didn't even do. It hasn't soaked in my brain yet that I might not be getting out in a long time. What am I going to do in here until then? Will I survive? I'm not going to make it in here. This cell stinks and I'm already tired of being around all of these women.

"Williams, let's go! You're up for trial!" The guard yelled through the bars as they opened up. He put the cuff's on like I'm going to take off running.

I'm so nervous, what if they give me life? I'll never get out and if so, I'll kill myself. I refuse to endure in this place. Hopefully they'll see that I'm innocent and let me go. I hope Tyrome didn't lie on me cause that would be low down and dirty. And if I find out that he did, I'm going to get him.

It's about 12 noon and the court room is just up ahead. Why are there so many people standing around? I know they're not waiting on my trial? Sure enough they are. The court room is crowded, not a seat left in the room. Everybody seem to be upset. Some are fussing back and fourth, while others are crying. I'm trying to understand.

They brought me out from the back, away from the crowd and led me over to my lawyer which is an average built black man wearing big glasses. He has a thick mustache, a beard, and a small speckled grey fro'. He can pass as a doctor real quick. He looks real smart. I hope he's good, I guess I'll see soon.

"Was there a trial right before mine?" I asked him as I took a seat in the chair next to his.

"Yes there was. It was the Tyrome Jenkins trial." He said, as he gathered up his papers, pulled them out of his brief case, and set them on the table next to me.

"What happened? Why are the people so upset?"

"Because he only got probation."

"Probation!" I yelled.

"Now calm down before they carry you out of here. They feel as if he deserved worse than what the judge gave him. I bet he paid someone off with all that crime money he has. I would not be surprised." He tried to whisper. His proper accent can be mistaken for an up coast accent.

"Well if they gave him probation then what are they going to give me?" I whispered back to him.

"Don't worry, this is your first offense so I'm sure they'll give you the same thing." He tapped his pen on his papers.

The size of the court room seems quite large. It probably seats about 100 people.

The judge just entered the court room. "Please stand! Now entering Judge Anderson!" The attended shouted over everybody as the judge came in and sat down on the Bench.

"You may be seated." The judge said as he motioned bringing his hands down. "This trial is set for Ramona Williams. It says here that you were caught in a stolen vehicle, aggravated robbery with a deadly weapon, possession of narcotics, speeding, and resisting arrest. How do plead?"

"Hey that's not me!" I yelled as I jumped up out of my seat. "I didn't do all that!" My lawyer tried to pull me back down but I jerked my arm from him.

The judge hit the table with his wooden hammer. "You're going to give me order in my court. It's not my fault that you can't abide by the law and do the right things! Now you're going to give me respect in my court or this trial is over. Do you understand me?"

I calmed down unwillingly. "Yes sir." I slowly sat back down in my seat looking at my lawyer like he better get me out this mess.

The trial went on for a couple of hours.

Things came out that I didn't know. And things I never did. It's like they gave me somebody else's rap sheet.

The decision is finally here.

The judge came back out from the back and sat back down on his Bench. "Arise! Jury do you have a verdict?"

"Yes sir, we do." One of the jury spoke out. "We find Ramona Williams guilty of speeding in a stolen vehicle, guilty of aggregated robbery with a deadly weapon, guilty of procession of narcotics, and resisting arrest."

I sunk in my seat and cried with disbelief.

The judge left and went back into his office and stayed another thirty minutes.

He came back out and sat on his Bench again. "Miss. Ramona Williams, please stand." I stood up. "You do realize that you will be in jail for along time. I'm going to make an example out of you. Hopefully others will see this and learn from your mistakes. I'm giving you seventy five years serving twenty before any chance of parole." The hammer hit the table. "Court is dismissed!" He turned and left out the court room faster than he came in. He didn't even give me a chance to plead my side again. It's like somebody just hit me in the throat with their fist. I'm starting to feel dizzy. My life is shattered and crumbled into pieces. Where are you God? I know I turned my back on you but you're still supposed to help me? My dizziness is getting worse. My parents didn't come. And no sign of Michelle either. I know they heard about all the action on the news. I wouldn't have wanted them to come anyway. I got seventy five years in prison with twenty years before I can get parole. I can't even imagine it. I won't imagine it. I'll be fifty something years old before I ever see freedom again.

They escorted me out of the court room. Just that quick they're transferring me straight to the penitentiary.

It's a long country ride. They have about thirty women besides myself on what looks like a school bus. They have our feet and our hands tied down with chains. We couldn't escape if we wanted to. There are two police guards sitting in front of this long white bus with dark metal barred windows, and two police guards sitting in back. It's excruciatingly hot and they don't even care. They got the windows down just a little bit. They would pick a hot rainy day to transfer us, not to mention the sun's out to. Specks of rain showered my face as the bus sped through the excruciatingly hot country roads. I feel like I'm boiling. There's no radio. Nobody's making a sound. They told us not to say one word. I guess we're all thinking about the same things. What have we gotten ourselves into. What's going to happen to us when we get there. How are we going to make it in there. Will we live to see our paroles, and what are our families thinking. And I'm sure some don't even care, probably been in here more than once. This is the real thing. This is not TV anymore.

The 3 hour ride seemed like a 2 day ride.

It seemed forever getting to the prison. It's one of the largest prisons I've ever seen. It's got top maximum security. I heard the guards talking about it on the way here. They told us that we better not even think about breaking out because we would never make it pass the fence. If we last that long. They also told us we'll do good to survive a week because they're killing each other like flies in here everyday. I wanted to throw up when they said that.

Inside looks just like it looks on TV, but worse.

They're now processing us in. This is the most humiliating process, feels like they're invading my privacy. I thought, as they checked me all over my body for weapons again, threw me some orange husky pajama looking jumpsuit, a white long sleeve shirt, some white socks, some thin black sandals, and told me I had two minutes to put them all on.

When I finished, another woman directed me to the camera room. "Right over here Williams. Stand right in front of the camera and hold up these numbers. This'll be your name for the duration of your time up in here."

Another guard met me at the door. Gave me a sheet and a thin pillow. Then he escorted me through about five or six different halls. Every door we entered, we had to wait until they opened them. I always saw this on TV and would think, how in the world can they live inside of their? But never in my wildest dreams would I have ever thought I would be locked up in here to. Just hearing the bars open and shut scares me. They shut like I'm never coming out.

We came to the last hall which is the place where I'm going to be. Everybody's loud. Shouting all kinds of sexual, immoral, degrading words from behind their cell bars. I just ignored them and kept walking. I'm so scared. I have never been this scared in my life. I never had to. I can't let them know I'm scared. I've got to think of something or they're going to beat me crazy in here.

My jail cell is about the size of a 6 x 8 small bathroom with brick walls and one barred door that locks from the outside. The window is like looking through a miniature picture frame. It has one toilet and one tiny sink that looks like it hasn't been cleaned in years. Two bonk bed's on top of one another with two very thin mattresses on each bonk. How in the world am I going to be able to last seventy five years on that?

I've been in my cell for about an hour. Which makes it about five o'clock. I've just been awakened by a loud siren. Now all the cell doors are opening up all at the same time. Everybody's coming out of their cells like it's a normal routine.

"Let's go Two Ton or you're going to starve for the rest of the day!" A voice yelled, passing my cell. Who's Two Ton? I thought, jumping up and running out of the cell like my life depended on it.

The food was awful. Everything was imitation. It wasn't a real meal. I hated it. Wanted to complain but was too scared.

I ate this for about a month and I've lost so much weight already.

It's almost noon and they got us shoveling some dirt in a fake garden. It must be about a hundred degrees out here. I heard one of the guards say that they're re-designing the front of the prison, so I guess we're doing the dirty work.

I'm still determined to kill myself. I said that if I had to stay up in here for all these years I was going to kill myself. It's not like anybody cares anyway. I'll do it quick, that way I won't feel the pain. My mama and daddy don't love me. I haven't seen them in I don't know when. And probably never will. No friends. Michelle, yea' right. No man to comfort me. Tyrome, yea' right again. He better be glad I'm going to kill myself cause if I could just get out of here right now, I would kill him without any remorse.

During the time we were shoveling dirt, nobody saw me but I took one of the tools and shoved it into my shoe. The tool is used for cutting weeds, so that means it's very sharp.

The rest of the day was a long one. The cell doors have finally shut for the night. And all lights are out. No roommate and I'm glad.

I know I have to do it quick if I'm going to successfully kill myself without giving the guards time to come in and save me. My minds on my family. I ask myself, what will they do when they have to identify my body? My life's a living hell. It feels like I'm already in hell. I didn't ask to be here. It's like the guilty goes free and the innocent gets locked up. I don't understand this stupid world and I'm not going to try and figure it out. I have no friends in here. Nobody cares whether you even breathe. In fact, if you breathe, that'll give them something to beat you up for, or even kill you. Heaven is nowhere to be found in here. It's been a living hell ever since the first day I stepped foot on these grounds. I'm tired of being touched on. I'm tired of feeling alone. I'm tired of watching my back so that I won't get stabbed for no reason. Either join a gang or God. It's just not worth living. I don't have anybody who would care whether or not I live or die. I've done so much to God that He wouldn't accept me into Heaven no way. I picked my head up from off the pillow, grabbed the garden tool from underneath my mattress, held it in my sweaty hand, and then got on my knees between the toilet and the bed. My under arms are perspiring and sweat's running down my face. I admit, I'm nervous. I've never done anything like this before cause I never had the desire to. I'm sure it's because I believed in a God that I knew would punish me if I did. But now it really don't matter what I believe in anymore. They call me fat and ugly. They shout nasty things to me none stop. I really think they're trying to make me go crazy. Well it worked! Nobody have to worry about me cause I'm a done deal.

The sweat has become more rapid. It's falling down from my face to the floor. My hands are shaking, my legs are trembling. I can hear this voice in my head telling me to "just do it." It's constantly telling me to shove the knife inside my heart. But then I can hear another voice saying, "I love you no matter what you have done. And yes I will accept you into Heaven if you repent and come back to Me. Don't do it Ramona, don't do it." I can now hear the other voice saying, "Nobody loves you because if they did you wouldn't be up in here. So just kill yourself and get it over with. The guard won't be able to get to you in time if you place the knife right in the middle of your heart and shove it in real hard." The voice kept repeating itself over and over again while getting louder each time.

That's true. If they really cared, I wouldn't be up in here right now. There's no point in me living.

I put the knife up to my chest, shaking uncontrollably and drenched from sweat, I raised up the knife counting backwards from five down to one. My hands are shaking so much that I can't keep it to my chest. When I got down to one, a bright light suddenly appeared through my cell from out of nowhere. In the mist of the bright light there's a Man clothed with a robe which reaches down to His feet and with a gold girtle crossed over His breast. His head and his hairs are like wool, as white as snow. His face is like the sun shining in full power at midday. His feet glowed like burnished bright bronze, and his voice is like the sound of many waters. He held his right hand out and said, "Here, come to me and I will give you rest for your soul." When I saw Him I fell at His feet as if dead. But He laid His right hand on me and said, "Do not be afraid. I am the First and the Last… I died, but see, I am alive forevermore… I am Alpha and Omega, the first and the last… the beginning and the ending, saith the Lord, which is, and which was, and which is to come, the

Almighty…." (Rev. 1:8-18). His glory blinded my eyes. Godly sorrow is filling my heart. All I can do is weep, repent, and beg for forgiveness. "Lord, I am a backslider. But you said that You're married to the backslider. I want to rededicate my life back to You and serve only You. I confess with my mouth the Lord Jesus, I believe in my heart that You were raised from the dead, You said I shall be saved (Romans 10:9). And You said that whosoever shall call upon Your Name shall be saved (Romans 10:13). I'm calling on Your Name to save me tonight Lord!" I yelled out as voices from the other cells told me to shut up. "I'm sorry for the things I said against You and for the things I did against You! Save me Lord, please save me I'll never try and kill myself again! I'll never speak evil of others again! If You save me this time, I promise I'll get right, I will! There's no other god but You!" Just that quick I felt a release in my spirit. "Thank you for receiving me back! Thank you for saving my soul. And I will tell of Your goodness! Now Lord, please deliver me from all of my sins…" Still on my knees, I lifted up my arms towards the light with what strength I have left. An enormous amount of heat is building up in my body, as if it's burning the sin out of my mind, body, spirit, and soul. All I can do is say, "thank you Jesus for healing me! Thank you Jesus for delivering me! Thank you for healing my mind. Thank you for healing my body! Thank you for renewing in me a right spirit! You're an awesome God! I worship You Father!" There's a sensation in my spirit. A renewing if that's what you want to call it. The power is so overwhelming—it's awesome. "If you get me out of here I promise I will serve You as long as I live! Show me what You have called me to do." I cried out, pouring out all my soul. As I looked up into the light, fear started welling up within me, and suddenly the light disappeared.

I laid there on the floor for the rest of the night until early morning.

It's the next day and I'm in my cell staring out the window, thinking about what the Lord did for me last night. I can't believe I said all those things about You Lord. You're so merciful. You showed yourself and You didn't fail me, You did save me and I'll never forget that experience as long as I live.

I had to learn the prison life real quick. What to say, what not to say. What to ask, what not to ask. When to talk, when not to talk. There were many long cold nights. I would wake up and my pillow would be soaked from my tears. I cried every night for about a month. It seem like since the time I tried to kill myself and God stepped in and saved me, things got so much better within me. God has truly been doing a mighty work in me and He's been taking me through a process which has caused a total change within me. He's been healing, purging, cleansing, and washing me. He's been delivering me from all the old things I used to do and say. He's been crucifying my outer self and putting in His love and all of His precious fruits (Galatians 5: 16-26). He's been teaching me how to see things in the spirit and not in the flesh. He's been teaching me how to trust Him even when I can't see the out come. And because of these things, it has caused my faith to go to a whole new level. I've learned that trials and tribulations come just to make me strong. It hasn't felt good going through them, but I know it's all worth it in the end, and it's all for my good. He's made it easier for me to survive up in here. And trust me, it hasn't been easy. I've needed His strength everyday and still do.

Chapter 11

It's been four years since I've been in here. I didn't think that I would have lasted this long. One thing I've learned is that you have no friends and everything is yes mam no mam, yes sir no sir. And if you slip up and say or do the wrong thing, you're in solitary for a month. You stay in their twenty four hours a day with a fifteen minute recess with no exceptions. The meals aren't Thanksgiving meals either. And it's pitched dark. I've been in their before for something I didn't even do. During my time in their I learned to release my fears by constantly praying so that I wouldn't go crazy, and each time, God delivered me. Things started becoming real clear to me. I've lost over a hundred and fifty pounds in the past month. I'm malnutrition. Most of the time I go days without eating. It's been a struggle for me. This inner confined world could care less about you. I've seen them die hard up in here and everybody just looks normal when it happens because it happens everyday. It's like a fad or something. Monkey see monkey do. Every woman for herself. I've seen them get raped repeatedly. I've seen them get stabbed for nothing. This is one place nobody should ever come. Nobody cares. You can scream forever and nobodies going to

159

come to your rescue. I've seen them crack up and go crazy. It's a mad world up in here.

"Right this way Two Ton." Two Ton became my prison name. They've been calling me that for about four years now. When I first got up in here, I was really over weight. Everybody up in here has a nickname. If you don't name your own, they'll do it for you. The guard motioned for me to follow him as the cell doors opened.

"What's going on now?" I asked the guard.

"You have a visitor."

"A visitor, I really don't want to see anybody."

"You should be glad, most of you guys don't get visitors at all."

What if it's Tyrome? He wouldn't take a chance coming here. I don't want to see him no way! I don't want to see anybody! I thought as I followed the prison guard.

The visitor's room is just right up the hall.

The cell doors opened. I can see about twenty five inmates sitting and talking with their families at different tables. As I looked across the tables, I could see this brown image of a slim woman standing with her hands wrapped around one another, bald up to her chest.

As I got closer I can clearly see who it is that's come to see me. I'm unhappy on the outside but very happy on the inside. Maybe because I haven't had a visitor since I been locked up.

She screamed, "Ramona is that you?" She teared up in disbelief as I got closer. "Hey girl, what's up?! You look like you haven't eating in years!" I sat down at the table across from her. She sat down as I did. "Wow, you've lost so much weight even in your face girl. I didn't even know that was you when you walked in. What are they feeding you up in here? Soup? You know I heard that soup does the body good!" She laughed but I didn't. There's fear and excitement in her eyes. I'm sure it's because she's convicted because she knows that she was wrong.

"So what do you want Michelle?" I asked.

"What do you mean what I want? I came to see you and to see how you were doing."

"After all these years you want to see how I'm doing? I don't think so!"

"I thought about you everyday Ramona. Trying to figure out what I was going to say when I saw you. I knew I was wrong and I didn't know how you would react. I missed you a lot." She wiped her eyes as a couple of tears fell. "What happen with you and Tyrome? Why did he do you like this?" She looked down at the aluminum table as if it was me.

"I don't want to talk about it."

"See, this is one of the reasons why I couldn't find it in my heart to come and see you because I didn't want to see you in this place. I cried every night for months. I didn't come to the trial because I had warrants and they would've put me in jail. But I saw it on TV though. And that was so wrong how they just let him walk off free and gave you all these years. What I want to know is what happened?" She asked, looking up at me.

I always knew that Michelle was all for herself. But at least she came to see me. So much I can say for everybody else. I guess I can talk to her in a civilize way. "It all happened so fast. One minute we were riding in the new Land Cruiser he had supposedly just bought me, and then the next minute the police was taking us to jail. And I haven't seen Tyrome since that day. The day of my trial is when I found out that he got off free. I was stupid and naive. He used me Michelle." I said, looking up towards the high security barred windows in the room.

"I always knew it was something about him that wasn't right Ramona, but I didn't want to say nothing because I knew you had it in for him." She reached to touch my arm.

"Don't touch me. You were the one that was pumping me up, telling me to give him a chance. How could you sit there and lie like that?"

"You're right, but it was because I couldn't see anything wrong then but when he jumped you, I knew that he was no good for you."

"Alright Michelle whatever, I don't want to talk about it anymore. Let's change the subject."

"How is it in here?" She broke in and asked after a quick moment of silence.

"It's the best place you would ever want to be. Fit for a queen." We both looked at each other and laughed. "You don't ever want to know. It hurts so bad up in here. I can't recall not one exciting moment ever. Except for what happened to me about four years ago."

"What happened?"

"It was so awesome Michelle." I scooted my chair closer to the table. "I better leave it alone cause you probably won't believe me no way. You know how you used to get when I started talking about the Lord." I sort of smiled.

"Well, actually I haven't heard you talk about the Lord in a long time, even before you got put up in here. Go ahead, I want to hear what you gotta' to say girl."

"Jesus came and visited me in my cell room."

"Jesus? Girl get out of here. Jesus Himself? What did He look like? Did He say anything?" She tried not to laugh.

Fear's written all over Michelle's face. She sat back hard in her seat like she knew it was going to catch her. I'm debating whether or not I should tell her about me trying to commit suicide. I don't think she'd believe me anyway. "Girl it was amazing. There was this huge bright light shinning from the ceiling down into my cell. It was like the sun was shinning through the wall. The light behind Him was so bright. He had long beautiful shinny slightly curly hair. He was glowing, and He came through the light and reached out His hand and spoke to me. He was so beautiful Michelle. I had never seen this before in my life. I can't explain it. But one thing I do know is that the peace and comfort I felt was none that no man could ever give. And all I know is, I'll never forget it." I whispered.

"So, so you mean to tell me that He just showed up through your cell bars out of nowhere and for no reason? What did He want? Was He by himself? What did He look like? And wh…"

"Ok, ok all these million to one questions. Yea, He did show up for a reason. But I don't think you're ready to know why He came. You can't even imagine how it is up in here."

"If I didn't want to know I wouldn't have asked. I know I can't imagine how it is in here but at least I'm here and I'm trying. I didn't have to come. The reason why I'm asking all these questions is because things haven't been so great for me. Something awful happened to me. But right in the mist of it something good happened. It's funny how you described your experience because it's so similar to mine. I couldn't understand why, and maybe that's why I'm here to see you. I always knew that you were a Christian even when I tried to make you do things against what you believed. And even when you fell and had sex with Tyrome, I still knew you loved the Lord. Even though I judged you like crazy and didn't want to even hear God's Name when you brought Him up, I still knew that you loved the Lord, and I didn't. I have to be honest with you Ramona, I messed up big time." She started crying. "I'm real lucky to be sitting across from you right now. All this happened within the four years you been up in here. You remember how I used to brag a lot about my job and about having sex with all those different men? And how I used to say all I need is a man? Well all that's changed. I'm changed." She wiped her eyes with her hands.

"Michelle, I'm here and I'm listening." I put both of my arms on the table.

"Yes I've changed. And it took something terrible happening to me to do it. You know I used to sleep with a lot of men. Do you remember my boss that I worked for at Concept Designers? Well one night we had went out for some drinks at this club that was downtown not too far from the job. He and I would always go out for drinks so it wasn't no out the way thang. But this particular night he wasn't himself after we finished drinking. He drove to the club as usual and so it was obvious that he was going to drive us home. After the club he was driving me home and he made a detour going in the opposite direction. When I asked him where we were going, he just said that we were going for a ride. I knew he was drunk but he would always be drunk driving us home from the club. And you know I haven't ever been scared of no man. And surely what he could do to me while I was sleeping with him. He detoured off toward the south end of town. We came to this abandoned building where he forced me out of the car. He started beating me. All I could think about was no this is not happening to Michelle. This never happens to me I'm the one who gets the upper hand, not them." She paused and pulled some tissue from her pocket, wiped her eyes, and then blew her nose. "The way he was beating me was like I had killed his mama or something. He dragged me in this abandoned building, tore off my clothes, forced himself on me and raped me for what seemed like forever. He beat me while he was raping me. All I could think about was how he was going to kill me, because at that point he had done all that he could do to me except but kill me. I remembered how you used to witness to me, telling me about the Lord. One thing that struck my mind was when you told me that having sex with all these men was a sin. And that I was committing fornication and that God was not pleased with what I was doing (1 Corinthians 6: 18). And one day it was all going to catch up with me if I didn't stop and turn to God. I didn't believe what you were saying at that time. I thought something like this would never happen to me. I felt like I knew this man. He was the reason why I moved back in the first place. If I had known that he was going to do me like that, I would have stayed in Chicago. It hurt so bad Ramona. He didn't kill me. He just left me to die in that old building. While I was lying on the ground, this bright light came from out of nowhere, bursting through a broken window. I didn't know what to do, I was already hurting. I thought it was the police at first. I suddenly saw this man coming through the window. He was glowing all over. What I saw was an angel. And since I didn't believe in angels, let alone in God, I thought it was a man coming to save me. But when I reached out for his help, he quickly disappeared. Then there was this dark image that came from out of nowhere and was trying to pull me underneath the ground. It looked like the devil. It smelt so bad and was growling while telling me that I was going to hell because I didn't believe in God and that God would never forgive me for all the wrong I had done. It was pulling me so fast. I screamed the Name Jesus. But He didn't help me right away. I guess because I was only calling on Him to help me, but still in my heart I didn't believe in Him. Then the devil told me that the Lord didn't help me because I had done too much wrong to be helped. But girl when he started showing me what hell looked like, and all the people that died and went to hell that we knew from High School, my heart quickly turned towards God. At that point, all I remember was calling, screaming, and begging for Jesus to help me with a true heart and I repented for all the things I had ever done wrong. I asked Him to give me another chance to get right. I really don't remember what else I was saying because I was so scared. That's when I came back to the building and the devil disappeared. This man came out of nowhere with a cell phone and called the cops and the ambulance. When they finally got there, the man was nowhere to be found. I asked them did they see a man out there and they said that there weren't anybody out there. It was an experience that I'll never forget. When I was finally able to go back to work, I realized that I had no job. And because he told me that he would kill me if I told the police, I never tried to press charges on him. Nobody would have believed me anyway. I just accepted the fact that I was going to have a horrible secret for the rest of my life. I've gone back out there since the time I gave my life to God. I had no job and I had to make a living some kind of way. It's just temporary until I find a job. I know I've changed cause now when you ask me something about God, I'm ready to listen."

"I'm really sorry that that happened to you Michelle. You know, I've learned that everything happens for a reason. No, it wasn't your fault that he did all that to you. But when you live in sin doing things you know you shouldn't do, eventually it's going to catch up with you. It's like you reap what you sow. Look at the outcome, God had to show you hell in order for you to believe how real He really is and that He wasn't playing. Either you get right or hell is where you're going to be just like the others from High School. And that's why He didn't save you right away because He wants your whole heart not a fake heart. He knows our heart, and that's why we can't hide from Him nor can we even begin to out smart Him. Now what if He would have left you in hell for real? What would you have done then? And you say since then you've gone back out there. Now what if He comes back today? Would you be ready? Stop playing with God Michelle! I don't mean to come off hard but…"

"No you're not coming off hard. I need to hear what you have to say."

"But you need to know the truth. There are so many unbelievers out there who still don't believe in God. But now you can tell your testimony of how He saved you cause you do know you should have died and went to hell in that building? But He gave you another chance. Now you're back out there like He never did anything for you. Don't you have the fear of God?"

"I think I do. Look Ramona, I just got to do what I got to do right now. I'm practically out on the streets. It's just for a little while. I'm sure God'll understand."

"How many chances do you think He's going to give you? He could come back today, and you would be left behind. When Jesus came into my cell room, I gave my life back to Him, and I know He forgave me. All of my sins were washed away in the sea, never to be remembered anymore. And this is what He wants to do with you. Are you ready to come back to Him again? You can't stay out there living for the devil because if you're not living for God, you're living for the devil. But if you come back to God, He will help you. He'll give you a home to stay in, food to eat, and a job to work at. He'll accept you just like He accepted you in that building that night. Look Michelle, God is no respect of persons (Romans 2: 11). He doesn't treat anybody no better than the other. It don't matter that you left Him and now you need to come back. He'll still forgive you and accept you back in right standing with Him. So are you ready? All you got to do is confess with your mouth and believe in your heart that God was raised from the dead, you will be saved..." The guard broke in on me.

"Hey, let's go times up." He came quickly.

"Can I just finish asking her this question? It's very important that I get a response from her."

"No, let's go. You know the rules."

By the time I turned to tell Michelle bye, she had already vanished around the corner. Maybe she got intimidated by the guard? Or just maybe she was convicted? I hope she comes back soon because she didn't get a chance to rededicate her life back to God. So now she's back out there on her own, without God. I hope she comes back soon.

All night long I thought about what Michelle said to me. I even cried a little at the thought of her even getting hurt. I don't want to see her get hurt even if she did put herself in that position. I'll always remember what my mama told me, that you reap what you sow, good and bad. And that thought has always stayed with me and will continue to stay with me as long as I live. I know now that I'm reaping what I sowed. I was disobedient to God because I feel in love with a married man, and allowed him to come into my heart and rob me of my precious gift from God. My virginity. And now I'm paying for it.

I always read it in the Bible that adultery was wrong and I knew it was when I first found out that he was married. I don't know why I didn't see that it wasn't ever going to be nothing, because he had nothing to offer me from the beginning. But a bunch of emotions. The thing I regret doing was falling in love with him. He was a smooth talker and it didn't take much for him to have his way. Yea I admit, I was lonely, stupid, desperate, and crazy. But I never had a boyfriend practically all my life. Except in elementary when this boy name Johnny hugged me with his eyes closed on the playground by accident, when he was really trying to hug this other girl named Amy instead. That hug made my day even though he wasn't trying to hug me, I always considered him as my boyfriend. I know that sounds crazy. But o' well it's the truth. I got plenty of time to think about all those times. I have approximately seventy one more years left up in here. What a lot to look forward to. Will I survive that long? I think I will, I've lasted this long. But you never know what to expect up in here. You just pray for the best.

Chapter 12

Well another three years have passed and if you ask me what I've learned, I'll have to say not a thing. The new year's just come and go up in here like it ain't nothing. I haven't had a great experience since the last time the Lord came and paid me a visit. And that's been a little under seven years ago. I haven't seen nor heard from Michelle either and that's been about three years ago. I hope she's alright. The way we left off was one I'll never forget. Her words we're so real and true. She was healing herself right up in this joint. She was crying so hard, I wish I could have helped her. But the help she needed could only come from God. I hope she knew that in her heart even though she didn't get a chance to rededicate her life back to Him.

"Come on Two Ton, you have a visitor." The guard yelled through the cell bars as they opened up.

What? I have another visitor after three more years of being in this place? I hope its Michelle or my parents. I'm sure they know I'm in here by now. I thought as I turned the last corner leading into the visiting room.

Whoever it is hasn't come in yet so I'll take a seat at this table over here and wait. I'm sitting at a table that sits right in front of the door so I'll be able to see who it is right a way. As long as I've

169

been in this place I never noticed how hard we're being watched. They're cameras set up everywhere. That's a trip.

This voice yelled from out of nowhere as she came from around the corner. "Hey my snookum' pookum'! How's my lil' neicy piecy?!" She shouted as she always do.

"Hey Auntie LolaMae!" I shouted back, leaning over to get a good look at her as she came towards the table. I'm so glad to see her. Look like she done gained some more weight. I hope it's just the clothes she's wearing.

"So how you doin' in this ol' nasty place?!"

Every word that comes out of Auntie's mouth is so loud that you almost have to hold your ears when she talks. And don't tell her something private, she'll repeat it in a heart beat. I can remember one time when I tried to whisper something to her about one of the ladies in church one Sunday, and she repeated everything I said so loud that the lady heard her and now that lady's still not speaking to me. I guess I shouldn't have been talking about her anyway. What a laugh. "I'm doing alright. It's been seven years since I've been in here." I looked at her as if to say why haven't you come to see me before now?

"Seven years?! Dawg, that's a long time! So what cha' eat up in here cause you lookin' like you ain't ate since you been up in here?! You look like one of them ladies I see on TV talkin' bout' they need to lose some weight, and they already weighin' sixty pounds!" She laughed and leaned over to one side of her chair and back.

"I don't look like I eat Auntie?"

"No you don't! I promise you look like you on strike from eatin'!" She laughed. "No, no, no, I know what chu' look like, you look like you scared to eat cause you scared of gettin' gas like me all the time!" She laughed so hard, she passed gas right in her chair. It was so loud everybody turned around and looked.

"Auntie, you're embarrassing me, will you act right?" I laughed underneath my breath. "You're still the same. Still that old country girl that loves to have fun and act crazy. And that's what I always love about you. You don't care what nobody think or cares." I started laughing with her.

"Show don't, and ain't gon' never change either cause' I'm me. And if I got to get this air out of me, I'm gon' do it!" She passed gas again. This time louder and longer. "You know what they say, if you hold it that's when you're in trouble. And I ain't triyn' to be in trouble all off up in here!" She burst out laughing again. "So have you found you somebody in here or what?!" She said, trying to hold back her laugh.

"Are you crazy? Come on now, you already know I don't roll like that."

"Yea, I know but seven years is a long time and I just don't think I would be able to do it. Well I can't say that because I'm doing real well. You know me and Mr. Walter don't talk no mo'?!" She smiled as she closed her eyes, and turned her head in the opposite direction.

"No I didn't know that." I laughed so hard, tears started falling from my eyes.

"Now you know I'm just playin'. That's my hubby I'll never give that up. He's too good to me. You know he bought me a big smoked hog for Christmas? Yea' girl we ate that thang all night long too!" We both laughed.

This is what I miss about my Auntie, she makes me laugh non stop. I could always be myself around her. She's the one that really encouraged me when times got real tough. She knows how it is to have her lights turned off with no food to eat and six mouths to feed. With no phone to use because they turned that off too. Just making ends meet. So she knows how to encourage a person real quick. I guess that's why she's here today. Her timing is always right. "When you talk to him, tell him I said hi Auntie."

"I'll be sure to tell em'! He ask bout' you everyday! Na' I'm lyin', he hardly ever ask about you. Shoot he better not ask bout' no woman as much as he asks about me!" She closed her eyes and smiled. "So have yo' friend came to see you?! What's her name?!"

"You're talking about Michelle. Yea, as a matter-a-fact she came to see me about three years ago."

"Hum… Yo' mama and the rest of em' are doing fine. Yo' daddy still working those long shifts as usual. I don't see how yo' mama can take it. He ain't never home to take care of her needs! I couldn't do it! I'd have me a back up plan see! Home by yourself?! Nobody lookin' over yo' shoulder?! No cameras?! Come on now, talk to me somebody!" She threw her hands up in the air as if to high five me. "Oh' you not gon' give me five?!"

"It's not that. We're not allowed to do all that touching."

"You mean to tell me I can't touch my own niece?! They gon' make me go crazy on em' all off up in here!"

"Come on Auntie, don't create a scene. All you'll do is hurt me. They'll put me in isolation for a long time."

"You better be glad I love you cause I would go straight to the president of this prison! And you know I can cut up?!" She swung her arm's round and round hysterically as she swayed back and forth in her seat.

"No that won't be necessary Auntie. Hey don't forget you're saved now? You don't want to go back to those old ways of how you used to be" (Ephesians 4: 22-24).

"Who you talkin' to like that?! Now I know you not tryin' to preach to me?! Ain't that somethin', this girl's tryin' to remind me bout' the Lord and she stuck up in prison! I should be remindin' you! Let me go cause I'm not gon' be judged by how I talk! God knows my heart and I'm not gon' change for nobody!" She stormed out of the room, and vanished around the corner without saying bye. You can still hear her fussing. It's kind of funny. Anybody else would probably have gotten offended but because I know how Auntie LolaMae is, I just learn how to ignore her. I know she loves me. She'll probably send me a card or write me a long letter telling me how sorry she is. Oh' well, back to this boring cell...

I've learned how to make use of my time by reading books, visit the chaplain for church, and meditate on the Lord. I wonder where I would have been if I hadn't been put up in here? Tyrome probably would have ran me crazy and Mr. Kevin would've made me pop him one.

I wouldn't have chosen this place to put nobody in but that's why I'm not God. The Bible says that nobody can be God. He's God all by Himself. So I don't even think about worshiping other god's cause' God is a jealous God and He will take vengeance. That means don't put no man in higher esteem than God because then you'll start to idolize and that's putting other god's before the real true and living God above. I can remember when I was so into Tyrome. I was so into him that I put him before God. I would sometimes miss church to spend time with him because he never wanted to go to church. Every time I would ask him, he would tell me no. That should've been my signal to leave him alone then, but I didn't and that's why things got worse rather than getting better. I stopped reading my Bible and was going out to eat with him almost every night. I would eat and sleep Tyrome. If I even heard his name I would jump. I put him before God. I even put Michelle before God. There were times when Michelle and I would go out all night and wouldn't get home until five or six o'clock in the morning. And getting up for church was not happening for me. I would never make it to church. I neglected God for a minute thrill. I put my ex-boyfriend and my best friend before God and that was wrong (1 Corinthians 10: 19-20). I was really out there and didn't know how to turn back to God because He was my first love. I was owned by the devil and what he wanted me to do. Like having sex with a man I wasn't married

173

to. Let alone the fact that he was already married to somebody else. There was no conviction at all. That is when I knew I needed help. But when I repented and accepted God back into my life, he became my new owner. He became my Father and friend again. God is so merciful.

The cell bars opened up. It's recreational time. A girl I work with in the kitchen told me to meet her in the library cause she knows that I love to read. I wonder what she want?

The walk from my cell to the library was rather long, considering all the doors we had to go through. But we finally made it.

"Hey girl what's up? What did you want to show me?" I asked.

"Nothing, I just wanted to show you what I wrote today. Read this poem." She handed me a sheet of paper.

I read it while she watched me the whole time. "That's nice, what are you going to do with it?" I handed it back to her.

"I'll probably send it to my baby's daddy back at home. His mother is taking care of one of my baby's. This is the least I can do huh'?

"I guess girl I really don't like to comment about issues like that. Just pray about it that's what I would do."

She put the poem on the table. "Yea, I guess you're right."

"I'm going outside to exercise do you want to come?" I looked at her, then turned and walked towards the door.

"Nah', I'm a go and write my boyfriend a letter. I'll talk to you later."

She's an ok friend for in here. She throws all of her burdens on me too much cause she won't trust God. Instead she looks to me for all of her answers. I have to constantly remind her that I'm not God and to put her trust in Him and He'll make the right choices for her (Proverbs 3:5-6). But anyway, enough about that...

Today is a beautiful day! The sun is shinning so bright without a cloud in the sky. It's just the right kind of day for a miracle. Everybody is out doing their own thing before they call us in for the day. Some are lifting weights, some are running around the dirt track, some are playing dominoes and cards, some are playing basketball, while others are just standing around talking and smoking. They call it back home, just wasting time.

"Hey Two Ton! You got a visitor! Let's go!" The guard shouted from across the field.

"Alright!" I shouted back as I ran towards the guard at the front gate.

When I got to the visiting room, I couldn't believe my eyes. It was Michelle. I knew she'd come back to see me. She looks real sad. Look like she came to tell me some more bad news. I hope nothing has happened to her again.

"Hey girl!" She said very nervously as she jumped up out of her seat to greet me.

"Hey, how you doing? Long time no see?!" I sat down.

"I know, I know. Things have been going so fast that I hadn't had time to get back up here to see you. But I can say that it hasn't been long since I thought about you." She sat back down in the seat across from me.

"Why are you looking like that?"

"Looking like what?"

"Looking like you got something to tell me."

"Well actually I do have something I need to tell you. And I should've been told you this but I wanted it to be the right time to explain it to you the right way."

"Oh' I know what you're about to tell me. You're about to tell me that you're sorry that you haven't received God as your Lord and Savior right?"

175

"No, I wasn't about to say that. I have something to tell you that have been bothering me for along time which is the real reason why I had to come back up here and get it off my chest. What I'm trying to say is if I can ever get it out is that I've been seeing Tyrome." She quickly turned her face as if I was going to jump up and hit her.

"What did you say? I can't believe that you would have the audacity to do something so backstabbing like that?! I thought you was my friend?!" I got loud and the guard came walking toward my table.

"I am your friend!"

"No you not, shut up! You were always the main one who said that he wasn't no good and that I needed to leave him alone because he was hurting me too much! But what it was, was all you wanted me to do was leave him alone so that you could get with him and have him all to yourself! You would think you would have learned your lesson by now!" I yelled, pointing my finger in her face.

The guard broke in. "Two Ton I'm warning you, If I hear you yell like that again, your visiting hours are over."

"Ok, I'm sorry. It won't happen again."

"Good." He said, as he walked off.

"And another thing." I lowered my voice. "You always had all the men and I would always encourage you even when I knew that they were no good and was using you all over the place. And when I found me what I thought was a good man, you couldn't take it so you took him from me. You are so messed up in the mind. You better be glad…"

"Now you wait a minute."

"No you wait a minute. There's not anything else you got to say to me."

"I do have something to say. You lucky I came to tell you cause I could've kept it a secret and you would have never known. And it ain't like you've been the perfect angel either cause

176

look at cha', you up in here and I'm not. So who's the lucky one now?" She paused. "That's what I thought. Now snap back to that." She stood up and then quickly sat back down. "We've been seeing each other for over seven years now, before you got locked up in here. I was going to tell you eventually but I was waiting on the right time. Look Ramona, I don't want us to lose our friendship over something like this which is the reason why I personally came to tell you instead of writing it on paper."

We were quiet for about five minutes and then I said, "I'm not moved by that. I'm not moved by that at all. I don't receive anything from you. You got a problem. The devil has totally taken control of your mind. I'm trying to figure out when you and Tyrome had time to see each other? I wouldn't be surprised if you and him set me up. In fact I know you did. And that's why you wouldn't come riding in the new truck because you knew it was stolen. And that's why you wouldn't come and bail me out of jail when I first got put up in here. And that's why he got off with only probation so easy. It was a set up. It was all for me to take his wrap. You and him planned it that way. How could you Michelle? How could you?" Tears are falling fast from my eyes. "I want you to know one thing, you will never get a way with doing evil. I thought you would have learned by now. Tyrome's going to do you worse than he did me. He don't love nobody but himself. So what makes you think he's going to love you better? Why because he can buy expensive gifts? Why because he looks good? Why because he dress nice? All that junk doesn't mean nothing. He looks good on the outside but is a walking dead man on the inside and you better get away from him while you can. I tell you what Michelle, how bout' you never come to see me again? I just want you to go on about your business and don't worry about being friends anymore because you know in your heart that you're not my friend. You never was my friend cause friends don't do what you did. You think you got me looking

177

crazy because I'm up in here, but one day the Lord's going to bless me to get out of here and it's going to be a different story all together. You will definitely get yours. God bailed you out of that situation that happened to you a long time ago. He spared your life. That man could've killed you, but God was there protecting you even though you didn't believe in Him nor about Him. He's shown great mercy towards you and you still continue to be evil and sneaky. Well this time you messed with the wrong one. I feel for you Michelle. I'll be praying for you." I motioned for the guard to come get me. I never looked back. I could just hear her yelling.

"Whatever, say what you want to say! You don't scare me! I'm oughta here!" She got up and quickly ran out the door.

My eyes are red and my face is swollen from anger. Even though I got used to hearing the worse of things, I still found a sensitive side that I still had not dealt with. Tyrome and I been over with. Maybe if it was anybody else it wouldn't hurt so bad, but I thought I had this honest, loving, and caring friend that was just like family. But I'm finding out that she's a wolf on the inside and was waiting on the chance to eat me up. I'll never be able to trust her again.

I'm lying on my bed thinking about what Michelle told me. I got set up. They were seeing each other all along. How could I have not known that? He played me and now he's playing her. Now I know for sure he never did love me. All he wanted was a ginnie pig. Somebody to get him out of trouble. Well it worked. It's amazing how you can physically see but still be blind. I need Your help Lord! I don't know how You're going to help me but I pray that it's soon. I know I made some mistakes in my life and I feel like I'm paying for them now. But when is the payment over? When do you show mercy? How much repenting do I have to do? Is it something I'm not doing? Is it something I'm not saying? Please help me! Now I know how it feels to be punished for something I didn't do. I remember when I used to laugh at those people in prison and talk about them because I felt that they were crazy for getting themselves put up in here. But now I've found out that everybody in prison is not guilty. There are many people put in prison everyday and they're innocent. And I'm one of them. Lord if You'll help me this time. I know there's a scripture in Your Word that says something about favor. I need supernatural favor right now! Bless me much indeed. I want back everything that the devil stole from me! You said You are no respect of persons (Romans 2: 11), so I know if I just ask You and believe it, I will receive what I'm asking of You (Matthew 21:22). Please help me. If You let me out of here, I'll do Your divine will...

Chapter 13

This morning seems different. I don't know why, but it just seems different. I've been locked up for over 7 years now which seems like a million years. To say that I haven't gotten killed yet is a blessing. Since I've been in here there have been on an average of 3 deaths per day. Either by murder or by suicide. Wow! I don't know why I feel so strange today. I've never felt this way since I been locked up in here. They just opened the bars for breakfast, but for some reason I'm not hungry. I can't seem to shake this feeling I'm having this morning. I hope it means something good is about to happen. Thinking to myself. I really don't feel like going to breakfast but we really don't have a choice. I have to admit, I do have a stash put away underneath my bunk so if I get hungry later. I'll just naw on that.

The guard yelled inside my cell. "Let's go." The cell bars are already open so they didn't need to open them. "No, not that way, this way." He pulled me in the opposite direction of the cafeteria.

"Where are you taking me? I didn't do nothing wrong?" I looked back at him.

"You right, you didn't do anything wrong. You have some visitors."

"You said visitor or visitors?"

"Visitors."

I wonder who can this be? I don't know that many people, and the people that I do know wouldn't come to see me at the same time.

It was a long walk to the other side of the prison. Something's not right because we just passed the visiting room. Where in the world are we going? Ok let me think, did I do something wrong and forgot about it? I know I'm not up for parole? Shoot, they did tell me that my parole was coming up. And they told me to get letters of recommendations from friends and or family members. I didn't do neither one because I don't have any friends anymore, nor am I even talking to my family members except Auntie LolaMae and she's mad at me right now. And anyway I never have thought about what I could say to them but the truth. And you don't have to rehearse that. So I'm not worried, it's probably for something else.

We came to this beautiful huge wooden door with a gold door knob. You can tell not too many inmates come down this way often because even the hallway got carpet. I remember when we used to live in the projects when I was a little girl, which was right before daddy got his good job and all. And anybody living in the projects knows there ain't no carpet. You don't even get a rug. I thought, smiling to myself.

The guard opened the door. There's a crowd of men and women sitting around this long table. Looks like it should be in one of those big time executive offices.

"Come in and have a seat." One of the three men confidently said from behind the table. It's about seven people up in here. I'm so intimidated. I feel like a little ant in front of seven gigantic dinosaurs. Just about all of them have their arms folded, their wearing nice expensive suits, and each of them has folders sitting in front of them.

I sat in the cold seat that's directly across from everybody. I don't know whether to cross my arms like them or just put them in my lap. This is crucial. I feel like I'm about to break off in a sweat as cold as it is up in here. Must be my nerves.

"Do you know why we called you in here?" One of the ladies asked but never looked up. She has long blond curly hair and long nails. She's also wearing a dress suit probably from some big time designer store for the rich folks.

"Um', no I don't know why you've called me in here."

"You have been incarcerated for a little over 7 years, is this correct?" A different woman asked.

"Yes, that's correct." I nodded my head.

"What have you learned through these years? Have you learned your lesson? If we let you back out in society do you plan on coming back? Why should we let you out? You may answer these questions in any order you wish."

"Well um'. I um', um'… I've learned that you must pay for what you do wrong… And once you have paid for doing wrong then… Um' then you got to find a way to change your life so you won't go down that same road again. I made a big mistake in my life. First of all for falling in love with somebody who cared less about me. Then for committing a crime that I knew nothing about. But I figure if I had not been with him, all this would have never happened. So I'm paying for it now. My mama always told me that you reap what you sow good or bad. I've learned to never let someone see inside your heart without talking to God about them first. And that I did not do. I didn't pray about this man nor did I pray about this friend I allowed myself to hang around when I knew she wasn't the positive friend I needed. See, I just took it for granted that they were going to treat me right and everything was going to be perfect. Well it happened just the opposite of what I had planned. They turned on me and as a result I got caught doing something that I didn't even know anything about. And of course they got off free. If I had another chance in society today, I would follow after the vow that I made with God a little after the time I got put up in here. I promised God that I would get my life right and that I would get back in church and serve Him like I used to serve Him. And if He granted me with that, I definitely would not come back up in here. The only way possible would be to minister to the inmates, and let them know that they don't have to stay the same way. Even though they made some mistakes they don't have to give up. God can change anybody, and He's changed me. And I would also tell them that God is a forgiving God. No matter what crime they've committed, no matter how many people they've murdered, no matter how many cars they've stolen, no matter, no matter, no matter. And people think that every inmate that's inside of here is dangerous and will never change. That's not true. I'm not dangerous and I have changed since I've been up in here and I will continue to change even more if I'm ever let out of here. And if I don't get out right now, it must mean I'm not ready yet because God would permit it to happen. So I have hope that one day I'll be free to get out but it'll totally be left up to God." I threw my hands up as if to say I'm done.

"Thank you, you may leave now." One of the ladies quickly motioned with her hand for the guard to take me out.

It was a long quiet walk back to the cell. Could this be the open door? Could this be the favor that I asked God for? I don't know. Maybe I went a little too far, but I was only telling the truth.

It's a long night. I can't sleep thinking about that meeting and how it came about so quick. That was weird. That wasn't supposed to happen so soon. It wasn't time for my parole yet. I'm not up for parole until about another 13 more years. I never

184

knew that God would open doors for me so fast. Maybe I'm doing something right cause He allowed this to happen? I asked myself. I'm reading this book that's talking about having an abundance of God's blessings in your life forever. It's awesome. It's describing how you can literally break through to the blessings in your life that God has for you to receive forever. Ever since I've been reading it, I've had miraculous blessings to happen in my life. Most people would ask how could you have blessings and favor in prison? Well it can happen. I got hooked up with free snacks. One of the inmates didn't want her snacks because she was allergic to them, so she gave them to me. And then I got extended recess time. When I asked why, they didn't answer me. God's got to see if He can bless us with the little things first. And if we pass, then He'll bless us with the large things. So I just believe that my large blessings are here and I'm not turning back because I want all my blessings. And one of them is to get out of here.

I thought myself right to sleep last night. Now it's a new day and I'm wondering what it's going to be like. Breakfast is over. It seems as if it's going to be a long hot day. I'm out working in the field's today and I really don't feel like it, but I have no choice.

It's hot just like I said. And it's only 8 o'clock in the morning.

"Two Ton! Two Ton! Let's go! Put down your rake and come with me! You won't be needing it anymore!" The guard yelled from a distance as she came closer.

What is she talking about? I thought.

"Come with me, you have another meeting to go to."

She smiled.

This guard was always nice to me ever since the first time I got put up in here. I believe God has given me favor with her. I know she wants me to get out.

I'm right back in the same room, in the same seat, and sitting in front of the same panel of people. I just hope the outcome is a positive one.

"Good morning Miss. Ramona Williams."

"Good morning." I nodded my head.

"We have reviewed your file and we must say that we are very impressed. Especially with your behavior and your patience towards us. You stated on yesterday that everyone makes mistakes and that they are not to dwell on them but to move forward. Those were your words right?"

"Something like that, just not in those same words."

"We understand. What we are trying to say Miss. Williams is that we have made a terrible mistake with you being in here. You should have never been put in here in the first place. There was a mix up in our records. You have been awarded clemency. We are truly sorry. You're free to go."

"I can't believe this, are you sure? I mean, this isn't some kind of joke is it?"

"No mam', you are free to go." They all started getting up out of their seats.

"Thank you Lord! Thank you Lord!" I shouted with tears in my eyes. If you just keep the faith and keep believing, the Lord will deliver you in due season. Thank God this is my season." They all just looked at me. Some stayed and listened while others quickly left out.

What in the world am I going to do first? Where am I going to go? I know all the stuff in my apartment is gone and the apartment itself. I'm sure they re-rented it out years ago. My parents are still not talking to me so I can't call them. Even though I had the fight with my mama, daddy pretty much does what she wants. So if she's not talking to me, he's not either. Not to mention Michelle and I are no longer talking so I can't call her. And Auntie LolaMae is not talking to me either. But when we were talking, she put me on her address so that I wouldn't have to go to a halfway house. And now that we're not talking, I wish that she had never done that so I could at least have somewhere to go. So basically I have nobody to turn to.

"Ok, are you ready? Let's go so you can get cleaned up and checked out. I'm happy for you, and I know you will make an impact on the outside world. Have a great life." The guard said.

"Thanks I really appreciate the encouragement. And I want to tell you that you have looked out for me since the first day I got put in here. And I just want you to know that God is going to bless you for your love and support towards me." I said, as I fought back the tears.

After I got myself cleaned up, a couple of guards walked me to the release room to get my stuff, gave me some cash that I had accumulated over the years, and walked me out. There was a city bus waiting on me that took me to the local bus station.

I'm now waiting on a late cab I called over an hour ago. I only got $75 dollars from all these years I spent in the pen and I don't know how long this is going to last me. They gave me a free ride to the bus station but I got to pay the rest of the way. I don't know how much this cab's going to charge me. I hope I have enough to get where I'm going. I guess I'm headed back to the big city. I don't have anywhere else to go. It feels so good to be free. I don't know how to act. This'll always be memories to me and I'll never forget it. But certainly I won't ponder over it. I thought smiling to myself. I don't know when was the last time I smelt fresh air from the outside world. By the sun's shinning as bright as it is, anybody would think it would be hot out here but it's not, it's actually kind of cool with the wind blowing and all. It' feels like early fall weather. I can see myself at a beach right now. Laid back on my towel, drinking my cool ice tea, and twitching my toes threw the sand. I closed my eyes, raised my head up towards the sky, and took a deep sniff as if to imagine it.

The bus station is not that far from the prison. Actually it can be seen from the bus station. It's too far to walk but not too far to drive. The cab is running so late it was supposed to have been here over an hour ago and my nerves are starting to act up. Not to mention the bus station is just too crowded and people are everywhere. You would think they just got off a plane. Some are laid over their luggage asleep, while others are up walking, talking, and standing in line to buy a ticket.

The cab finally came roaring through. Sounds like something's wrong with it. "Where you headed?!" The cab driver screamed over the loud engine. He's an Hispanic guy which looks to be in his early forties with a Southern accent. His cowboy hat, checkered shirt, and blue jeans caught my eye immediately.

His engine sounds real raggedy, maybe he doesn't realize that it needs to be checked? Sounds like it needs a new everything. I thought as I bent down towards the passenger window. "Back to the city!" I screamed over the engine while looking in through the window. "I'm going back to the city?!"

"Ok, get in!" He yelled.

"Your engine is so loud it sounds like it's about to blow up at any minute! Are you aware of this?!" I yelled over the seat as I got in and closed the door behind me.

"Oh' don't worry, it's been doing this for months!"

I got quiet.

I looked back towards the prison as we drove out of its view thinking, I won't miss that place at all. The only way I'll come back is to do prison ministry. Hopefully God will use me to save all of them. And I mean all of them, even the workers.

We're about an hour away and things are starting to take a turn for the worse. The motor is sounding crazier than it did when he first came to pick me up. "What's that noise?!" I screamed towards him with the greatest fear I've ever had.

"I don't know!!... Oh' my God nooo...!"

Our screams went for what seemed like forever as the car tumbled and turned. Darkness, glass, and debris quickly shattered my eyes as I threw my arms up to try and shield my face and that's when I blacked out.

"Come in she's awake." Someone said with an echo that sounded far away.

"Hi Ramona, can you hear us?" A nurse asked softly.

"Yy- yea. I can hear you." I struggled to answer.

"Do you know where you are?"

"I hope I'm in Heaven." I tried wiping my eyes but couldn't because of all the bandages.

"No not quite, you're at St. Agnes's Hospital and you have been in a coma for going on two weeks. We're happy to see you awake." She said.

"What happened to me?" I pulled at the bandages around my head.

"You were in a car accident. You hit the freeway wall going eighty miles per hour. The car was totaled. Nothing was recognizable. It didn't even look like a car. You should be grateful."

"What do you mean you?"

"Well we mean you and the driver. You were in a cab do you remember that?" The doctor broke in and asked.

"Yes I do remember that, what happened to the driver?"

"We're sorry but he died at the scene. They couldn't recognize him. He didn't stand a chance. We're still trying to figure out how you made it." The doctor lifted up my arm to check my blood pressure, and took the bandage off from around my head.

"I'm so sorry for him." I said trying to get my vision to come in clear but everything was so blurry.

"Why are you sad? His body doesn't go to Heaven, only his soul." He took the blood pressure strap from around my arm.

"That's just it. I'm sad because I didn't get a chance to witness to him. I don't know if he was saved or not. Therefore I don't know if his soul went to Heaven?"

"You don't have to worry because he was a devoted deacon at one of the local churches here. And yes he was saved. I knew him personally. So you don't have to be sad. If you're going to be sad, be sad because of all the war and pain down here on this earth. And everyday it's getting worse. I know God is not pleased." He pulled the cover up and tucked it underneath my neck as my arms rested on top of it.

"I'm glad. And you're right, I'm sure God isn't pleased with all the war and pain down here. Hey can I ask you a question?"

"Sure go ahead."

"Are you saved? Do you know the Lord?"

"Yes, I'm very much saved. I'm not only saved but I'm filled with God's Holy Spirit. And you better believe if it had not been for His Holy Spirit, I wouldn't be here speaking to you today. Because there have been times in my life when after I got saved, I went back out and did those things I used to do like having sex with a bunch of women, getting drunk with the guys, smoking marijuana, and stealing from stores. But some how I couldn't keep doing it. The Holy Spirit would convict me every time. I thank God, because I made it and I don't have to worry about those things anymore. I'm glad you asked, I knew you would though." He smiled pleasantly. "Now you get you some rest and I'll check on you later. It's amazing how you've recovered so quickly. You just came out of a coma. It's like you were never in one. God planned it all. Hey don't you worry about your eye sight. You'll get it back fully. And don't worry about where you're going to stay. God's going to take care of you and he's going to bless you in a huge way." He smiled and left out of the room.

"Wow that man knew exactly what was on my mind. He had to be a prophet. Some don't believe in them, but I do. I'm wondering what's up with all these strange things happening to me. I don't understand, maybe one day I will.

It's been about two days now and I'm so ready to get out of here. "Ok Miss. Williams are you ready to get checked out?" A nurse came in and asked.

"Yes I sure am." I should be sad about my eye sight but I'm not because that could have been me instead of the cab driver. I can't believe I didn't die in that crash. They said that the car was totally ripped apart. It didn't even look like a car. How in the world did I survive? What in the world am I supposed to do on this earth? There must be something because it's too many miracles happening in my life. I see people on TV all the time talking about how they survived a car accident or some type of accident that they know they should've been dead. And all they say is something saved me I don't know who it was, or that it was luck that did it, or that they can't believe that they're still alive, and they would like to thank the person who helped them without ever thanking God. I won't ever understand how quick we are to give credit to man and not to God. He's the one who allowed me to live through that and nobody can ever take credit but Him. And I'm proud to give it to Him.

Now I'm thinking where do I go from here? I wish I knew. It would've been great if I was reunited with my parents again. They probably don't want to have nothing to do with me anymore. I can see partially but it's hard for me to recognize certain objects. I can only see them when they're close up.

Stephanie Franklin

Leaving this hospital is the hardest thing to do because I don't know where I'm going from here. I need to go buy me a coat, it's really cold out here. I wish I had somewhere to stay. I wonder what they did with all my stuff. Probably sold it all, my clothes, jewelry, furniture, and ain't no telling what ever else.

Chapter 14

I've been out here going on two weeks and I've been wearing the same clothes I had on when I left the hospital. My body stinks so bad. I'm glad it's cold cause anybody would probably be able to smell me from a mile a way. The temperature is almost freezing, it's gotten colder since the time I left the hospital. The days are going by real fast.

It's going on 9 o'clock and the downtown night life is on fire. So many lights and so much action. People are going in and out of bars, couples are walking hugging one another, crowds are rushing the clubs, and pimps and prostitutes are in action doing their thing. The wind is blowing so hard I can hardly walk. Every step is in slow motion. My lips are bleeding from the cuts on them because of the cold. I can't believe people are still out despite how cold it is.

As I walked a little further down and looked through a department store window, I can see the stores haven't changed. Prices are still too high. I see a blouse for a hundred and sixty two dollars. I could go to a thrift shop and get the same blouse for about $5 dollars.

The night seems so long and the streets are so cold. It's about twenty degrees and dropping and I need to find me an abandoned building to sleep in. I tried going to all the shelters but they were all too full. I never would've imagined that I would be homeless. Just like I never imagined that I would ever go to prison. I used to see homeless people on the corners begging for money and I would say to myself that I'd love to help them. And now, I need help. Just like they say, never say never cause you never know when you'll be in that same position. I'm freezing, I'm hungry, my body aches from the cold, and I feel like I'm about to give up. "God You got to do something!" I screamed out with all the energy I have. "Are You punishing me for something?! What am I going to do Lord?! I thought when I repent and asked You for forgiveness, You would forgive me and remember my sins no more?! I don't understand?! Please help me I'm cold and I'm so lonely out here!" My yells and my cries are so loud, some people are stopping to look and listen while others are still walking past as if I'm not saying anything. "What about this doctor telling me that I'm going to be blessed?! But now I'm homeless?! I thought when I gave my life to you, things were going to get easier, but I see it's just the opposite! They're worse! And I'm supposed to be saved! What I look like trying to witness to somebody and I'm worse off than they are?! They gon' say, where is your God? Why isn't He here to help you?! How can I answer them?! I can't! You gotta' do somethin'! I'm out of money! It took almost all my money tryin' to get here! And when I got here I had to buy me somethin' to eat and that took the rest of my money! But that was two weeks ago! You know I've been eating out of trash cans and stealing candy from stores just to have somethin' in my stomach! And you know I don't have nowhere to brush my teeth and wash my face! I forgot how I look! I can barely see where I'm going! Is this the way it's supposed to be for the rest of my life?! I'd rather had stayed in prison! At least I had a decent meal everyday! I'm not gon' make it out here Lord you gotta' do somethin'!" I screamed into the air hoping all America could hear me. Smoke from the cold blew from my lips and nose. My hands and feet feel ten times larger. I can't hardly walk because numbness is starting to set in. "Oh' God! I feel like I'm about to die! I can't breath!" I grasped for air, threw myself to the cold ground, and scooted against a brick wall.

People are walking all over me like a dog. I guess because I'm bald up against a department store in the heart of downtown. It's late at night and I can hardly see a thing. Everything's so blurry. My eye sight have yet to come back to me. If I can only see more clearly.

"Say baby what's up? You need some help? I can help you if you want me to? I can give you a warm bath and a warm bed to lay in? And you won't owe me a thang. What do you say?" I didn't answer him. "Now I know you not gon' say no to a brotha' especially not to an offer like dis', cold as it is?" I still didn't respond to him. "What happen, yo' man put you out?" He asked, leaning over me. "What's wrong cat got cho' tongue?"

I have to admit, it does sound very enticing and I can use a warm bath and a warm bed to lay in right about now too. He said I don't owe him anything. Maybe this is God's way of saving me? Oh' why not?… "Where is your place?" I looked up at him, only able to see the outline of his body.

"That's what I'm talkin' bout'. This was real easy." He stepped back so I could get up.

"What do you mean this was real easy?"

"Oh' now baby I'm talkin' bout' gettin' you off these streets and into a nice cozy warm bed." He pulled me up off the ground. "A fine beautiful sexy woman like you don't need to be on these crazy streets, somebody just might take advantage of you. Here, drink some of this. Dis'll warm you up real quick."

I'm so hungry and thirsty I'll try anything. "Thanks… Pew! What in the world is this stuff?!" I spit the drink out on the ground.

"Say you crazy girl, don't be wastin' my liquor. That cost me some money you fool! Now come on drink it, it'll make you real warm!" He pulled me closer and shoved the bottle into my mouth.

I gulped it down so fast I didn't realize that it's liquor and not water. I have to admit, it was nasty but I'm getting warm real quick. "Is this supposed to make me hot this quick?" I held my forehead while tilting my head down towards the ground as it spun round and round.

"Look woman, I ain't got time to baby you. Come on, follow me."

"Can you hold my hand, I can't see that well?" I waved my hand trying to find him.

"You mean ta' tell me you blind?! I can't do nothin' with you!" He turned and looked.

"No I'm not blind. Things are just a little blurry at night that's all." I said, pointing my finger in his face. "I can hold my own. I don't need no hand outs!"

"What?! Woman you so stupid!" He grabbed my arm but I jerked it back. "You actually think somebody's gon' give you somethin' free?! Look I'll give you free room and board but you gon' have to pay for it!" He started walking off slowly.

"Like how?" I followed him.

"By runnin' the streets for me." He pointed in the opposite direction as if he was pointing at something.

"Look I'm not a prostitute! I'm sold out for the Lord you got the wrong one! And furthermore it's too dawg-on cold to be running up and down these streets!"

"Don't look like it to me! You not gon' make it out here dumb woman! Look at you, you all dirty and don't look like you gon' last the rest of the night! And I won't even talk about you darn near drinkin' up my whole bottle of liquor!" He laughed so loud people passing by turned and looked.

"Look I slipped up ok?! But that don't mean I'm not…"
Shoot, I can't say a word. I started walking off with shame. I
turned and yelled back at him. "What do you want me to do?!"

"That's my girl!" He ran back and caught up with me. "Who
needs the Lord anyway. You make mo' money without em'. I
need you to make money for the both of us. The money you
make from yo' customers you gon' share with me and that'll
cover yo' room and board. And some nights I might need you to
add me to yo' list if you know what I mean?" He smiled, then
looked me up and down.

What am I doing? I don't even know this man and I'm going
home with him. All I know is that his cologne smells real good
and he's wearing a loud red pen striped suit with a pimp hat to
match. The kind with the feather sticking out. He's a very slim,
short, scanty looking guy. Short men is not my first choice. I've
been close enough to see this much. And I think he's missing all
of his teeth in the front because he talks with a hiss. Just like little
kids talk when they're missing their front teeth. I laughed to
myself. I'm asking myself, why am I thinking about taking this
job? One, because it's too cold to stay out here, and besides I'll
never make it if I did. Two, because I don't have nowhere else to
go. And three, because at least I'll have a warm place to stay. I'll
have free food and I can save me some money and get out of
here and get my own place. You got to start some where. "When
do I start?" I asked, looking in his direction.

"Now." He quickly pulled some clothes from his coat and
handed them to me.

"These sure are some skimpy clothes?" I asked, as I felt what
was supposed to be the top and the bottom. There only two
pieces. A strapless top and a skirt that would obviously cut across
my butt if I was to put it on. "Now where do you expect me to
wear this?! It's too cold out here for this?! I'm not wearing this, I
might as well stay out here with what I got on! You better go find

me some better clothes than this or you can forget it!" I tried walking off fast but my feet wouldn't let me.

He yelled as he trotted towards me and grabbed my arm. "Alright, alright let's go to my crib and I'm a let you pick out what you wanna' wear!" He sounds like a real pimp.

"Ok, ok let my arm go! You don't have to grab me like that!" I jerked my arm away.

He pointed his finger in my face. "Look woman I'm not bout' ta' treat you like you somebody special. I got too many of ya'll to look after and I don't have time to baby sit! Either you in or you out!"

After a moment of thought, I finally gave in. "I'm in, but just for a little while." He walked off while I was talking.

He laughed underneath his breath. "Um', that's what you think."

It was a long walk to his vehicle. He has a clean black four door Suburban. The rims on that thing is bigger than the tires. They're sparkling even in the cold. Now I want to see what his house looks like. I bet he lives in Lake Forest. That's supposed to be one of the riches neighborhoods in the city.

"Come on woman, get in!" He opened his side and got in. The inside is as clean as the outside.

It took a minute to get to his house as fast as he drives. And not to my surprise his house looks like an apartment building. It's just that huge. I knew he stayed in Lake Forest. This neighborhood is so rich, we had to go through a security guard before we could even enter into the neighborhood. It looks like a dream land. My vision seems to be coming back to me a little at a time. The lights are beautiful! Lakes and trees are everywhere. I see why they call it Lake Forest. "Hey what do you got running here? Is this really your house?" I asked, jumping out of the truck.

"This' my house and ain't nobody runnin' this but me. I got about ten rooms in counting, but I can always add some mo'. You not the only one who got free room and board." He smiled. "I have a water fall pool, a tennis court, a basketball court, a work out studio, and a lil' ol' track to walk around. Of course you don't need all that cause you lil' enough. Come on, my house is this way." He said, as he guided me towards the front door and then opened it.

Oh' my God, look at all these people! The music is so loud! People are everywhere! Some are walking around with bathing suits on, some are carrying trays of food and liquor, some are hugged up with each other, and the rest are standing around smoking cigarettes and marijuana. I can barley see the people for the smoke and it's starting to choke me. Seem like everybody got a drink in their hands.

"What's up! Party over here, party over there!" This guy came over and shouted in my ear and walked off into the smoky crowd.

It's got to be over a hundred people up in here. "Now I know he didn't just take off leaving me standing here all by myself?!"

"Hey sweet thang', you better get in where you fit in!" This tall skinny guy said as he continued to sit by the door. He act like he's the door man.

"Where do I find my room?!" I asked, trying to yell over the music. Now I know this skin and bones is not trying to ignore me?! Let me ask again this time I'm going to yell in his ear. "Hey! Where do I find my room!" I screamed in his ear.

"Look lady, you don't have to scream! Anywhere you lay yo' head is your room! Look I'm blowed so leave me alone!" He yelled, as he tilted his head back on the back of his seat and closed his eyes.

Let me go up these stairs and find me a room, I'm sure they're plenty of empty ones to choose from. I guess I'll try this room, it seems pretty quiet in there.

"Wait!" A woman shouted from behind the door as I opened it and quickly closed it back.

I walked a little further down the hall only to find that one of the bathrooms was the only room left to sleep in. And it isn't the perfect luxury spot either. Smells like everybody down there been up in here. But at least I'm warm. Actually I was pretty warm right before we got here. Whatever that was he made me drink, made me feel real high above the clouds. I figure at this point anything's better than being out there on the freezing streets. There wasn't any cover to be found so I just covered up with the bathroom mats instead. I'm so tired. There's no way I'm going back out their tonight...

My eyes eventually closed by themselves...

My life has made a 360 degree turn for the worse. Again. Four month's have past and I have to admit, I've become what anybody would call a prostitute, a drug user, and an alcoholic. Anything to take the pain away. The promise I made to God have yet to come true. It's like I never knew Him. I fell... I know it... And I really don't know how to come out of it. I feel worse than I did when I was doing all the wrong things with Tyrome. I've been making a lot of money but it's been swallowed up by my boss cause time I get it in my hand and walk out the building, he's right there with his hands out to take it all away. I don't have feelings anymore. I just think about other things while they do their business and then I get my money when it's all over with. With no feeling. But this is the last time I'm doing this. My body is so tired even though it's only been four months, but it feels like a life time.

I never thought I'd stoop this low. So low that I'm so desperate to survive and quick to degrade myself. I'm weak and worn out. I haven't had a decent meal in over a month. I've lost more weight. I probably weigh about a little over a 100 pounds now. Bulimia and anorexic would be some of the words to describe me. I have a fear of gaining my weight back. Everything I eat I throw it back up, even though I don't have an appetite most of the time anyway. Drugs and alcohol have been my meals. I hope I don't have Aids or any other type of diseases because they didn't always use protection. I'm so ashamed. Maybe it wouldn't be so bad if I had always been like this and never knew what it was to live right. But that's not the case, I was on the good side showing everybody how to live right. Being the Godly example for them. The sad thing is that I experienced God's wonderful Spirit and I felt on top of the world, and chose to run away again. The question that anybody would ask a backslider is why run away from something so unexplainable and miraculously wonderful? Well, the only answer I can give at this point would be that I allowed satan to come back in and take charge again. And I'm worse off than I was when I was out there before. I remember reading in the Bible where it says that once you've been delivered and then you go back out there doing all those wrong things again, those same demon spirits come back in you 7 times greater. And then you're worse off than you were before you got delivered in the first place. I don't know what I've been thinking.

Lord I hope You're listening to me all that I have done. I've made so many promises that I've fell to keep. I'm in it so deep that I don't know how to stop. If You just get me out of this... I don't know what to say or what to do or who to turn too anymore. I just want to be right, and I just want to feel right again. I'm tired of everybody taking advantage of my body. And I'm tired of feeling dirty and useless. It's a war out here and I've lost the battle along time ago. Now I got my white flag up. I surrender all. Take all of me Lord and do with me as You please. Satan made me feel like I wasn't going to make it if I didn't do what I'm doing right now. He had me looking only at the money and not at the sin. Some nights I make over thousands of dollars, but hardly see any of it. That's why he's living in this huge house, cause he's ripping us all off. I've made him my god, but not anymore, I need your help Lord. Only if You find a little more mercy somewhere in Your heart... I cried myself to sleep...

Chapter 15

I **feel so dirty.** I can't do this anymore! I pushed him off me, jumped out of the bed, threw on my clothes, and ran as fast as I could down the hall.

"Hey! Where are you going? I haven't gotten my money's worth yet! I'll get you for this! You gon' give me my money girl!" He yelled from behind the door as I ran out the building.

I ran and ran and ran until I couldn't run anymore. Tears are streaming from my eyes. As busy as the downtown life is, nobody noticed me crying uncontrollably as I rushed threw the crowd. I ran like I had a destination to reach. Which was nowhere.

I've walked for about a good two miles now. The sun is shinning bright in this cold weather. I'm hungry and no money to get me nothing to eat with. All the money I did make, Mr. Pimp took it from me talking about I owed him for some past bills. Which was a lie. I thought, while looking down at the ground. "What's this?" I picked up a piece of paper that I can barely see. It's lying on the ground all torn, wet, and nasty from everybody stepping on it. Some of the words have bled off, but what I can read says: "A Revival for those... slipped away from Christ! God is still able to heal and deliver!..." And at the bottom it reads: "The revival crusade starts on Monday, May 28th until June 1st." Maybe this is the way out of this mess I'm in? I don't know. I thought, as I tried reading back over the rest of the flyer but couldn't because it was too blurry.

A car skidded behind me. Before I can turn around, my boss came running up behind me, grabbed my arm, and jerked me around. "Say woman what's wrong with you?! I just got a complaint from one of yo' customers that you didn't finish yo' job! Now you gon' go back over there and finish the job you started or I'm gon' mess you up real bad! Yea' you heard me right, I'm a kick yo' a#& up and down these streets! Now get back over there and finish. I don't do bad business wit' nobody!" He tried slapping me, but I blocked it with my arms.

"I'm not going nowhere! And I'm not doing anything!" His eyes got big. "I'm a grown woman and you don't own me! Nor are you going to tell me what to do anymore! You not my daddy!" I yelled, as I took off running towards a small grocery store.

"Come back here, you don't run from me!" He caught up with me, picked me up, and body slammed me on the ground.

I thought every bone in my little body was broken. I can't move. I'm thinking it's over and he picks me back up and slams me on the ground again. "Stop! Leave me alone!" I yelled but it didn't work he then reached down and started punching me in my face. "God make him stop!" I screamed.

"Hey you! Leave her alone before I call the police!" An elderly Caucasian man came running out the store with a bat in his hand.

He turned around and jumped up. "Man whatever, she ain't even worth it!" He pointed his finger in my face. "Don't let me catch you in my territory again or I'm gon' kill you! Do you hear me?! I'm gon' kill you! You real lucky! Women don't make it out of my house! Once you in you stay in. Somethin' must be helping yo' a#&...! You the weirdest thang I've ever seen!" He pointed at me again while walking backwards down the street. He then got in his truck and drove away.

"Are you alright?" The elderly man asked, as he raced over and reached down to help me up.

"Yes sir, I'm alright. How could I ever thank you for saving my life?" I grabbed his hand allowing him to pull me up.

"You don't have to thank me. Here let me get you a towel to wipe your face. Sit on this bench, I'll be right back." He sat me down and went inside to get a towel for my bloody nose and lip. It's funny because I don't feel any pain at all. Even when he was hitting me, it didn't even hurt.

"Here you go. I wet it with warm water. I hope that's alright?" He asked, as he handed it to me.

"Yes sir, it feels ok." I took it and dabbed the blood off my face. Where did that flyer go? Don't tell me I lost it? "Do you see a flyer around here?" I looked down on the ground as if it was right in front of me.

"What kind of flyer?" He looked down as if he would never find it.

"It was part of a flyer to this revival at some church I found on the ground. I couldn't see the address, that's the part that's torn." I said.

"Oh' yea', I bet you're talking about the revival at a church about fifteen blocks from here. I was invited to visit by a friend about a month ago. But just never had time to go see what it was all about. I heard it's a spirit fed church I reckon'. I'll probably go soon." He said.

"I think he strained a muscle in my lower back so I know I'm not going to be doing a lot of walking for a while. Plus I can't see that well either. My eye sight is very blurry from a car accident I was involved in a while back ago."

"What happened?"

"You really want to know?" I looked up at him.

205

"Why sure I wanna' know darlin'."

He makes you feel like you can tell him your inner most secrets. It's like he's the white grandfather that I never got a chance to get to know. "You're not going to judge me are you?" My throat tightened up as the tears clouded my eyes.

"Of course not sugar, believe you me I've done a lot of things in my life time that I'm not proud of either."

"Ok, well I had just got out of prison. I got put up in there for something I didn't even do. I was with an old boyfriend that was wanted by the police and I didn't know it. I was so stupid, he had supposedly bought me a brand new Land Cruiser. While we were riding in it, the police stopped us because I was speeding. Well, I thought they were going to give us a ticket and let us go. But that wasn't the case. They took us in. Come to find out he had so many warrants out for his arrest. They had been following him way before that day, and the truck was stolen too. But when they stopped us, I couldn't understand why they were taking us to jail. It wasn't until my trial when I saw how crooked he was. He got out on bond and I got the wrap for all his wrong. He blamed everything on me. Because of that, I spent a little over 7 years in prison for something I didn't even do. The day I finally got out, a cab picked me up and was bringing me to the city, but we never made it. I complained to him that the engine didn't sound right when I first got in the car. He insisted that it was ok. Then later on down the highway is when it happened. The cab hit a wall going eighty miles per hour. The entire car was shattered into pieces. The cab driver never stood a chance. They rushed me to the hospital where I was in a coma for about two weeks. I was talking the minute I came out of the coma. The only thing I was effected by was my eye sight because of all the glass and debris. It's a little blurry but in time I think I'll regain it all back. You may ask how did I make it through all of that? Well maybe my mission here hasn't been completed. That's the only way I see it."

I wiped my eyes with the towel. "I know I should've been dead right along with him."

"You're right, God must have a great work for you to do. Wow that's a story within itself. I'm honored to be talkin' with you right now. Seems like we both need to get back right with the Lord so we can see what it is that He really wants us to do. It's not by accident that I'm still livin' on this earth. I'm an ol' man. My wife of fifty years died about eight years ago. We only had one child and he died before she did. He caught a bad case of the flu and what we thought was minor was really major. He died two days after we took them to the hospital. He was only forty one years old. So I've been alone ever since. My wife and I built this building and business from the ground up when this downtown didn't even look like it looks today." He turns and looks at the buildings around us. "And we've been open ever since. I hope somebody can take it over after I die." He turned back around. "I grew up as a lil' boy knowing the Lord quite well but never accepted Him. My mother and father were devoted Christians who didn't believe in missing a day of church. You name a day they were there. And as long as I've lived in their house, I was goin' to do the same. So I basically played church. You know what I mean?" He winked at me.

"Yea', I hear you." I smiled tearing up.

"As I got older peer pressure got the best of me. I started runnin' with the wrong crowds, doing things to degrade myself and my parents. They were well-known in our town and well respected. My mother used to sit up and pray for me every night. Sometimes she would fast from eating for days. I could feel her prayers to, but I still just couldn't do right. The more she prayed, the more I wanted to do wrong. It was like the devil was controlling me. To make a long story short, she died praying. It must've worked cause God's kept His hand over me. I guess I should be more thankful. He allowed me to meet my beautiful saved wife of fifty years. I can remember when she would try to minister to me about the Lord and I wouldn't listen. And she tried numerous of times to get me to go to church, but I just didn't want to go. She knew I wasn't saved and she was praying so hard for me before she died. One of the last things she said right before she took her last breath was, she hope she see me again. That stuck with me for a very long time. In fact, for years, but I still never gave my life to Him. I figured if I read my Bible, give and help folks, and watch church on TV that should be enough to go to Heaven. And I sometimes still feel that way. He's done so much for us. He allowed us to own our very own business when I was twenty one and she was nineteen, and it's been prospering ever since it first opened up. And because of it, I've given so much free food away to needy families. And I've shipped food and clothes over seas to other countries to help with starvation. I felt like I owed God that much because He's done so much for us and I wouldn't even go to church to show it. Nor would I even pay my tithes off my income and my business." He wiped his eyes with his hands. "I don't want my wife's and my mother's prayers to be in vain, hopefully I'll get saved before I die."

"Wow, that's a story within itself. One thing I'm led to tell you and I hope you don't take this wrong?"

"I won't take it wrong. Go right on ahead darlin'."

"Good. Well, no matter how good you've been and how giving you've been if you haven't confessed God as your Lord and Savior, then you're not saved. And if you were to die today, you would go to Hell (Romans 10:9). See people get it twisted, you can be the most popular person, you can be the most giving person, and you can even be the most helpful person, and still go to Hell. You must confess with your mouth, meaning that it has to come out of your mouth. And you must believe in your heart that God raised Jesus from the dead and it says in the Holy Bible that you will be saved. So that's all the more reason why you and

I need to go to that revival. I'm a backslider. I accepted God into my life and then turned away from Him so many times. I didn't tell you this earlier, but right before you saved me from that guy, I had just ran away from a guy who I had just been with. I, well, I was prostituting. And I got tired of abusing my body so I ran away. The guy told my boss, and he came after me and that's when you came out and stopped all the commotion. I used to have a great relationship with the Lord, but I let sin come between us. So I know I need to come back to God. And you need to come to God. So we both need to take care of our business." I turned, looked at him, and smiled.

"I can agree to that." He said as we both laughed. "Where you goin' to go now?" He looked at me then looked away.

"I don't know. I have nowhere else to go."

"You can stay here til' you get on your feet. You can work in my store and that should help you save some money."

"Are you serious? Thank you so much. You know, I just met you and it seems like I've known you all my life." We both laughed again. "As long as we've been talking I don't even know your name. One thing I do know is that you're Heaven sent." I reached out to hug him.

"Awh' that's nice. Mr. Kelly's my name, and I'm glad to help just don't go back out there in those streets no more. You here?" He said as he reached to hug me back. "Now let me make you some hot coco. I know you'll like that won't cha'?" He smiled as he got up and walked towards the store.

"I sure would!" I said, as I followed him.

"Looks like I'm a have to fatten up those bones. Looks like you're way under your normal weight?"

"I am. But I don't want to get back to how big I used to be." We walked on into the store.

Mr. Kelly's a blue eyed Caucasian man in his late 70's. He's about six feet and has a slim slumped over built. Some how or another it's quite handsome. His hair is a dirty blond color and looks to be slicked back with moose. He seems like his favorite clothes are overalls, cowboy boots, and country checkered multi-colored long sleeve shirts. I laughed to myself.

Four days have gone by and I can't seem to stop thinking about how my situation changed so quick. By this time I would've been out in the streets still prostituting, drinking, and drugging. It's funny because when a person gets sick-en' tired of doing wrong, that's when help is staring that person right in the face. Fortunately for me my help came in the form of Mr. Kelly. I'm sure there are many other ways I could've been helped. But I thank God for this one.

Tonight is supposed to be the last night of the revival. I've been so busy working in the store that I hadn't had time to go the other nights. And I guess the same goes with Mr. Kelly. I know it's the devil doing us like this. "Mr. Kelly, are we going to the revival tonight? You know it's the last night?" I looked at him while handing a shopper their bag. "Now look, the devil has stopped us from going for the past four nights but we really need to make it to this last night."

"You're right. What time does it start?" He asked, while looking down at his watch.

"I think it starts at seven."

"The only thing is that all the customer's aren't out of the store yet. You know sometimes they don't leave until after seven thirty. I know, that's why we didn't make it all the other nights. If they leave out on time, I imagine we can go. Hey gal, that doesn't stop you from going, you're welcome to go by yourself. I'll just go some other time." He smiled.

"That'll be good. Are you going to dock my pay?"

"A boss gotta' do what a boss gotta' do." He smiled again and walked off.

"I'll just wait and see what happens at seven then." I sighed with frustration, trying not to look at him.

Now this is what I can't understand, why he has to dock my pay? He's the owner, he can simply tell the customers to leave and come back tomorrow? Sounds like an excuse to me.

It's a quarter til' seven and there's about eight customers left in the store roaming around like they don't have nowhere else to go. I haven't even gotten dressed and I still have to take a shower. Frankly, I don't think we're going to make it. Mr. Kelly's over there watering the fruits. Not even bothered. He's been away from church for so long that it's a routine for him not to go. I see right now I'm a have to pray for him. See he don't understand that it's urgent that I go because I made a vow to the Lord while in prison that I must keep. Probably why I can't get ahead now? Let's see here I can start cleaning off the counter, that'll save me some time.

The last customer has just left and it's way too late to go to the revival. It's the last night and no tellin' when they'll have another one.

The days are shooting by so fast that sometimes I don't even have time to think. Eight month's have passed and I can truly say that I'm drug and alcohol free. I know that God has delivered me because I haven't even desired it. Nor do I desire degrading my body anymore with a bunch of no good men either. But right now I'm seriously affected by this huge void in my life. I have come to the conclusion that we may never get to the destination that God wants us to be. We have yet to get to church. No time to do anything. And the customers can be so rude. I can't see myself doing this forever. Bagging groceries, yea' right, what a life. All I can think about is what that doctor said in the hospital, something to the fact that I don't have anything to worry about. And that I'm going to be blessed. Hum'. I'm still waiting for that to come true. I don't even go nowhere. All I do is work all day and night and then watch TV until I fall asleep every night. Again, what a life. I know Mr. Kelly means well and would let me stay here forever. But I can't be bound. I feel like I'm trapped inside of a hole with no way out. If people knew my situation they would probably say that I'm being selfish. And that they would love to be in my position right now. A free meal and a free place to stay as long as I'm working in the store. You can't beat that. Normally I would agree, but somehow I don't. I know my parents are out there somewhere and I would like to see them some day. I guess they still live here. I don't know. I haven't tried to look since I got out. Maybe it's because I don't have the courage. They probably wouldn't accept me back anyway. They both had expected oppositions of me by me being the only child and all. My mother wouldn't let me wear certain clothes because she would always say to me that I was more mature than the other girls and she didn't want me to get unnecessary attention. And not to mention daddy, he was stern all the way around. I couldn't go nowhere. I couldn't sing at the table while eating. Could barley have friends because he thought they would all hurt me one day and cause me to rebel against them. Well I'm not proud to say this but he was right, and yes the friendship thing did affect my life in its entirety. Even though he was never home to see it. Honestly, I don't see how mama did it. She was alone so much. At night I would hear her crying and I would walk to her bedroom door that she always had closed, and listen. I wanted to open the door so bad and cry with her. I think to this day he doesn't know how much he's hurt her not being there with her. He needs to know that money's not everything, and for sure I wouldn't sacrifice my marriage for it. Hopefully their still together.

Ever since we missed the revival I've been waking up in the middle of the night reading my Bible. Almost like somebody's been waking me up at the same time every morning. It's weird. I heard this minister say this same thing on the Christian channel once. They were saying how God wakes them up in the early hours of the morning to seek Him, or to pray for themselves, or simply for somebody else. Like having a personal time with God. And then I heard this powerful woman of God talk about being purged and how God would wake her up in the early hours of the morning and have her to pray. During this time she was fasting and praying that God would deliver her from depression and alcohol. She wasn't out there caught up in it anymore, but she still had a desire to do it in her mind. And she said that God was purging it all out of her. She said she started reading the scripture Malachi 3:2-3 out loud, which talks about the refiner's fire. How God will purge you so that you can offer up righteous and clean praises. She even went to Psalm 51:7 where it says: *"Purge me with hyssop (to purify), and I shall be clean: wash me, and I shall be whiter than snow" (KJV).* She was saying that the scripture is not talking about taking a bath and then being clean, even though everybody should do that anyway. But what the scripture is saying is that we should be clean on the inside. Meaning in our hearts, minds, and spirits. And allow God to take out any and everything inside of us that's not like Him. For example, like somebody committing adultery and trying to praise the Lord with clean praises, which is impossible. Because in James 4:4 it says that *"the adulterers and adulteresses know ye not that the friendship of the world is enmity with God? Whosoever therefore will be a friend of the world is an enemy of God" (KJV).* Once God has saved you He doesn't want you going back out there doing those things you used to do before you got saved, like having all these different kinds of lovers and ungodly relationships. That's like being a friend of the world. We live in the world but we're not of the world. There's a difference. She

213

was also saying that God wants us to worship Him in spirit and in truth (John 4:24). And not with fleshly lusty desires.

I have learned so much just by watching the Christian stations. I thank God everyday for them. I didn't realize the Christian station on TV could be so powerful until I moved with Mr. Kelly. There are a lot of great men and women of God who come on the station to minister to so many people like me, with so many spiritual needs. And I also like that they also have singing, praise dancing, game shows, cartoons, and so much more on the station. Anything you name in order to get Jesus Christ across to the nation. And because of this, billions of people have gotten saved, healed, and delivered. And have come to have a personal relationship with Christ. Mr. Kelly believes that we're fine as long as we got the Christian station, we really don't need to go to church. And that we can just give our tithes to the needy instead of giving it to the church. And all I could tell him is what the Bible says in Malachi 3: 8-10, *"will a man rob God? Yet ye have robbed thee? In tithes and offerings. 9. Ye are cursed with a curse: for ye have robbed me even the whole nation. 10. BRING ye all the tithes into the storehouse (the church), that there may be meat in mine house (the church), and prove me now herewith, saith the Lord of hosts, if I will not open up the windows of Heaven, and pour you out a blessing, that there shall not be room enough to receive it" (KJV).*

I'm just sitting here reading this in the Bible and it is true. Nothing can be added and nothing can be taken away (Revelation 22: 18-19). I don't understand why people try to change the Bible. All we have to do is ask God for understanding and knowledge of His Word, and He'll give it to us. We can't change or manipulate the Word of God no way. It is what it says, and it means what it says.

Mr. Kelly's been complaining that he doesn't feel good lately. I'm starting to get worried about him. Maybe I need to take him to the doctor. We did eat a lot last week so maybe he has a bad case of intergestion. Who knows. He'll be alright.

It's a beautiful day outside. The sun's beaming down so bright, birds are singing, and there's a slight breeze. Nobody should be cooped up in the house, that's why I'm sitting outside at one of the table's on the front patio, enjoying me a hot cup of coffee and watching the city life unfold for the start of the day. People are already starting to crowd the streets which doesn't take very long. I love the city life and all but I can see myself at somebody's beach right about now getting a tan. Ha! Yea right! If anything I'm running from a tan. I thought, laughing to myself as I ran into the store to meet Mr. Kelly's coughing hysterically. "Mr. Kelly are you ok?!" I asked, out of breath from running in to check on him. I put one arm around him to comfort him.

"Awe' yea' darlin', I'm ok. Darn cough keeps me up all through the night!" He said, as he got choked up with another cough. "Reach over there and get my cough medicine over on the counter." He pointed towards the counter behind the cash register.

"Don't you think you need to go to the doctor?"

"Awe' gal, don't start worryin' me bout' no darn doctors. I'll be just fine. You run along, you got a customer that needs to be checked out. I'm going upstairs and take me a nap." He said, as he slowly vanished behind the wall leading to the stairs.

Mr. Kelly's house sits on top of the store. It has two bedrooms, one bathroom, a kitchen, a small living room, and a walk-in pantry. It's rather old looking on the inside. You can tell it's been here for decades. The wall paper looks like it's from the thirties, and the wood smells like old pine from the early twenties. Mr. Kelly likes to collect antiques so you can imagine what it looks like in here. All the furniture's old fashion. And even smells old fashion to. Even in both of the rooms. They probably haven't changed the furniture since they first moved up in here. Which could be a good thing. I'm sure all the furniture is worth a lot of money. And now that I'm thinking about it, some people love the old fashion look and smell anyway. When you first walk in, you walk through the kitchen into the living room. And to the right is a short hall leading to the master bedroom on the right, and my bedroom is on the left, with the bathroom straight ahead. It's not what you call a mansion, but it'll due for just the two of us.

Mr. Kelly had a funny look on his face like he's keeping something from me. I hope he's alright. He's a good ol' man and I know that if it was something wrong, he probably wouldn't tell me anyway.

I woke up to hysterical coughing. Almost as if somebody was being choked. It's 4:16 in the morning with no sound of life moving around outside. I jumped out of the bed afraid that somebody might be in the house, grabbed the stick I keep by the bed, tip toed to my closed bedroom door and listened. Sounds like the noise is coming from the bathroom. That sounds like Mr. Kelly! I threw open the door, ran into the bathroom only to find Mr. Kelly choking and gasping for his life. Blood is everywhere. On the sink, the toilet, the counter, and all over the floor. You would think he got stabbed. "Mr. Kelly! Mr. Kelly! Are you alright?!" I screamed as I shoved my hand's under his arms and tried to pull him up. "I can't pick you up, just lay there I'm a go call 911!" He didn't even respond back to me. He just held his throat and kept on coughing and choking as blood kept coming from his mouth. "Don't try to move, you're going to be alright!" I screamed as I ran to the phone in the front room. Shaking with fear I could barely dial the number. I ran back into the bathroom after calling 911. "You're going to be fine!" I yelled. "The ambulance is on it's way! Everything's going to be alright! You're going to be fine! I'm right here! I'm not going anywhere!!" I screamed as I grabbed him and held him with all of my strength. "Don't you give up on me Mr. Kelly! Don't you give up! I don't know what I'll do without you! Somebody help me! Please!…"

My screaming voice faded out like a song that was about to end…

Chapter 16

Mr. Kelly's been in the hospital for going on three weeks now. The doctor's diagnosed him with cancer and they have already started the cancer treatments. I guess all those years of smoking have caught up with him. Since he's been in the hospital I've had to take care of all the important business. I'm so glad that he showed me this way before now. We've gotten so close. So close that I see him as my father. He didn't only save my life, but he closed the gap that was starving to be fulfilled.

I haven't been living here long but already he's helped me with my self-esteem. For many years I felt like a big fat nobody. But now I finally feel like somebody. Thought I found the love of my life, somebody to make me more than happy only to find out that he was a woman beater, a cheater, and a crook that was already married. I feel sorry for him because of what happened to him as a child, almost like he's getting back at everybody because of it. Not to mention the friend I thought had betrayed me, set me up, stole my man, and now is running around here enjoying all of it. But I always felt that a person with a lot of money without the Lord is sad on the inside. And a person without a lot of money and has Christ, has a lot of peace on the inside. And I believe that

that's what's happening to Michelle and Tyrome where ever they are.

Hospitals are always so cold and always have a funny smell to them. To this day I can't figure out where the smell comes from. All of them smell the same. The hall leading to Mr. Kelly's room is so long you would wonder if he's even in the hospital. They told me B-420, which seems like B-1,000,000. I laughed to myself. My heart goes out to each patient up in here. I can't imagine having cancer. I wish I could help each one of them, and they all would be fine. And I wish I could help Mr. Kelly to. I have to keep telling myself that he's going to be alright. I'm trying not to tear up. I'm at 418, two doors down from his room. I hope he don't start feeling sorry for himself because of the position he's in. Mr. Kelly's the type of man that has a lot of pride like most men do. I mean he's a humble man, but sometimes that pride will rise up in him and I have to open rebuke him and get him straight. I smiled to myself. They think they can do everything by themselves with no help from nobody, not even from the Lord. If anything went wrong around the store or the house and he couldn't fix it, he wouldn't call for help he would keep messing it up until it was finally fixed. He wouldn't even let me help. He feels that a woman's place is not to do hard labor. His idea of hard labor is replacing the seat on a toilet. I laughed as I finally arrived at his room.

"Hey what's up my man? How are you feeling?" I asked, running over and planting a big kiss on his cheek.

He whispered slowly. "I'm ready to go home so I can replace the toilet. That ol' toilet's been giving us problems since I've been having the house." He sipped on a cup of water as if it was hot coffee.

That's funny because I was just thinking that about him and the toilet. He doesn't look good at all. In fact, he looks worse than he looked when they came and picked him up from the house. "Do you need me to do anything really important for you?" I asked, lowering my tone and fluffing up the pillow behind him.

"Yea' I need you to do something really important for me. Can you do it?" He whispered as if it was hard for him to speak.

"Yes, anything just name it." I whispered back, trying to hold back the tears.

"Go in my room, look in the back of the closet, pull the strip of wood up, and get the piece of paper from out of the hole. Can you do that for me?" He slowly turned to look at me as a tear unbearably rolled from his left eye.

I wish I could make it all better for him. "Yes sir. I can. But what is this about?" I asked, as I reached for his hand.

"It's my funeral plans and my will. It has everything in it that you need to know. I want my funeral to go just how I have it on the paper. And everything in the will stands, don't let nobody change it. Both of them have been notarized." He said, slightly squeezing my hand.

"Don't talk like that you're not going to die. I won't accept that cause you not going to die."

"Accept it darlin', and do what I asked you to do. You'll be alright, don't worry. I've lived a good life and now it's about that time for me to hang up the ol' boots."

"What I'm going to do without you?" I asked, reaching to hug him with tears falling from my eyes. "You took me in and helped me get back on my feet. You gave me so much confidence in myself and I'm so thankful for that. Your my guardian angel, and my guardian angel can't die! No!" I yelled so loud that the nurses came running in and carried me out of the room. I was hysterical as I left the hospital in tears.

I took the first bus available. And it's crowded as usual. Some are getting off and some are getting on. Getting a seat is almost impossible. I can't stop crying. All I can think about is Mr. Kelly lying in that bed helpless. Everybody that's sitting by me is staring at me, even this little girl that's sitting in her mother's lap. She haven't looked away yet. I'm sure they're all trying to figure out what's wrong with me. I don't even care, they can stare all they want. They don't know me. They don't know what I'm going through. If they had a heart of God, they'd come over and see if I'm alright.

"Mam', are you alright?" Someone standing over me politely asked as I looked up. He paused for a moment and then said, "I see you're not in the mood for talking. I saw you crying and I couldn't just sit there and watch you cry and not come and ask you if you were ok. If there's anything I can do for you please let me know, no matter what it is. I'm sitting about nine seats behind you." He said, as he staggered away because of the moving bus.

I couldn't say a word. My mouth wouldn't allow me to. His smile was incredible. I could hardly keep my eyes on him he's so handsome. When our eyes met, they connected. I felt it deep down in my stomach. That was so weird. I can't remember the last time I seen a man that good looking. Except when, well, unfortunately Tyrome. He looks better than Tyrome though. Much better. His caramel color makes his skin look so smooth. You can tell he takes good care of it. His mustache is neatly trimmed and his hair is full of waves. It's more wavier than Tyrome's. This man has a lot of class. He looks to be about six feet. He's wearing some fitted blue jeans that's not too tight, a black twisted belt with a silver buckle, a blue jean button down shirt, and some all black steel toed boots. He's also more toned than Tyrome. And his eyes are so warm and friendly. They twinkled while his smile glowed to be unnoticed. There's no lust about this man. There's something special about him that I've never felt before. Not even with Tyrome. That was a bunch of flesh anyway. But not this, this is spiritual. I want to ask him if he's a minister. The presence of God was all over him. I better hurry before the bus stops again and that'll be where he gets off.

I can't believe this man took my mind off of Mr. Kelly just that quick. I forgot I was even crying, and I know I love Mr. Kelly.

Reaching up to grab the seat ahead of me, the bus made a wild turn and threw almost everybody out of their seats and on to the floor. Some are screaming like they're really hurt, while others are yelling and shouting talking about they're about to get paid. It's kind of funny because the turn wasn't that hard. This elderly lady is lying on the floor screaming whiplash while laughing at the same time. I have to wonder. I laughed to myself. I'm not hurt at all. I got up and sat back down in my seat. Some did the same while others stayed on the floor still screaming like we ran over a cliff. My seat is toward the front half of the bus.

The bus quickly came to a stop. The bus driver is now motioning for all of us to get off. I guess as a caution routine. Everybody practically ran off the bus while some stayed. Pushing and shoving each other like the bus was on fire. We're now waiting for the ambulance and the police. Where is he? I wonder if he got off before me? The bus has two doors. One in the front and one towards the back. It looks like two buses stuck together. I came out through the front and I guess he must've came out through the back. I hope he didn't get hurt and is still on the bus. Let me go back in their and see. Everybody has vacated the bus. It's too hard to find him outside with people lying on the ground, while some are sitting along the curve and in the grass. All of them seem to have something wrong with them. I'm looking around, and he's nowhere to be found. Shoot, I missed a chance to talk with him. Oh' well, I'm sure I'll never see him again. If I do, then I know it'll have to be destiny.

We've been out here for almost an hour. And it's so hot out here. I guess they're sending for another bus for those who weren't hurt and still need to ride the bus. I've got to hurry up and get back to re-open the store. I closed it to go see Mr. Kelly.

It took an hour to get back to the store.

Let me go up here and get this paper for Mr. Kelly. Ok... he said to go to his room, look in the back of his closet, pull up the wood from the floor, and get the paper from the hole. Here it is, I got it. Now let's see what he's talking about. Wow, there's a check for thirty thousand dollars attached to it. Now let me read this paper and see what he wants me to do with it. He has it outlined with everything he wants me to do with the money. From the place where he wants to be buried which is in the same place as his parents, his son, and his wife. On down to the color he wants his suit and coffin to be. It's kind of hard to read this and I don't want to accept it but I'll do just as he asks...

It's slow around the store today. Three o'clock in the evening doesn't seem late but it makes it real boring when there haven't been a customer in almost an hour. You have to wonder if the Super Bowl's on, or some kind of festivities are going on around town. Let me go back here to the stock room and get some more bags of chips while things are slow. We've been running a little low on them. The door ringer will let me know if I have a customer or not.

How in the world did we get all this food back here? This stock room isn't that big? Mr. Kelly must've done it while I was gone one day.

The door ringer rang, a customer must've come in. Let me hurry up and get from back here. I thought as I ran towards the front and scooted behind the front counter. Whoever came in is in the back doing something. They're getting something from the freezer and laughing with one another. Let me get this paper from off the floor while they're still back there.

"Hello! Is anybody here?!" He yelled, as they walked up to the counter.

I rose up and to my surprise it's Jerry and Sandra. Some old high school classmate's of mind. They have always been close ever since they been in high school. Everybody actually thought they would one day get married. But come to find out, he wasn't what she was looking for. She was looking for somebody more feminine. I can see she's still pretty bulky. She's always worn her hair short. Caps seemed to be her favorite attire along with matching basketball jerseys, jeans, and the latest tennis shoes. Jerry on the other hand- Mr. Pretty Boy, was always conservative. The dress pants and dressy button down shirts with some penny-lofa's. They're two totally different people. But they say opposites attract. Since I've been looking at the Christian station and reading my Bible, my eyes are more open now. God allows me to see so many things I couldn't see at first. I want to tell her so bad that she can be delivered from that life style. Maybe you'll open the door for me to say it Lord? Anyway they fell out with each other but later became closer friends and been friends ever since. They're made for each other. Still messy, mean, and full of gossip. That saying is so true, you hang with who you are. If you're messy, you hang with mess. If you're mean, you hang with mean folks. They have always teased me and called me names. So I won't be surprised if they do it now.

"Wait a minute Ramona?! I know not! What's up Miss. Thang? Long time no see! I hardly recognized you. You done lost so much weight! It's been years since we seen you! What? A little over twenty years?!" She asked, as she put her hand over her mouth as if she was in shock.

"Yea! What in the world have you been doin' with yo' self girl-lee?" He glanced over at Sandra, then back at me. "You look skinnier than those pencils you sellin' over there. I can't lie, you do look good. I beat you sayin' to yo' self, thank God I'm not fat anymore!" He said, as they both looked at each other again and burst out laughing.

"I've been just fine." I said calmly without one smile on my face.

"So what's up?" She threw up her hands. "Do you work here? Cause you know we know you spent all those years in the pen. I can't believe you workin' cause you know it's hard to get a job after spending all that time behind bars!" She asked with a sarcastic expression. She then turned around as if to be looking for somebody in the store.

After God delivers you, people got a way of trying to bring back up your past. They try to treat you like you still the same. But little do they know, I'm not the same. Lord please forgive me for what I'm about to say. "No, actually I own the place." I said with a smirk.

"No way, not Miss. Ramona ownin' no store? You out of all people we would have least expected. But maybe not, you was kinda' nerdy. No maybe it was the fact that you were so fat that it cluttered up your brain?! Which one was it?!" They both laughed hysterically. "But look like you anorexic now! What's wrong?!" He asked, as they both bent over and laughed again so hard that it pierced my ears.

"Well Miss. Thang we know you heard the big news and all?" She leaned over the counter.

"What big news?" I asked.

"Oh' come on save us the breath, we know you heard?" He asked leaning over her shoulder.

There was a pause. Then she said, "girl you still the same. Miss. Daydreamer. You heard us ask you a question and you still want to wait forever to answer. Still the same huh' Jerry?" She asked, looking at him for his approval.

"I'm tellin' you!" He answered as if to be intimidated of her. He's always been afraid of her, and almost everything else.

"No I haven't heard the big news!" I slammed my fist down on the counter as both of them jumped. "Would you please tell me?!"

"No she not gettin' an attitude?!" She yelled, as she rose up off the counter and looked at him with her face full of anger.

"Look like it to me! What chu' gon' do about it?!" He yelled back while pointing his finger towards me but looking at her.

"She not gon' do nothin' but hear what I have to say! I'm sick and tired of you two after over twenty years thinking you can just come in my store and talk to me like you used too! Now I let you get away with it earlier cause I could've kicked you out of the store! But enough is enough! You think you can get away with laughin' and gettin' off on how I used to be! Yes, I said used to be! I'm not the same! But what you two need to be worryin' about is your own souls! God is not pleased with you two going around hurting people, and sinning like it's ok! Because it's not ok! Look at you Sandra, you are a very attractive woman, but the lifestyle you're living is going to send you straight to hell! And you two sin with no shame. You talk to people all evil and just full of hate." I grabbed a Bible from underneath the counter, opened it up, and turned to Romans 1:24-32 *KJV* It says: *"Wherefore God also gave them up to uncleanness through the lusts of their own hearts, to dishonour their own bodies between themselves: Who changed the truth of God into a lie, and worshipped and served the creature more than the Creator, who is blessed for ever. Amen. For this cause God gave them up unto vile affections: for even their women did change the natural use into that which is against nature: And likewise also the men, leaving the natural use of the woman, burned in their lust one toward another; men with men working that which is unseemingly, and receiving in themselves that recompense of their error which is meet. 28. And even as they did not like to retain God in their knowledge, God gave them over to a reprobate mind, to do those things which are not convenient; 29. being filled with all unrighteousness, fornication, wickedness, covetousness, maliciousness; full of envy, murder, debate, deceit, malignity; whisperers, 30. backbiters, haters of God, despiteful, proud, boasters, inventers of evil things, disobedient to parents, 31. without understanding, covenant breakers, without natural affection, implacable,*

227

unmerciful: 32. who, knowing the judgment of God, that they which commit such things are worthy of death, not only do the same, but have pleasure in them that do them." And you two sit there and try and cover up how you're really feeling inside. But you can't hide it because God knows everything, even those things done in secret. It says in Luke 8:17 *"For nothing is secret, that shall not be made manifest; neither anything hid, that shall not be known and come abroad."* See, God knows everything. Sandra and Jerry, the way you two are going is only going to end you up in hell. In Romans 6:23 it says: *"For the wages of sin is death; but the gift of God is eternal life through Jesus Christ our Lord."* But the good news is that you two can be saved from going to hell by simply repenting of your sins and by confessing God as your Lord and Savior. Many people believe that you cannot be delivered from homosexuality, but you can Sandra. God sees sin all the same. There's not one greater than the other. It's all wrong. If you want to be delivered today just admit that you have a problem, then renounce that sin out of your life (1 John 1:9), and receive your deliverance. Because God is a forgiver and a deliverer. And today He's come to set you two free. Sandra, you've always bullied people around just to hide the fear that's really deep down on the inside of you. Not to mention the gang banging and the stealing from stores. You were molested by your uncle and that's why you're so mean towards everybody. But God wants you to know that you don't have to stay that way. He can save and deliver you. He can stop the tears from falling in the middle of the night."

"How did she know about all those things, we haven't seen her in years?" She bewilderingly turned and asked Jerry.

"I don't know." He answered, shrugging his shoulders.

"God knows and He's using me right now to speak into your lives so that you can believe that He is real and that He can save you. It's call prophesy. And it only comes from God. Look, it's not about me, it's about you two getting right with God. Are you ready to do that today? This is the real reason why you two came here today. Will you let God complete the mission?"

She turned and looked at Jerry again. "I know this has to be God because I haven't ever told anybody what all she just said. I know we didn't tell her about us stealing from all those stores. And didn't nobody know that I be cryin' at night either? And she's right, I was molested and have a lot of anger in me because of that." She looked back at me. "And I do have feelings for the same sex. But I'm tired of this lifestyle and I want to be free. I don't want to live like this anymore. Inside, I always wanted to be delivered but just didn't have nobody to talk to. I couldn't trust nobody. I was afraid people would judge me and not like me. That's why I put up a front and it worked for many years. But I'm tired and I'm ready to change. I'm glad you said that God will forgive me because I always thought that He would never forgive me for everything I did wrong, and for everything I do wrong to people and for the lifestyle I'm living in. So maybe God is tryin' to tell us somethin'?" She looked at him again. "And she used the scriptures out of the Bible and everything. That's one thing I don't do is mess with the Bible. I believe what it says. I don't live what it says, but I always believed it. Yea', I do wanna' be saved." She turned back to me. "And yea', I do wanna' be delivered from this lifestyle. And from all the other things that I do and have ever done wrong." She said, putting her head down as her eyes started tearing up. That's the first time I've ever seen her cry. Thank you Lord. Please continue to have Your way.

"Man, girl you cryin'?" He put his hand on her back. "Ok you right, this is real I wanna' be saved too." He started crying. "Nobody knows but I never wanted to do the things that I did to people either. Like gang banging, robbing stores, beating up everybody because I was mad. I was jealous and fighting my parents because they wouldn't let me do what I wanted to do, like going out all hours of the night. I got turned on to an occult group by one of my friends. We would kill animals and then drink their blood. I was told that it would give me supernatural powers. And I always wanted to be powerful. I got so deep in it that they started making gestures of killing me and drinking my blood. I feared for my life and got out of it. It wasn't easy to leave at first because the witches that was in it was so demonically powerful, they would torment me day and night. They would send demons to growl in my ears. Telling me I've drunk the devil's blood, and now I'm a devil and I could never turn to God and go to Heaven. Sometimes they still haunt me to this day. If God is who He say He is today, then He'll save me from this fear and torment, and deliver me from all my wrong. You did say that He's a God that forgives, right?" He asked, as he balled his fist together in front of his face and shook them as if to beg.

"Of course He will forgive you. All you two got to do is lift up your hands and repent of your sins." They did so with their eyes shut. "Now repeat after me. Lord, I know that I'm a sinner." They repeated. "I have sinned against Your Word, and I confess with my mouth and I believe in my heart that You were raised from the dead." They repeated again. "And now I make You my Lord and Savior and my Redeemer." They repeated. "I thank You today for saving me" (Romans 10:9). They repeated again with tears falling from their eyes. "Now Lord, I renounce satan completely out of my life. Come into my heart, come into my mind, come into my spirit, and my soul, and wash me with Your precious Blood." They barely repeated because of the brokenness that God is doing in them. "Now say, Lord deliver me from everything that's not pleasing in Your sight." They barely repeated again. They're waving their hands with tears falling uncontrollably down their faces. "Now just receive your deliverance!" God, Your Spirit is in this place. All I can do is weep with them because not only are they getting delivered, but I am too. I have just rededicated my life totally back to God. I can feel Him delivering me from all the things that I thought I was already delivered from. But wasn't. He's delivering me from loneliness and gluttony (Excess in eating or drinking, greedy or excessive indulgence). I've had this problem all my life. I'm not big anymore but the thoughts are still there and I can feel God taking the desire away. Thank you Jesus! Even the feeling that I could never love someone again, and the feeling of never being able to receive love by anyone. I can feel Him taking it all away! The hate, the anger, the unforgiveness, the bitterness, the oppression and depression, the shame of what people thought about my past. The condemnation, the jealousy, and my ungrateful ways. God's doing a great work in this place! I ran from behind the counter, threw my hands up, and began to worship God. I began to thank Him for delivering me. All three of us are weeping uncontrollably with their hands lifted to the ceiling. The Lord is filling us with His precious Holy Spirit. And He's washing me all over again! Thank you for washing us whiter than snow. Thank You for creating in us a clean heart and renewing in us a right spirit, thank You for purging us, thank You for restoring and reconciling me back to You. And upholding us with Your free Spirit! I love You Lord! I need You Lord! I can do nothing without You Lord! I worship You Lord! Thank You for never looking at our pasts again!! Thank You that our names are recorded in the Lamb Book of Life (Revelation 20:15)! Thank You for Your glory falling down in this place! Thank You Jesus! Thank You Jesus! Hallelujah! Hallelujah!!" I shouted, as we laid out on the floor like new born babies...

We were in the presence of God for over an hour. We have cleaned our faces, embraced one another, and are now standing next to the front counter.

"I can't believe all this just happened to me. I, I never expected to come up in here and get saved, let alone delivered. I

231

feel like a free woman! I'm so excited! I just wanna' thank you." She hugged me. "Look Ramona, girl I'm so sorry for how I treated you in high school and in the past. And for how I talked to you earlier. You really don't look anorexic, you look good. And I know I used to bully you around at school and make fun of your weight, but I just want you to know that I'm truly sorry. I was wrong, will you forgive me?" She asked.

"And will you forgive me too? All these years I teased you and picked on you not knowing that you were such a loving person. I guess that's why it's not good to judge people and to pick on them because you never know, you just might need them one day. Like today. You care about us this much to see our souls saved and our lives changed. I thank God that the fear and torment is gone. I feel like a new person now. I'll never treat my parents wrong again. I'll never rob another store. I'll never be apart of another gang. Nor will I ever paint graffiti on buildings and beat up people. Thank you Ramona and I hope God uses you with many more other people. Because you've truly changed my life." He said, as he hugged me over Sandra.

"I forgive you two but don't thank me, thank God because He's the real reason for this. He just used me to do it. He could have chosen anybody. This is why you two came here in the first place." We let one another go as I continued to speak. "He has so much planned for you two. He has a purpose and a plan for your lives. And now that you two are saved and filled with His precious Holy Spirit, you need to go and join a church that God leads you to, and get active so that you won't go back out there doing those things that God has delivered you two from today. And don't stop there, go out and witness to all those that you know and don't know, and tell them what God did for you and that He can do the same for them." We all smiled in a agreement.

"We're going to do just what you said." Sandra said, looking over at Jerry as he agreed.

"What we were trying to tell you earlier was that Michelle and Tyrome got sent to prison with life, without parole." Jerry said, as he jumped up and sat down on top of the counter.

"What?! How did that happen?" I leaned against the ice cream machine that sits in front of the counter.

"Michelle caught Tyrome in the bed with another woman and she pulled out a gun and shot her in the head. She tried to shoot him too but the gun jammed, and he took off running. She tried to catch him but couldn't." He said.

"How did he get life?" I asked, as I shrugged my shoulders.

"Well a week later he robbed a liquor store and shot and killed two clerks that was working that night." Sandra said, as she broke in.

"God, that's sad! One thing I always said, you reap what you sow, good or bad." I dropped my head. "After hearing that anybody would be glad, but I'm really sad." I feel the change in me already. "Most people would probably be happy especially if they had to spend all those years in prison for something they didn't even do."

"You spent all those years in the pen and you were innocent?!" He asked. "Something told me you we're innocent! See I told you Sandra." He said, as he quickly turned and looked at Sandra.

"Yea', how you think I got out so soon? I just knew you guys knew. I'm sure everybody knew."

"No we didn't, but go ahead and keep talking." She said.

"But I'm really not happy to hear this. Just knowing that a person will never be able to see life again is sad. Both of them got a lot of baggage from their past. Michelle never had parents to love her like she needed to be loved which is probably the reason why she always felt like she didn't need nobody. I can say that she did have a loving and caring grandmother who loved her a lot. But Michelle didn't receive her love. Instead she tried to find that

233

love in different men that she never did get from any of them. And so did Tyrome. He didn't have loving parents at all. He was a foster child and was passed from home to home. He lived in abusive and unloved homes. He was betrayed and so he himself had betrayal built up inside of him. He didn't know how to love even if he tried. And that's why he felt the need to control women. And when he lost control or was about to lose control, he wanted to beat on them like he was beat on. How could I have ever thought that he could love me like I needed to have been loved? Impossible. I guess I was real lonely at the time, and then just maybe I really cared for him. I was saved then, supposed to have been living for the Lord but I let this man in my heart and a so called friend who enticed me to pursue him. Even though he was still married. I dealt with my weight and my self-esteem all my life and when he came into my life, I thought he was the one. Even after I was brain washed into thinking that we could ever have something someday. Not so. You can never have something with a man that's already married. It only ends up in destruction. Like it did in my life. It took me so far away from God and my family. I didn't think I would ever turn on God, but I did. I was in a car accident after prison and was in a coma for two weeks, and the only result I have is not being able to see that good. Everything's still a little blurry. Which is good because at first I couldn't see at all. I still believe that God's going to heal my eyes totally. After that I got out there on the streets because I got into it with my mother before I got put in prison, so when I got out I didn't have nowhere to go so I was homeless. I started prostituting just to have money and food to eat. I got hooked on drugs. I used dirty needles, pills, marijuana, cocaine, and syrup. I was also an alcoholic. I couldn't take the pain and the stress I was in. The pain of the memories and the stress of fulfilling other people's needs. My life was in shambles. I became num and cold hearted on the outside, but was torn in many pieces on the inside. Bitter would be the word. I stopped eating. I weighed a little over a 100 pounds. Most of the time I would smoke and drink myself to sleep. But one day I got tired of the life I was living and said to myself that I wasn't going to degrade myself anymore. I called out to God for help and he sent Mr. Kelly out of the store with a bat to help me because the pimp I was working for, was beating me up. He ended up running away. And from there Mr. Kelly took me in and I've been here ever since. I thank God for loving me enough to give me a another chance at life. I'm not trying to get people to believe in any type of religion, I'm trying to get people to believe in God. And to know that He is real, and that He will live within you if you let Him. He has truly changed my life! I've learned that we all fall down, but we don't stay there, we get back up and keep on going. We all make mistakes but we don't give up, we shake them off and try again. I'm so happy that I kept on going even when I wanted to give up and attempted to commit suicide. I now feel like I got it going on with God again. It's like I got my groove back from God. And nothing can come between us again. He's my main Man. He's my Lover and my Friend and I wouldn't trade Him for nothing in this world."

"That's awesome. That's so awesome Ramona. I hope you share your testimony with many more people. They need to hear from you. I never knew you went through all that. And I know it's more you haven't told us, but what you did share is touching. That inspired me when you said about falling and getting back up again. I feel like I did that today. I got back up again. And I too feel like I got it going on with God again. Like I got my groove back from God. That's awesome. I'll always keep that thought within my heart no matter where I go. You're going to make it Ramona and God's going to use you in a powerful way. You have such a good heart." Sandra said, as she wiped her eyes and reached and hugged me again.

"Hey, this'll be a great way for you to go in there and talk to Michelle and Tyrome. And maybe they can get saved?" Jerry said, as he jumped down from off the counter.

"You're right, I'll just continue to be lead by the Lord."

"Well look, we don't mean to run because we really wish we could stay all day talking about what the Lord has done, but we got some important business to take care of. We hope God continues to use you especially with Michelle and Tyrome. They need it bad. By the way, they're at the city jail right now. But you need to go before they get transferred to prison." She said, as they both started walking towards the door.

"I'm sure God will have His way with me as always. Alright I'll be praying for you two and I hope you two won't be strangers." I said, smiling and squinting my eyes as I followed them to the door. "Oh' and by the way, I don't own the place, I'm just taking care of it for Mr. Kelly." I smiled.

"Fa' sho'! We'll be back by to see you girl! And we knew you didn't own the store cause we know Mr. Kelly personally. We used to come through here all the time. He's a nice ol' white man." We laughed, as they walked out of the door and down the side walk on into the distance. When I couldn't see them anymore, I closed the door behind me.

Wow Lord, You really know what You're doing. They both looked totally different from when they first walked up in here. Even their skin has gotten lighter. And what's so amazing is that You didn't let not one customer come up in here while all that was going on! You're the greatest! What they were saying really made since about going in there and ministering salvation to them.

But, I don't know how to do it. I mean I still don't have a church home. And I don't want them asking me no questions that I can't answer. I just want it to be right. Maybe it's not the right time yet. If it wasn't the right time, you wouldn't have used

Sandra and Jerry to come in here and tell me that. So I, well, I don't know maybe I'll see them one day…

Chapter 17

Today is a stormy day. It's been raining off and on all day. The thunder is so loud, it sounds like an earthquake. It came again but this time it felt like it shook the entire hospital room. It's funny because I'm looking out of the window of about three stories high and I can see this cute little chubby dog, which I'll call him Chubby. Because he's as big as the Big Dipper in the sky. He's soaking wet and he's running underneath this parked car when ever he would hear the sound of the thunder. Once it stops, he would come from underneath the car. That's too cute. I smiled to myself.

It's been three weeks since the last time I seen Sandra and Jerry. I hope they're doing alright and have joined a church. I can't seem to shake off what God did for us that day. He filled me with His precious Holy Spirit. Before that, I was so sad and depressed on the inside. I used to struggle with my spirituality. I struggled just to stay free from all those things I had already been delivered from. And now I don't have to do that anymore. Today's a strange day. I just got this feeling that something good is about to happen to me. I don't know what it is, but I do know that it's sure not the rain. The bus is probably going to be too crowded, it always is on rainy days. Taking the cab won't be so bad I got a couple extra dollars on me.

Mr. Kelly is sleeping now so I'm going to go ahead and leave him resting. I've been up here since 5 o'clock this morning, and it's now 12 noon. It's sad that he doesn't have any family members. It must be a lonely feeling to be up in here all day everyday and not have any family come to see you. This is the time when you really need somebody the most. They said Mr. Kelly's not getting any better. They've given him two months to live. He's lost a lot of weight. He wasn't very big in the first place, just tall. He's now on a breathing machine to help him breath better, and all of his hair is gone. I brought him his favorite hat from the store yesterday. He had it on when I came this morning. I guess he was thinking about me. I smiled at the thought. He still knows who I am and can still somewhat communicate with me. He just talks slow with the oxygen tank in his nose and all. But I can pretty much understand what he's saying. Especially about the store. He's got to know about his money. Don't mess with an old man's money. I don't know why some elderly people are like that. My grandmother was like that. Even though she had Alzheimer's disease, she could still keep count of her money. She didn't play that. She would put a stick pin in her little wallet and if the pin was moved, she new somebody had went in it. One time mama told me that my grandmother accused my dad of going in her wallet, and tried to chase him all around the house with a switch. He was a grown man then. Those were some hilarious moments of listening to the stories that mama would tell me. I'll never let those memories go.

Well, let me see what I'm going to do. I'll probably come back later after I close the store. I've been closing the store while I come up here. He hasn't told me to hire anybody else so I'll just spend some time with him and then I'll go and open it up.

Seems like we're not getting that much business lately. I know it can't be the hours. And I won't talk about paying any tithes either. Maybe your trying to tell us something Lord?

The cab is taking so long. It's kind of cool out here, I guess from the rain. You would think I'd be scared to ride in cab's considering what happened to me a while back ago. I thank God for delivering me from all that fear. I can't be afraid for the rest of my life. If I die, then I just die and see Jesus. If I live, then I have a chance to bring more people to Christ. I thought, as I flagged down a cab driver from the busy downtown street.

The downtown life is so rush rush. People are blowing their horns for nothing. Screaming at one another from car to car. You can even hear the sound of construction work going on. You would think after raining like it did earlier, the streets would be deserted. But not downtown. It'll always but crowded and congested no matter what.

The cab driver sped up to meet me as I flagged him down. "Where to honey?!" The driver asked peeping over his shoulder.

"To the downtown city jail sir!" I answered. Oh' my God, where did that come from? I said it before I realized it. I meant to tell him to take me back to the store. Well if I messed up, then why am I not telling him to turn around? Maybe it's your will Lord so I guess I'll go ahead and go. I hope Michelle and Tyrome are still there before they transfer them to prison.

It was a long ride to the jail because of the lunch traffic. Everybody goes out to eat lunch, and it's always so crowded. I remember how I used to be in a hurry to eat lunch while at work. Meeting Michelle in the cafeteria and watching her gobble down all the good food while I did the salad thang. Well at least I tried. It never worked long cause the food she was eating smelled too good. And her smacking in my face didn't help either. Knowing

241

her, she probably was doing it on purpose cause she knew I was always attempting to be on a diet or on some kind of fast. Ha', yea' right! Out of all the wrong she's done to me, I kinda miss that girl. I feel so sorry for her.

We finally arrived at the jail. I paid the cab driver and sent him on his way. The lines are long as I would expect. Looks like I'm going to be here awhile.

"Well look a here! I know this' not who I think it is?!" A woman yelled as she ran towards me from the front of the line. She gave me the tightest bear hug I've ever had.

I can't believe who I'm looking at, it's Auntie LolaMae! "Hey Auntie LolaMae!" I said, trying to yell back but couldn't because she was hugging me too tight.

"Now who done snuck you out of prison?! I bet not say that too loud, might get cha' caught!" She said, laughing as she put me back down. She laughed so loud people are turning around and looking.

"Nobo…" I tried to say, but she cut me off.

"So did you escape? You know I thought you had done got killed up in their?! I hadn't heard from you I guess you still mad at me?!" She shouted.

"No I didn't escape nor am I mad at you." I said, trying to hurry up before she cut me off again.

"Well that's good. So how'd you get out?!" She asked, putting her hands on her hips.

"They made a mistake so they let me go free. They charged me for something I didn't even do." I said, smiling because I remembered what she said when I was up in there.

"You mean to tell me that they had you in there all that time for nothin'?! You got to be crazy! I would sue they butts! They wouldn't get away with puttin' me up in there all that time and I'm innocent! No mam'!" She shouted.

Auntie LolaMae has an answer for everything. I know she didn't think I was innocent but now all of a sudden she does. But that's how she's always been. She'll change her answer quick when it looks like she may be right. She's so funny because she always has to shout when she talks. I guess it's because she likes a lot of attention. And trust me, she gets it every time she opens up her mouth. "I'm just glad to be out." I said, throwing up my hands.

"I know that's right! You know your Auntie loves you and I'm glad ta' see you!" She reached out and gave me a big kiss.

"I know you love me Auntie. I know you love me. Hey what'a you doing up here?" I asked, stepping back from her.

"Baby I know your feelings might be hurt but I'm in here to see Mr. Walter!" She said, wiping her eyes.

"What did he do?"

"They caught him stealing some tires down at the junk yard to go on his truck. But that's not why he's in here though. They just gave him a warning and told him not to go back down there no mo'. But later on that day, I told him I wanted to eat some cat-fish. He didn't have no money but cha' know he always wanna' make me happy, so he went down to Grocery Lane and stuffed about twenty pounds of frozen cat-fish in his shirt and pants! They wouldn't have caught him if he hadn't kept shaking his leg and one of em' fell out! They ran up to him and took him straight to the back to wait on the police! He already had warrants so they just went on and kept him and took him to jail! I didn't tell him to go down their and get twenty pounds of fish! That's a crazy man! But that's my baby, he always told me he would do anything for me!" She shouted while laughing so hard, she bent over and held her stomach.

"Auntie, you so crazy! I'm sorry to hear that!" I said, laughing so hard, tears are falling from my eyes.

"Awe' girl sorry for what?! He won't be up in there but only about six months. They really got him cause of those warrants from all that drinkin' and tryin' to drive! Look you can come get in front of me, I got one person in front of me before I get to the window!" She said, as I followed her as she walked back towards the front of the line.

"So where you staying?!"

"I'm staying with a new friend of mine."

"I know that's right! Finally got cha' somebody! That's good, I hope he treat you right! Better than that one you had! Look here, don't be no stranger! You know where I live! And I'm prayin' for you and yo' mama's relationship! It's gon' be alright. Now gone you next up to the window!" She shputed as usual, as she pointed towards the window. I didn't even bother telling her the whole story about Mr. Kelly because it's just too long. Maybe I'll tell her when we have more time alone.

"May I help you mam'?" The clerk asked, as she re-positioned the glasses on her face. She's a Hispanic woman which looks to be in her late twenties. She has long reddish hair, kinda' reminds me of some actress with all that red hair.

"Um', yes mam' I need a pass to see two different people." I answered.

"You can only see one person at a time. The women are on a different floor than the men. I'll give you one pass and you can come back down to get the other one after you visit with one. What is the name of the person you wanna' see?"

"Excuse me mam' this line is very long, is it possible if I can get both of the passes at the same time?" I asked, bending closer to the window.

"No! You'll have to do like everybody else. If I make exceptions for you then everybody else is going to want them." She answered, with a slight Hispanic accent while never looking up.

"I'm not trying to cause no trouble. I haven't seen these people in a long time and if it's possible I would like to see them both today? I'm not asking much." I said, as Auntie broke in.

"Look you don't be talkin' to my niece that way! She better be glad she behind that glass, cause' I'll buss through it like a locomotive!" She shouted, squeezing me against the counter.

"Calm down Auntie, I'll handle this!" I shouted back trying to calm her down before she squeeze the breath out of me. I thrust my elbow in her side motioning for her to back up.

"Well she ain't got to be talkin' to you that way! People's get their little ol' jobs and forget where they came from!"

The clerk broke in and said, "You better quiet her down before I get security to make you two leave." She pointed towards the guards at the entrance.

"Mam' that won't be necessary, she's going to act right. But as I was saying all I want to do is see my two friends and…"

"Look I'm going to do this, this one time but you better not come up here expecting it again!" She yelled through the window cutting me off. "Now what are their names?"

"Michelle Jackson and Tyrome Jenkins." I spoke back through the little opening in the window.

"Spell their names." She asked while writing at the same time.

"M-i-c-h-e-l-l-e J-a-c-k-s-o-n and T-y-r-o-m-e J-e-n-k-i-n-s." I spelled their names out letter by letter.

"Just a minute." She said, as she typed in the names on the computer. "Here are your passes, go right to the left and up the elevator to the seventh floor. You'll be visiting Mr. Jenkins first." She said, pointing towards the elevators.

"Thanks mam' I really appreciate this." I said, as I started walking towards the elevators.

"Before you go let me give you mines and yo' mama's new phone numbers!" Auntie shouted behind me. She took out a piece of paper and wrote down their numbers and handed it to me.

"I'm so excited, I didn't even think about getting this information from you. I'm glad you said something." I said, taking the piece of paper from her hand.

"Now you can come to church! You know Pastor still preaches the church house down! The membership has gotten' bigger since the last time you been there! We even got a new minister in the church. Al' right I'll tell yo' mama I seen you and call me sometime!" She shouted as she waved me off and started talking to the clerk.

I thought about giving her Mr. Kelly's phone number but she wouldn't do nothing but start mess by saying that I'm staying with an old man. It would be too much drama. I already know she can't wait to tell mama and them that I'm out of prison. I'm not worried, I got their new number I'll call them myself. I'm kind of excited to see them, I guess because it's been so long. I wonder what they look like?

I'm waiting on the elevator which seems to be taking it's time by coming back down.

The elevator doors finally came down and the ride up to the seventh floor was a long one. The thing moved slower than a snail.

There's a whole new environment up here. I thought as the elevator door's swung open. Solid blue walls and bars are everywhere. Reminds me of the prison life. Up ahead there's another check-in counter. But before I can check-in, I have to go through another metal detector. They then patted me down, and led me to the front counter. After checking in, the guard told me to go around the corner and Tyrome should be waiting on me. They probably called him before I got in the elevator. Anyway, he's waiting for me. Lord help me...

When I came around the corner, his eyes got so big, his mouth flew open, and was followed with a smile. He grabbed the phone and motioning for me to do the same. "I had a feeling you would come and see me. You sho' lookin' good, I see you've lost all that weight. Me personally I liked it when you was big." He said.

"Don't start with your smooth talking words because they don't work with me no more." I spoke sternly into the phone.

"Are you here to be nice or are you here to fuss like somebody nagging mama? It's your fault we're not together anyway. I know I wouldn't have been locked up in here if you had of never broke up with me. We would've never gotten caught in the truck because I wouldn't have had to steal it just to get you back." He said, tilting his head.

"I'm not here to argue with you. Nor am I here to go back to the past. I know exactly what happened so I don't need your lying opinion." I said, as the phone got quiet. Ok, now Lord You're going to have to help me. I can't do this by myself. You're going to have to show me why You led me up here, because right now I'm wondering why I ever came. I thought to myself as I paused for a moment." Tyrome, I'm here to let you know that I'm here for you if you need me." I spoke through the phone. By now I'm staring him straight in his eyes.

"What you mean you here for me? You not here for me. Ain't nobody here for me. So you can just drop that. And further mo', how'd you get out of prison anyway? You need to go back cause you talking real crazy."

"Look, ok fine. I'm not here for you. And don't worry about how I got out, that's not your business. But one things for sure, when you're innocent, you're innocent. You always feel like nobody's here for Tyrome. Nobody's ever been there for Tyrome. You always got all the answers that's why you're in here right now. If you would just shut up and let somebody care about

247

you and stop rejecting them, then maybe you would be a better person. And I'm sure it would've saved you from half the trouble you got yourself in already. I'm here to let you know that no matter what you've done, God will forgive you. But you got to repent."

"Why? I'm not sorry?" He threw his hand up.

Ok Lord, You sho' got to give me the words to say. He has a stony heart, but I'm going to say what You would have for me to say. If he don't listen then, he can't ever say that he wasn't told and that You didn't try to help him. Now Lord, give me the words to say... "You should be." I said.

"Why should I be?" He asked, holding up one hand, hunching his shoulders, and holding the phone with the other.

"Because you not only hurt me, but you hurt yourself and many others. Remember how you told me the story about your past? How you were abused and many other things happened to you that wasn't your fault? You said that you would never hurt nobody like you were hurt, and that the things that you saw, no child should ever have to experience? Well, you're doing the same thing, just different situations. Let me take that back, some are the same situations." Tyrome just stared through the window as if he was listening, with one hand holding the phone and the other resting on the table. "You abused me for nothing. You were abused. You controlled my life. You were controlled. Can't you see the vicious cycle? Can't you see that's a generational curse put on you by satan? I know your foster aunt hurt you when she raped and molested you and it felt like she destroyed your life forever. I know your foster father hurt you when he abused you and killed your mama for nothing. I see all the hate, the anger, the bitterness, and all the unforgiveness that you're still holding on to from your past. It took a long time to get over you Tyrome. It took a long time to forgive you for all the things you did to me. And how you degraded me and destroyed my life. I had to let you go out of my heart and out of my spirit in order for God to take away all the pain and unforgiveness from me. I have forgiven you for what you did to me, and I have completely moved on. But I'm here to help you. I want to let you know that God has a purpose and a plan for your life and He wants you to fulfill it. But He can't do it when you're being evil and doing evil things. You can't go back to your past, nor can you change the things that you've already done. But you can change where your life is going. God has truly changed my life. I'm not the same person you met years ago. Actually you did me a favor by coming into my life because I'm a whole new Ramona. With the evil things you did to me, you allowed me to find myself and the destiny that God has for my life. It helped me to grow and to see life more clearly. I got my common sense back, I got my dignity, I got my mind back, and most of all I got my heart, mind and soul back. I've learned how to love myself, and I've learned how to give love and receive love. I know you're thinking that God won't forgive you for all the things that you've done. But I'm here to tell you that He will. I'm a living witness." He wiped his teary eye with his fore finger. "God wants to heal you from all the hurt and pain from your childhood that you've gone through that wasn't your fault. And He wants to deliver you from the things that isn't right inside of you right now. But before He can do that, you must be saved. Are you willing to let God save you so that your life can never be the same?" I said, as I watched him cry with his head down. I never knew he could cry, I never knew he even had feelings.

After a moment of silence he said, "I um'…" He sniffed. "You know? I know this is the good Man above cause I was just praying that He would send me somebody to help me, and to get me right so I can stop goin' through the same things over and over again. I'm tired of sellin' drugs, chasing women, gettin' drunk, gettin' high, stealing and robbing folks, beatin' up people, and all that stuff. I'm ready to give God all of me. I'm ready to do right. How can a man like me be saved? All that I've done wrong? I've done too much against God and I'm not going to play with Him either." At this point his eyes are blood shot red. His face is swollen from all the crying. I can see he's really sorry. I can see God breaking him. I just hope Tyrome's heart is touched and not his emotions. God is not about emotions, He's about the heart.

"It's simple Tyrome. All you have to do is confess with your mouth the Lord Jesus and believe in your heart that God raised Jesus from the dead, you shall be saved (Romans 10:9). But you must say it with your mouth and you must believe what you're saying in your heart. I can't say it for you because you're responsible for yourself." I said, as I whispered back into the phone.

"Oh', I believe what I'm saying. So that's all I got to do? I thought it was more to it than that like running around the jail cell and turning flips? A preacher told me that one time. And I told him I'm not running around no church in order to get saved." He whispered back, sniffing his nose.

"God wants us all to be saved. When different people get saved, they react in many different ways. Some may run around the church, some may lift their hands, close their eyes and weep and cry, while others may not do any of that but just thank God afterwards. Just like you're crying now and you may be crying afterwards. That's if you choose to receive Him as your Lord and Savior. However, that's what different people may do. But there's only one God and He's the only way, there is no other way. I thought you said that you got saved before?"

"I lied, I ain't never been saved. I was tryin' to get you." He said shamefully.

I sort of smiled, trying not to ruin the mood. "So are you ready now?"

"I think so." He answered as he hunched his shoulders.

"You think so, you got to know for sure. There's nothing to be afraid of. God hasn't given us a spirit of fear, but he's given us power, love, and a sound mind" (2 Timothy 1:7).

"Alright. Yea' I'm ready." He said, as he closed his eyes then put his head down.

"Repeat after me. I repent of all my sins." He repeated.

"I confess with my mouth the Lord Jesus and I believe in my heart that God raised Jesus from the dead" (Romans 10:9). He repeated again.

"I renounce Satan totally out of my life, and I now receive You as my Lord and Savior. Thank You now for saving me!"

He repeated. Tears are streaming down his cheeks as he raised one hand to the ceiling and held the phone with the other. I've never seen this man cry like this before. I know Your touching him right now Lord. "Just began to thank Him for saving you Tyrome. I believe God wants to fill you with his Holy Spirit."

"Thank you God, thank You." He whispered through the phone. "I didn't think... You would receive a man like me... All that I've done wrong." His word's chopped up because of the tears. "But I know You have received me cause I feel You touching me. Thank You... Thank You..." He continued to praise God for about another ten minutes or so.

Thank You Lord my mission is accomplished!

Out of all these years I never knew I would have to minister salvation to one of my worst enemies. That comes to show that God loves everybody, no matter what they've done in their past, they can still be forgiven and they can still be saved. And Lord You just proved that to me today. Wow, You're an awesome God! "Praise God Tyrome. Are you ok?" I asked, smiling.

"I'm more than alright. I'm just glad you came up here. I'm thinkin' about what you said earlier. You right about my past. Inside my heart I always wanted to get saved and live for Him. But somethin' just kept me from it. One of my foster mamas, you remember the one I told you about? The home that my daddy had killed in front of me? Well I think that's why she got killed cause she was so faithful in church, in fact she almost pulled me in there. That's where I got some of the teaching from before I strayed away totally. And my daddy didn't like her going all the time. All and all they were arguing and he started beating her up and then went and got a shot gun and killed her. I'll never forget what she told me though." He sniffed. "She told me to find a woman that loves the Lord. And when I found you, I just didn't know what to do with you. We was on two different levels. You were living so strongly for the Lord and I came along and messed it all up. Man! I let my ego get the best of me. And among some other things too." He said, as I cut him off.

"But Tyrome, God has forgiven you for all that. Don't let your mind go back to the past. You're not accountable for me. I allowed you to do what you did to me. That was all my fault. I messed up with God all by myself." I said.

"I know. I'm sorry Ramona and I know I could never repay you for all the pain I caused you, even what I did with Michelle."

"I forgive you." I said as I touched the glass.

"As much as I did wrong, I've never spent that many years in prison like you did, especially for nothing. Now I got a long time to think about it. At least I got a new life living inside of me and that's Jesus. I know He's going to see me through it. Ramona you a strong Christian woman. I've never had a woman that I did bad come back and minister to me. I really do hope you make it in life and that God will use you even more. You know? Maybe you can come and minister to us in prison one day? Have you ever thought about being an minister? Where do you go to church?" He asked, slightly smiling.

"I know God has a great call on my life, and whatever it is, that's what I'm going to do. No, I don't have a church home right now. But you better know I'm searching." I answered, attempting to smile.

"Let's go, visitation is up." The guard broke in.

"Hey, I'll never forget this day. God answered my prayers. I gotta' go cause my visitation's up. Come see me sometimes and get my address and write me. I'll put chu' on my list." He said, as he hung up the phone, then turned and walked towards the guard that was standing behind him.

During the entire ride down the elevator all I can think about was what just happened.

While thinking about all this, I totally forgot about Michelle. Tyrome and I didn't talk about him and Michelle much which I'm glad. One thing he did do that was good was apologize to me, which was something that I've never heard come out of his mouth. Ok now I need to gather myself. Lord You've got to give me the words to say and please fill me back up where I've poured out in Jesus Name.

"I'm here to see Michelle Jackson please." I said, after getting off the elevator and walking up to the counter where the guard is sitting. I'm now on the third floor where the women are.

"Go right in, you'll be in cubicle 12. She'll be waiting for you there." He pointed towards that direction.

As I approached the room all I can see is an image of a woman sitting with her head down and her hands in her lap. That can't be her, she's so little and dark. I think they got the wrong person or I'm at the wrong cubicle. I thought, while trying to focus my eyes. When I got up close to the window, my heart immediately fell to the floor. It's Michelle. She looks nothing like herself. She's lost so much weight. She was already little, well now she's even smaller. She looks like she's about eighty years old. How in the world am I'm going to do this without crying? Ok gather myself. I'll focus on the crack in the counter, yea' that's what I'll do.

I picked up the phone. Not one word will come to my mouth. Lord, I'm really going to need Your help. She's just sitting there staring at me. She has the phone in one hand and she has her head resting in the other one.

"I guess I better say somethin' cause you act like you can't talk. What's up? I can't believe you out of all people would come and see me? Well what you came to do, stare at me? You can talk I'm not gon' bite." She slowly said.

"How are you?" I asked with hesitation.

"I'm fine I guess. Basically waitin' to die off up in here, cause you know I got AIDS and I don't stand a chance of gettin' out no time soon? I know you heard. I guess you sayin' my sins have finally caught up with me. Well you right. I got AIDS through sexual contact. I've had it for quite sometime now. I got it from one of the men I was sleepin' with and don't ask me which one cause I don't know. See, I've never been able to see thangs how you always seen em'. That's what made you and me so different. That spirit that you have was always so admiring even in high school. I couldn't have put up with all that you did and still accepted and loved people. Inside I knew you were hurting and I hurt you even more and made it worse. All because I was jealous of the spirit you always had. How you were able to love and help people despite how they treated you. I hated that and that's why I talked about you behind yo' back. I didn't know how to be yo' friend. Even though it was an honor. Somehow in the back of my mind I knew you would come and see me. After all the wrong I've done to you, you still showing up in my face. I don't deserve this. I know you wonderin' why I'm sayin' all this. Well because I want to get all this out of me so when I die, I can die in peace." She spoke into the phone.

"Michelle I want you to know that I have forgiven you and I really want you to move on from all that." I said, slightly pointing at her. "But there's one thing that I want you to know is that you can't die in peace without the Lord. You must be born again (John 3:3). And you do that by giving your life back to Him. Then you'll have all the peace you need. You already know, this' nothing new to you."

"You right. I need to give my life back to him. I don't want to die and go to Hell." She said. Her voice is so brittle. It sounds like she's straining to get every word out.

"God doesn't condemn us, He convicts us (Romans 8:1). Yes you've done a lot of things that were not pleasing to God but when He forgives you, He's not going to remember them anymore. He's going to wipe them all out. Even what you did to contract AIDS. Are you ready to give your life back to God?"

"Girl you comin' with this God thang so strong and so quick." She got quiet for a moment. "I guess I should expect that from you cause you always been this way." She kinda' laughed. "Yes I'm ready." She said, barley raising her hand up.

"You know what to do first." She repented of her sins as she started tearing up.

"Now repeat after me. Lord I know that I'm a sinner. I've backslid against You, but You said in Your Word that Your married to the backslider." She repeated.

"Now I confess You as my Lord and Savior. And I do believe You died on the cross for my sins and then You were raised again." She repeated again.

"Thank You today for saving my soul and remembering the sins in my past no more." She repeated.

"Thank You that I'm born again and that my name is now recorded in the Lamb Book of Life." She repeated with tears running down her face.

Stephanie Franklin

"Now Michelle, God will give you the peace you need. You're going to be fine. You need not have to worry, your name is recorded in the Book of Life in Heaven. Remember that I'll always be your friend Michelle. No matter what was said in the past and no matter what was all done."

"Ramona I just wanna' say one mo' thang…" She broke down in tears again. "I just wanna' let chu' know and I'm gon' have to go. I'm truly sorry for what I did to you with Tyrome. I was out there and…" She said, as I cut her off.

"What did I tell you earlier? I have forgiven you for everything. It's all good." I said, as we both sniffed.

"Alright girl it's my time. I'm thankful for you and I thank God I'm saved. Will you write me? I know you will. I'll see you on that other side. Thanks for everything, I love you girl you'll always be my sista'." She said, as she blew a kiss, hung up the phone, and disappeared around the corner.

I held back the tears as I watched her walk off. Somehow I feel that that's the last time I'll ever see her again. At least down here. Thank You Lord for another mission accomplished.

All this praying, I need to be praying about my eye sight. I'm not worried, God's going to fully heal me one day.

It's about 4 o'clock in the morning. The hospital just called and said for me to come down. Mr. Kelly's not doing good at all. They're giving him maybe a couple of hours to live. What am I going to do without him? He's all I got.

The cab was slow as usual. It was supposed to be here 30 minutes ago.

I Finally made it up to the hospital and up to Mr. Kelly's room. It took me almost an hour just to get here. Mr. Kelly's lying on the bed so helpless. I reached down and gave him a soft kiss on the cheek. "Mr. Kelly can you hear me?" I whispered. He's lost so much weight I can hardly recognize him. He's had his right mind all this time. He still knows who I am he just can't talk that good with all the different pain medications and with the respirator over his mouth. "Mr. Kelly can you hear me? Mr. Kelly, Mr. Kelly?"

"It's y-ya' kid-o" He vaguely whispered back to me.

"Mr. K. I love you. You're going to be alright." He slightly nodded his head with approval. Things got quiet for a moment. "Mr. K. I love you enough that I want to see you saved. I don't think we ever got a chance to do that. Remember we were always putting it off? Well, I want you to know that you're going to make it in. Can you hear me? If you can, just nod your head yes."

He did it very slow. Then slowly said, "I... want to... thank... you... for taking... care of... me and... seeing... bout' me... I'll never forget it... You are... the daughter I... never had... Take care of the... store for me... You're a good... soldier, you... can hold... the fort down... Make..." He coughed as he took a breath after almost every word. "Make sure... you always... keep... those fruits... nice-in' fresh... Maybe you'll... get... yourself... a home and use... the apartment... for more... storage space." He slowly took a long breath.

"How am I going to get myself an apartment Mr. K.? We don't make that much?" I laid my arm across his pillow, behind his head.

"You'll... be able to... The business... is... going to... do great..." He slowly said, with a slight smile. "Hey, make my... funeral... nice and... pretty... for me... hear?... Follow... exactly... what... I have on... that paper... Give my clothes... to charity... and... don't forget... to donate... some money... to the cancer... organizations... And make... sure my... hair is nice... and... slicked back... You know... I have... to look

257

handsome... for the women... when... they come... around to... look at me..." He slowly said, barley smiling as he struggled with every word.

I know it hurts him to smile. I'm going to miss Mr. Kelly. I can't believe he still has his right mind. Most would have given up by now. I always knew he was a strong man. "Now Mr. Kelly you're going to stop talking like that. You're not going anywhere. You're going to get better and be out of here before you know it." I said, as I turned my face away from him so that he couldn't see the tears fall.

"Who... are you... kidding?... I'm ready... to go... I've lived... a good life... with... my share... of mistakes, but all... and all... I've lived... a good life... Now I'm... ready... for the pain... to stop... so I... can be free... I miss my... honey, I'm... ready... to see... her again..."

"Mr. K., you know you won't see her again unless you receive God into your heart, right?"

"Yea'... I know... I'm ready... let's do it..."

I can't believe my ears. He's actually ready to receive You Lord? "Ok repeat after me." I quickly said, as I held his hand. "Lord, I'm sorry for the sins I committed." He slowly repeated.

"I confess with my mouth and I believe in my heart." He slowly repeated again.

"That God raised Jesus from the dead."

He repeated slower than the first time.

"Now I receive You as my Lord and Savior. Thank You for saving my soul."

He stopped in between, but eventually finished. His eyes are full of tears.

"I'm so happy for you Mr. Kelly." I smiled. "Now you can see your parents, your son, and your beautiful wife again in Heaven." I smiled as he smiled with his eyes.

I guess he's saying to himself, if that was all he had to do, he could have done that many many years ago. And if so, I totally agree with him.

The heart monitor started speeding up. "Mr. Kelly, you hear me? Mr. Kelly?!" It's now making one long buzzing sound." Mr. Kelly no?! No don't leave me Mr. Kelly!" I yelled, as the nurses came running in and motioned for me to leave out the room.

After about fifteen minutes, the doctor came out and pronounced him dead at 6:15am. "I'm sorry mam', there's nothing more that we can do, he's gone." He hugged me, waited for a moment, and then walked away. Tears ran from my eyes uncontrollably. I wept like a baby in the hospital for about an hour as nurses came over and consoled me. I'm so glad he's at peace now. I'm sure going to miss him…

Chapter 18

One month has passed and I now realize that our days on this earth is shorter than I used to think. The store is still going in full affect. Considering in the past three weeks I had to go to four different funerals. Two in one week about two weeks ago and the other two just last week. The first two was Mr. Kelly's and Michelle's. Mr. Kelly's funeral went just the way he wanted it to go. From the funeral arrangements to his clean cut look for the women.

I couldn't bear to look at him in the casket, it would have brought back too many memories. Anyway I'm glad all that's over now and I can move on with my life. I miss him so much. I miss him fussing at me about keeping the store clean and the fruits washed off. That man was something else. It's hard for me to even think about Michelle's funeral. I never did go up to the casket. I just stayed to the back. I couldn't bear to look at her either, even though she gave her life to Christ before she died. Then just last week I went to Sandra's and Jerry's funeral. They went back to doing all the wrong things that God had delivered them from. Just to name a few, they started back gang banging and dealing drugs. They robbed a cleaners, but when they tried to get away, the owner ran out and shot them both before they could even make it to the car. It was all on the news. The first thing that came to my mind was what is a man profited, if he shall gain the whole world, and lose his own soul? or what shall a man give in exchange for his soul (Matthew 16:26)? I don't understand why would anybody want to trade Heaven for Hell? To gain this sinful world, but in exchange to lose their soul? Anyway those deaths taught me something, never to take life so casually. We can be here one minute and gone the next. Everybody don't get second chances. That's why we should do our work here on earth to the best of our ability and with the fear of God (1 Peter 1:17).

The mail man just dropped off a letter that has my name on it. Must be one of those bill collectors. Shoot instead of me given out money, I need to be receiving money. I don't know how I'm going to pay half of these bills. I'm not going to open it now, it can wait. They waited this long, they can wait a little longer.

Believe it or not I called Auntie about a week ago and told her that I was coming to church on Sunday. Considering that today is Friday and I really don't have much time to change my mind. So I guess it's a go.

It was busy all day around the store. I'm glad I'll have it closed on Sunday for church.

It's a pretty day for a Saturday. This strange looking man just walked through the door. "Hi, can I help you?" I asked, coming from behind the counter.

"Um' yes I'm looking for Miss. Ramona Williams please." He said with an envelope in one hand and a brief case in the other. He's a short thin Chinese man with hair missing on top of his head. His voice is rather squeaky and his suit looks to be a little too big for him. I'm sure it's because of his height. He might be a border line 5 foot guy. I have to admit, he's kind of cute though. I laughed to myself.

"I'm Ramona Williams."

"Hi Miss. Williams, I'm Mr. Kelly's lawyer and I was sent by here to give you this. Mr. Kelly left it for you but you must sign for it first." He said, as he reached in his coat and took out a pen.

"I'll sign but can you tell me what this' about?"

"I don't know mam'. He gave it to me before he went into the hospital. He told me not to open it, and to give it to you after his funeral."

"Well it's been a month, why have you waited so long?" I looked at him funny.

"He told me not to bring it to you right after the funeral. And the little extra time after that, I was tide up in the office. He wasn't my only client mam'." He said, smiling and stopped after he saw I wasn't.

"Thanks for bringing this to me. It's probably a letter he wants me to read. I'm sure another assignment." I said, as I walked him to the door, he turned and shook my hand, and then walked out. My eyes followed him through the window as he vanished around the corner.

"Now what am I going to do with all this mail? Should I just throw it in the trash? No, I know he wouldn't want me to do that. Might be something very important I need to know. I'll open it later.

Yesterday came and went so quick I didn't have time to think about what I was going to wear this Sunday morning.

I can't seem to find anything, I might not go. Nobody but the Devil. I wonder if Auntie LolaMae will understand if I don't make it this time? Let me call her and tell her. "Hey Auntie?!" I shouted over the loud music in the background. That's just ridiculous. She is too funny. She ain't nothin' but a character. I thought laughing myself.

263

"He-hello?! Yea' I worship ya' Lord on my soul!! Hello, is anybody there?!!" She yelled as she sang along with the music.

"Auntie! Auntie! Turn down the music so you can hear me!!" I yelled back into the phone.

"What?! Who is this?! Don't be callin' my house prankin'. I'll put Jesus on ya'!! Click..." She yelled, as she hung up the phone in my face.

I might as well go ahead and go because it's a waist of time calling her back. I guess I'll wear this dress suit. I don't know when was the last time I dressed up. All my other suits are too big considering that I wear a size 5-6 now. I'm so happy because I did reach my goal. Thank you Jesus! I don't ever want to gain all that weight again. It's easy to keep it off now because I've been delivered from that gluttony spirit that was making me want to over eat constantly. And I now watch what I eat. I know it was a generational curse that was place on my life. Heavy weight runs in my family. Thank God it's broken! And the only way it was broken was by first admitting that I had a problem, yielding my will to God's will, and then through praying, fasting, and deliverance. I also exercised while I was in prison, that's where I burnt off the calories and the fat which resulted in tone. I thought to myself. Ok, going back to what I'm going to wear. This suit has a spot on the jacket but they won't notice it unless they're really looking. They bet not be looking that close. I thought, as it took me over an hour to get myself together.

Let me get ready to go. I'm already 30 minutes late. Grabbing my door keys, I accidentally picked up the two letters that was underneath them. It's those two letters that came for me the other day. I might need to open them up before I go cause' ain't no telling what they're talking about. I got a little time while I wait on this slow cab, so let me see which one I'm going to open up first? I'll open this one address to me first. It says as I whispered: *"...This letter is to inform you that your settlement came through and on behalf of Cab Incorporated, we pay you 1.4 million dollars… Your check is enclosed and is payable to Miss. Ramona Williams. You may endorse it as you please… We apologize for any inconvenience we may have caused… Sincerely, Cab Incorporated."* I can't believe this. Is this really real? It can't be, I didn't sue their cab company? Did I? If I did I don't remember. Probably some telemarketer trying to get some money. Let me see what Mr. Kelly's got to say in his letter. *"…Hey kid-o, I hope this letter finds you in good health. This letter is my will. What you are looking at is real. And the check inside is real. I'm leaving you 3 million dollars. I've been saving this since I first opened the store. Through out the years it accumulated interest. This'll help you with the store and with buying you a new home and a new car. I know you're surprised. I'm just happy to know that I had you to leave it to. Go forth and spend it as you please but remember to be wise and reinvest it so you can get more. No, I'm not talking about gambling. (Smile)… And as for the other money you should have already received. I took it upon myself to take care of that when you first told me what happened to you. I went and did the research and I talked to my lawyer and we got you 1.4 million dollars. I hope that's enough. I realize nothing could ever replace a bruised body, but it sure does help to be comfortable while your healing. (Smile) I will always love you for what you did for me and remember, hold the fort down!… I'll see ya' on this side… Love Mr. Kelly…"*

As I finished reading the letter, tears ran down my face. "I can't believe he did that for me. I didn't think about doing that anymore after I got out of the hospital. How'd he do it without me knowing? I can't believe this! This is really real! This is a miracle from Heaven! Lord You said that I would be well taking care of. You weren't lying!!" I yelled. I jumped up and down and waved my hands in the air like a kid with a piece of candy. "I got a total of 4.4 million dollars! Church is going to be real good now!" I laughed and danced around the kitchen until I got ready to go.

Church service is well on it's way. There's no more seats in the front, so I'm a go ahead and sit in the back. The pastor is preaching. It sounds like he's toward the end of his sermon. It's been a long time since I've been in this church. Nobody recognizes me especially with all this weight gone. There's a little room left beside me and the ushers leading somebody over to sit beside me. I'm not going to even look, it's probably somebody I don't want sitting next me because they're going to be too loud.

I can't believe my eyes. It's the guy that was on the city bus that asked me was I alright. I thought I'd never see him again. I thought to myself.

He squeezed his way in between me and the person sitting beside me.

He looked around, looked at me and whispered. "Hey don't I know you?" "Seem like I've seen you some where before?" He's trying so hard to recognize me.

I whispered back and looked at him with a twinkle in my eyes. "Yes you do know me. I'm the lady that was on the city bus. You asked me if I was ok because I was crying. That was the day when the bus made a wrong turn and some of the people got hurt." He's so nice looking.

He whispered back as some people in front of us turned around and looked at us as if to say be quiet. "Oh' yea' that's right, are you ok? now even though that's been awhile ago?" He whispered back while looking at me with that beautiful smile of his. Nice teeth can make or break a man. Fortunately it makes him.

"I'm doing great." I whispered back. He don't know I'm a rich woman, so of course I'm doing marvelous.

"That's good. I was going to ask you that on the bus but I didn't want to bother you. This' got to be destiny because I thought I would never see you again. I looked and looked for you when the bus came to a stop. But I couldn't find you. When I say destiny, I don't mean that in a lusty way. I mean it in a Godly way." He said.

"That is so weird because I looked for you too but…" I said, thinking the same thing as he cut me off.

"Really?" He whispered, looking surprised.

"Yep really. But I couldn't find you. I even went back on the bus to see if you were still on their but you weren't. So I gave up, and I said if I see you again, it'll be destiny too."

"Well I don't want this chance to slip away from us again. I realize that we're in church but do you mind if I get your number?" He whispered trying not to disturb the people around us. But wasn't really working.

"Sure." I whispered back with confidence and excitement. "But first can I ask you a question?"

"Sure, go ahead." He smiled.

"Are you married?"

"No, I've never been married, nor do I have any kid's. What about you?"

"No, I've never been married and I don't have any kid's either." I whispered as we both smiled. I handed him my number.

I can't believe all this is happening to me at one time. I lose my weight like I wanted to. I got money to last me for the rest of my life. I just met the man of my dreams and most of all I got my groove back from God again. I got it going on with God again! I'm so happy! I shouted within myself. The Bible is so true, if you just be patient and endure your tests and trials, you will definitely come out on top. I've learned not to ever look at my circumstances and get mad and be jealous because my enemies seem to be prospering. Because the wealth of the wicked is stored up for the righteous. I'm so glad I got my wealth! And I'm so glad I got back everything that the devil stole from me seven times greater! I'm glad I went through what I went through, because it's made me who I am today, and now I know what to

267

do with it. Tell my testimony, win more souls with it! And touch more lives!

The pastor's doing the alter call now. "...Come, if you're heavy laden! God will give you rest and He will give you peace. If you want to rededicate your life back to Christ, come!" He's walking down toward the congregation. "You may need healing in your body, God can heal you! If you want to become apart of this church, come! The doors are open! Ministers please come up here, any ministers in the church please come up!" The pastor shouted across the church.

"Excuse me, that's me." He said, as he got up.

"You're a minister?" I asked, as I turned my body towards him.

"Yes, I am." He answered, as he smiled and walked down the aisle.

O' my God, he's a minister too? Pretty impressive. Let me come back to earth. I need to focus on why I came here in the first place. I need you Lord to heal my eyes and I need a church home.

"If you need a healing in your body, come! God is waiting to heal you!" He yelled, as he waved his arm back and forth motioning for the people to come.

Healing in my body? Yea' that's what I need! I jumped up out of nowhere and ran down to the alter. Everybody's clapping and shouting with excitement and praise.

As I turned around toward the congregation, my aunt came storming towards me with two people following behind her which I can't see.

"Hey baby! We are so proud of you!" She yelled as she gave me this big bear hug. When she finally put me down, I can see who the two people are. It's mama and daddy!

"I'm so happy to see you two!" We cried for what seem like forever. I didn't mind until Auntie stepped on my foot. This' a reunion in one, even though mama and daddy is separated.

The church got quiet as the pastor asked, "What do you want God to do for you my sista'?" Auntie, mama, and daddy went back to their seats.

"I want to join the church and I need God to heal my eyes. I'm having trouble seeing out of them." I said, facing the congregation with tears starting to run down my face.

After the pastor received me back in the church, he had one of the ministers to pray for my healing as my eyes were closed. After the minister finished praying it was like a load just lifted off of me. Something miraculous just happened in my eyes. I feel like I can see and I haven't even opened my eyes yet. Who ever is praying for me has a powerful anointing on him and an awesome gift from God!

"Ok you may now open your eyes and thank God for your healing!" The minister shouted, as the congregation started praising God!

As I opened my eyes, everything was totally clear around me! Thank God I can clearly see now! I turned, looked, and to my surprise the minister that prayed for me is you know who, Mr. Kevin. Who said that prayers don't come true?

There's another day and chapter to this story...

269

Recommended Reading and Prayer

Prayer:

If you are not saved or unsure of your salvation, just say this prayer out loud:

> *Lord, I know that I'm a sinner. I have sinned against You, but Lord I repent of my sins and I ask You to come into my heart, my mind, my spirit, my soul, and be my Lord and Savior and my Redeemer. I make a confession with my mouth and I truly believe in my heart that God raised Jesus from the dead. I thank You now for saving me! I'll never be the same! Amen.*

Praise God! Now your name is recorded in the Book Of Life (Revelation 13:8). God has wiped your past clean. He's not going to remember what you've done anymore (Hebrews 8:12) (Jeremiah 31:34).

Don't walk in condemnation or unbelief. If you believed what you just said, know from this day forward that you are saved and that you are a new creature (person) in Christ. Old things are passed away, behold all things have become new (2 Corinthians 5:17).

Recommended Reading

Salvation:

Romans 10:9- "That if thou shalt confess with thy mouth the Lord Jesus, and believe in thine heart that God hath raised him from the dead, thou shalt be saved."
   10:13- "For whosoever shall call upon the name of the Lord shall be saved."

Deliverance From:

Unforgiveness- *Matthew 6:14-15-* "For if ye forgive men their trespasses, your heavenly Father will also forgive you:"
   6:15- "But if ye forgive not men their trespasses, neither will your Father forgive your trespasses."

Loneliness- *Psalm 4:8-* "I will both lay me down in peace, and sleep: for thou, Lord, only makest me dwell in safety."
   Isaiah 54:10- "... my kindness shall not depart from thee, neither shall the covenant of my peace be removed, saith the Lord that hath mercy on thee."
   John 14:18- "I will not leave you comfortless: I will come to you."

Fear-*Isaiah 41:10-* "Fear thou not; for I am with thee: be not dismayed; for I am thy God: I will strengthen thee; yea, I will help thee; yea, I will uphold thee with the right hand of my righteousness."

Psalms 112:7- "He shall not be afraid of evil tidings: his heart is fixed, trusting in the Lord."

Sexual Sins- *Romans 1:24-32-* (fornication, homosexuality, adultery) *(1:24)-* "Wherefore God also gave them up to uncleanness through the lusts of their own hearts, to dishonour their own bodies between themselves:" *1:25-* "Who changed the truth of God into a lie, and worshipped and served the creature more than the Creator, who is blessed for ever. Amen."

1:26- "For this cause God gave them up unto vile affections: for even their women did change the natural use into that which is against nature:"

1:27- "And likewise also the men, leaving the natural use of the woman, burned in their lust one toward another; men with men working that which is unseemly, and receiving in themselves that recompense of their error which was meet."

1:28- "And even as they did not like to retain God in their knowledge, God gave them over to a reprobate mind, to do those things which are not convenient;"

1:29- "Being filled with all unrighteousness, fornication, wickedness, covetousness, maliciousness; full of envy, murder, debate, deceit, malignity; whisperers,"

1:30- "Backbiters, haters of God, despiteful, proud, boasters, inventors of evil things, disobedient to parents,"

1:31- "Without understanding, covenant breakers, without natural affection, implacable, unmerciful:"

1:32- "Who knowing the judgment of God, that they which commit such things are worthy of death, not only do the same, but have pleasure in them that do them."

1 Corinthians 6:13, 18- "...Now the body is not for fornication, but for the Lord; and the Lord for the body."

273

6:18- "Flee fornication. Every sin that a man doeth is without the body; but he that committeth fornication sinneth against his own body."

Matthew 5:27-28- "Ye have heard that it was said by them of old time, Thou shalt not commit adultery:"

5:28- "But I say unto you, that whosoever looketh on a woman to lust after her hath committed adultery with her already in his heart."

Jealousy- *James 3:14, 16-* "If you have bitter envying and strife in your hearts, glory not, and lie not against the truth."

3:16- "For where envying and strife is, there is confusion and every evil work."

Worry- *Isaiah 26:3-* "Thou wilt keep him in perfect peace, whose mind is stayed on thee: because he trusteth in thee."

1 Peter 5:7- "Casting all your care upon him; for he careth for you."

Feeling Unloved- *Isaiah 40:31-* "But they that wait upon the Lord shall renew their strength; they shall mount up with wings as eagles; they shall run, and not be weary; and they shall walk, and not faint."

Matthew 11:28-30- "Come unto me, all ye that labour and are heavy laden, and I will give you rest."

11:29- "Take my yoke upon you, and learn of me; for I am meek and lowly in heart: and ye shall find rest unto your souls."

11:30- "For my yoke is easy, and my burden is light."

1 John 4:16- "And we have known and believed the love that God hath to us, God is love; and he that dwelleth in love dwelleth in God, and God in him."

Low Self Esteem- *Romans 8:37-* "Nay, in all these things we are more than conquerors through him that loved us."

Murder- *Deuteronomy 5:17-* "Thou shalt not kill."

Abuse- *Luke 3:14-* "...Do violence to no man, neither accuse any falsely; and be content with your wages."

Friendship-*Proverbs 18:24-* "A man that hath friends must show himself friendly; and there is a friend that sticketh closer than a brother."

Temptation- *1 Corinthians 10:13-* "There hath no temptation taken you but such as is common to man: but God is faithful, who will not suffer you to be tempted above that ye are able; but will with the temptation also make a way to escape, that ye may be able to bear it."

From your Tongue- *Psalms 39:1-* "I said, I will take heed to my ways, that I sin not with my tongue: I will keep my mouth with a bridle, while the wicked is before me."

Gluttony/ Obesity (excessive eating)- *Proverbs 23:21-* "For the drunkard and the glutton shall come to poverty: and drowsiness shall clothe a man with rags."

Rape-*Isaiah 54:17-* "No weapon that is formed against thee shall prosper..."

Witchcraft- *Micah 5:12-* "And I will cut off witchcrafts out of thine hand; and thou shalt have no more soothsayers:"

Healing From:

Healing from your mind- *Philippians 4:7-* "And the peace of God, which passeth all understanding, shall keep your hearts and minds through Christ Jesus."

Romans 12:2- "And be not conformed to this world: but be ye transformed by the renewing of your mind, that ye may prove what is that good, and acceptable, and perfect, will of God."

Romans 8:6-7- "For to be carnally minded is death; but to be spiritually minded is life and peace."

8:7- "Because the carnal mind is enmity against God: for it is not subject to the law of God, neither indeed can be."

Healing in your body- *Isaiah 53:5-* "But he was wounded for our transgressions, he was bruised for our iniquities: the chastisement of our peace was upon him; and with his stripes we are healed."

3 John 1:2- "Beloved, I wish above all things that thou mayest prosper and be in heath, even as thy soul prospereth."

Healing from the flesh- *1 Corinthians 1:29-* "That no flesh should glory in his presence."

Romans 8:1- "There is therefore now no condemnation to them which are in Christ Jesus, who walk not after the flesh, but after the Spirit."

Receiving The Holy Spirit- *Acts 2:1-4-* "And when the day of Pentecost was fully come, they were all with one accord in one place."

2:2- "And suddenly there came a sound from heaven as a rushing mighty wind, and it filled all the house where they were sitting."

2:3- "And there appeared unto them cloven tongues like as of fire, and it sat upon each of them."

2:4- "And they were filled with the Holy Ghost, and began to speak with other tongues, as the Spirit gave them utterance."

More Scriptures:

Tithing- *Malachi 3:8-10-* "Will a man rob God? Yet ye have robbed me. But ye say, Wherein have we robbed thee? In tithes and offerings."

3:9- "Ye are cursed with a curse: for ye have robbed me, even this whole nation."

3:10- "Bring ye all the tithes into the storehouse, that there may be meat in mine house, and prove me now herewith, saith the Lord of hosts, if I will not open you the windows of heaven, and pour you out a blessing, that there shall not be room enough to receive it."

Strength- *Isaiah 40: 31-* "But they that wait upon the Lord shall renew their strength; they shall mount up with wings as eagles; they shall run, and not be weary; and they shall walk, and not faint."

Discouragement- *Deuteronomy 31:6-* "Be strong and of good courage, fear not, nor be afraid of them: for the Lord thy God, he it is that doth go with thee; he will not fail thee, nor forsake thee."

Pride- *Proverbs 16:18-* "Pride goeth before destruction, and an haughty spirit before a fall."

Suicide- *Psalms 118:17-* "I shall not die, but live, and declare the works of the Lord."

Alcohol- *Proverbs 20:1-* "Wine is a mocker, strong drink is raging: and whosoever is deceived thereby is not wise."

Drugs- *Galatians 5:21-* "Envying's, murders, drunkenness, revellings, and such like: of the which I tell you before, as I have also told you in time past, that they which do such things shall not inherit the Kingdom of God."

Women and Men In Prisons- *Psalms 142:6-7-* "Attend unto my cry; for I am brought very low: deliver me from my persecutors; for they are stronger than I."
142:7- "Bring my soul out of prison, that I may praise thy name: the righteous shall compass me about; for thou shalt deal bountifully with me."

Backslider- *Jeremiah 3:22-* "Return, ye backsliding children, and I will heal your backslidings. Behold, we come unto thee; for thou art the Lord our God."

Scriptures From the Book by Chapters

Chapter 2:
John 4:23-24   Philippians 4:19

Chapter 4:
1 Corinthians 7:2-3, 1:29,   Ephesians 6:11-19
15:31, 12:10   Romans 1:24-32, 2:11
Psalms 51

Chapter 6:
Galatians 5:19-21

Chapter 7:
Galatians 5:19-21

Chapter 8:
James 1:12-13   Psalms 110:1
Ephesians 6:1-2   1 Kings 16:30-34, 17-22
Romans 6:23

Chapter 9:
James 1:15   Hebrews 13:2
Romans 6:23   Proverbs 3:5-6

Chapter 10:
Revelation 1:8-18   Romans 10:13
Romans 10:9   Galatians 5:16-26

Chapter 11:
1 Corinthians 6:18   Romans 2:11

Chapter 12:
Ephesians 4:22-24   Romans 2:11
1 Corinthians 10:19-20   Matthew 21:22
Proverbs 3:5-6

Chapter 15:
Romans 10:9   John 4:24
Malachi 3:2-3   Malachi 3:8-10
Psalms 51:7   Revelation 22:18-19
James 4:4

Chapter 16:
Romans 1: 24-32   Romans 6:23
Luke 8:17

Chapter 17:
Romans 10:9   Romans 10:9
2 Timothy 1:7   Romans 8:1

Chapter 18:
Matthew 16:26
1 Peter 1:17

My prayer for this novel is that lives will be changed through salvation, healing, and deliverance. No matter what you have done. You don't have to stay there, get back up and try again. God is a forgiving God and He can deliver you from every stronghold that has your body or mind trapped or bound. It doesn't matter what sin or bondage you may be living in, God can save you and He can turn your situation around. All you have to do is repent, renounce Satan out of your life, then confess God as your Lord and Savior (Romans 10:9).

If God has promised you something, I pray that you will stand on His word and know that He will bring it to past.

Because "...God is not a man that He should lie, neither the son of man, that he should repent... (Numbers 23:19)" If he said it, it will happen in the right place at the right time. I pray that you will stay faithful and do not faint and that you will receive your blessing just like Ramona did! I decree it done in Jesus Name!

My mission while on this earth is to try to do the will of God and to finish it. Through this, there is not one thing I cannot accomplish (Philippians 4:13).

I look forward to seeing lives changed through this novel and that God will do a new thing in His people.

"... my meat is to do the will of him that sent me, and to finish this work (John 4:34).

1. When Ramona Got Her Groove Back from God

2. My Song of Solomon

3. My Song of Solomon *Prayer Journal*

4. Position Your Faith for Great Success

5. Position Your Faith for Great Success *Workbook*

6. The Purpose Chaser: *For Children Ages 5 to 12*

7. God Loves *Thugs* Too!

8. The Locker Room Experience: *For the Struggling Athlete & Coach, & Tips on How to Get Recruited in Sports*

9. Church Hurt: *How to Heal & Overcome It*

10. Winning Together: *His Needs Matter, Her Needs Are Important*

11. The Power of Healing

12. The Power of the Holy Spirit

13. REshape YOU: *A Fitness Guide to Teach You How to Create the New YOU from the Inside Out*

14. REshape YOU Elderly Fitness Exercises & Eating Plan Book

15. DO IT ON PURPOSE: *How to Respond When Challenges Try to Pull You Away From God's Purpose for Your Life*

You may purchase them at any Christian Bookstore, Barnes & Noble, Amazon.com, Borders, Books-A-Million, and anywhere books are sold.

Contact

To schedule booksignings, speaking engagements, group siminars/sessions, or ordering my books contact:

EMAIL: info@stephaniefranklin.org
WEBSITE: www.stephaniefranklin.org
WEBSITE: www.stephaniefranklinministries.org

Stephanie Franklin, M.A. (T.S.)

Obtains a Master of Arts degree in Theological Studies and a Master of Arts degree in Divinity. She has a vision to reach the world with her mentoring, teaching, life coaching, and preaching ministry. She has a heart to reach the youth and young adults along with the entire family, bringing them all together as a unified fold. One of her greatest desires is to be used by God in whatever capacity He chooses.